THE LETTER

FROM

ABERDOVEY

THE LETTER FROM ABERDOVEY

By
Prue Brand

British Library Cataloguing-in-Publication Data
A catalogue record for this book is available from
the British Library.

ISBN PB: 978-1-9998488-6-6

Cover design by Anna Trussler
with original letter by Samuel Brand,
Welsh landscape photographed by Nick Kenrick,
archive photograph: 'King County WA'/VisualHunt.

Typeset and design by Anna Trussler
www.annatrussler.com

Printed in the UK
www.Biddles.co.uk

CONTENTS

CHAPTER ONE

Judith

1974

I

JUDITH CHECKED HER uniform in the mirror: blue and white, crimped and starched. *It suits me*, she reckoned.

As she scanned the duty roster on the staff noticeboard, she saw that her name had been put down for Acacia Ward, a ward for acutely deranged women. Judith was not worried by this information because, as the Charge Nurse had already explained to her, 'the patients in here aren't dangerous because they are under medical supervision. It's the untreated people outside hospital you have to watch out for.'

As an auxiliary Night Nurse, Judith had become accustomed to caring for the old men who lived out their lives in Dickensian wards amongst cockroaches and tiny ants that got everywhere. Acacia Ward would be a new challenge.

The Staff Nurse on duty with Judith was young and slightly officious. There was little actual nursing for them to do, so they sat together in a small side-office from where they could keep an eye on the ward, a vast space subdivided into smaller wards and cubicles. Judith was bored. Time crawled by. She yawned, and looked at her watch. She still had four more hours to endure. It was hard to stay awake.

Suddenly there was a terrifying crashing sound. Judith jumped up, and she and the Staff Nurse ran outside the office and stopped, horrified. A woman was running down the ward towards them, smashing the huge glass partitions as she ran. She was very big, and as she approached them, she smashed yet another partition before coming to a sudden halt a short distance from where they were standing.

The Staff Nurse gave quick orders.

'*I'll* ring for help. *You* tackle the patient.'

Judith looked at her with horror.

'I can't tackle her on my own!'

'You *must*.'

'No, I *won't*.'

The Staff Nurse repeated the order in a furious stage whisper.

'*Go and tackle that patient*.'

'*No, I won't*,' said Judith.

As the Staff Nurse telephoned for help, Judith's whole body shook. She stood hypnotised as the patient made a sudden bee-line for her, coming to an abrupt stop so close to Judith that she could feel her breath on her face. Then, as she watched in horror, the woman casually opened up her wrist with a shard of glass. Judith thought of her husband and children asleep at home. No, she would *not* tackle this lunatic single-handed. That was not her job.

Almost immediately the door at the far end of the ward was flung open and two male nurses ran down to where Judith was standing. They grabbed the woman, and with difficulty half dragged and half carried her to a side-ward and put her on a bed. They needed to sedate her (clearly she had not been properly sedated earlier) but she fought and struggled, and it took both men to hold her legs down. Judith was elected to straddle the woman's chest and pin her arms down, but the woman was crafty and pleaded with her.

'I've got a tickle on my face – *please* let me scratch it.'

Judith kindly released her grip, whereupon the woman snatched at her face with bloody fingers: but there was worse to come.

'I'm feeling a bit hickory-dickory-knickory today,' the woman confided to Judith.

These words, enunciated through blubbery lips, flashed through Judith's brain like a thunderbolt. She examined the woman's face and immediately knew that those silly words could have only come from one person: a person she now started to recognise despite the wispy locks of greasy hair, the blood-stained face and crazy eyes.

Dear God, she thought; but whispered, 'Hello, Marcie.'

'Hello, you little twerp,' said Marcie, her eyes rolling back into her head as she lost consciousness.

Judith was staring into the eyes of her old school friend, Marcia Stanton-Gray.

II

A few hours later, as she walked home from the hospital, Judith tried to piece together the events of the past few hours. She knew she would never work there again, it simply wasn't worth it. The pay was too low, and the risks too high. The Staff Nurse was wrong to order a nursing auxiliary, or any nurse for that matter, to tackle a manic patient single-handed. What a shock, what a nightmare! For as it turned out, Marcie wasn't just any mental patient: she had once been Judith's dearest friend and ally. Judith shuddered as she recalled Marcie's physical strength and sporting prowess: she could so easily have killed her. She wondered what had driven her dear friend mad, when at school she had been so popular, so sensible, and so sane.

Judith's mind went back to the give-away words 'hickory-dickory-knickory' that Marcie had mumbled, recalling a silly joke that had meaning only for a small group of eight-year-old girls that had joined Brinkley House during the school year 1951–1952. At that time they had found the word 'knickery' so funny that even now Judith found herself smiling involuntarily as she unlocked her front door; but then she had a worrying thought. *Oh God*! Had Marcie recognised *her*? Was the remark 'Hello, you little twerp' directed at her personally, or was it just the drugs talking? Did Marcie know that it was her friend, Judith, straddling her chest and forcing her arms down? Aware of a sinking feeling in her stomach, Judith crept into the house, trying not to wake her family. She tiptoed upstairs, ran a hot bath, and scrubbed herself from top to toe.

Later, after Ralph had left for work and she had dropped the children off at school, Judith set her alarm clock and went to bed for a short rest. Lying in bed, she let her mind wander back to the Spring Term of 1952 and the day she first met Marcie.

III

That term there were only two new girls travelling from Paddington to the Welsh coast by train and one of them was Judith. Wearing the Brinkley House School uniform (grey coat, grey tunic, grey blouse, grey striped tie and grey hat), Judith had been deposited on the platform by her grandmother's housekeeper and left standing there. She was eventually rescued by a fat teacher who ushered her into a compartment where another new girl was sitting. Soon the train set off, and Judith and the other girl sat silently watching plumes of steam swirl past the window and listening to the happy shouts and laughter from pupils in the neighbouring compartments.

The train followed the route of the Cambrian Coast Express, calling at Banbury, Leamington, Birmingham, Wolverhampton and Shrewsbury to pick up more and more pupils, before venturing westward into the mountains of Wales and the coast beyond. Judith felt relieved when, after what seemed like an eternity, the train finally came to a stop at Penhelig Halt, where everyone alighted on to the narrow, windswept platform. Her relief, however, was short-lived. Starting to feel a bit queasy, Judith felt even queasier when she realised that the final leg of the journey was to be carried out by coach. She prayed that this part would be quick, but soon realised that the slow swaying of the elderly charabanc was going to be her undoing. Fearing the worst, she spoke to her travelling companion with urgency.

'I think I'm going to be sick.'

The other new girl immediately took action. She removed her teddy bear from her carrier-bag and put the bag on Judith's lap. Then, putting her arm around Judith to hold her steady, she looked around for help.

The fat teacher squeezed herself down the aisle.

'Don't worry, you'll be fine,' she said, just as Judith was sick into the bag.

The coach stopped, and Judith and the other new girl got out and stood together on the grass verge while all the other girls stared at them through the coach windows.

'Don't worry,' said the girl. 'It's not your fault. It could have happened to anyone.'

'Thank you,' said Judith.

The coach resumed its northerly journey towards Tywyn for a short while before turning down a winding lane leading to a large, grey building spread out over a promontory overlooking Cardigan Bay. As Judith looked at the school where she was destined to spend the greater part of the next ten years, her heart sank.

Relocated to Wales in 1941, supposedly on a temporary basis, Brinkley House School had been moved from Coventry to Aberdovey to avoid the German bombing raids. Thus it was that at very short notice the original hotel, the crumbling relic of a bygone era, had been given a cheap make-over and kicked into shape before opening its creaking doors to 150 lively schoolgirls, aged between eight and eighteen years old. Subsequently, and contrary to expectation, Brinkley House School thrived in Wales, so that by the time Judith joined it ten years later, it was as if the old Coventry school (which had been bombed to powder) had never existed.

Judith would always remember her first night at Brinkley House School. It was January and freezing cold, and as she lay in bed listening to the howling wind and driving rain she knew that it would be years before she would be reunited with her parents. She dreaded the thought of spending her holidays all alone with her grandmother and felt completely abandoned.

At breakfast the next day, struggling to swallow cold, lumpy porridge, Judith started to cry. The other new girl tried to comfort her.

'It's all right. Everything will be all right, *you'll* see!'

'What's your name?' asked Judith, wiping away her tears.

'Marcia Stanton-Gray. What's yours?'

'Judith McLeod. How old are you?'

'Eight, how old are you?'

'Seven, but I'll be eight in two weeks'

'Are you Scottish? Isn't McLeod a Scottish name?'

'My father's family comes from Scotland, but my parents live in India.' Judith started to cry again.

'Look, Judith, don't cry! We're nearly the same age, we travelled here on the same train and we sleep in the same dormitory, so you're not alone. You've got me.'

'Thank you', said Judith.

Judith wiped her eyes and examined Marcie's face properly for the first time. She saw two brown eyes brim-full of kindness and concern trained on to her face, and her heart warmed with the knowledge that she had a friend.

IV

During her first few years in the Junior section of Brinkley House School, Judith spent most of her free time skipping. Skipping was the craze. Those who had skipping ropes of their own shared with friends, and soon, whether inside in the gym or outside in the school grounds, skipping was the free-time activity that kept her year-group most happy and occupied. Soon they were able to carry out a variety of routines, often accompanied by skipping rhymes.

> *My mother said*
> *That I never should*
> *Play with the gypsies*
> *In the wood.*
> *If I did*
> *She would say*
> *Naughty little girl to disobey*
> *Dis-, dis-, disobey*
> *Dis-, dis-, disobey.*

On one never-to-be-forgotten occasion, a plump girl called Janey Collins was so determined to master a difficult skipping routine against the clock, she wet herself. So motivated was Janey, however, that she removed her knickers almost in mid-jump and carried on skipping, much to the delight of her onlookers.

> *Hickory dickory dock,*
> *The mouse ran up the clock,*
> *The clock struck one,*
> *The mouse ran down,*
> *Hickory dickory dock,*

Janey's friends were highly amused, but it was Marcie who made them all fall about laughing when she altered the rhyme from 'Hickory, dickory, dock' to 'Hickory, dickory, knickery', which stuck, even though it neither rhymed nor scanned. Later, one of the girls changed the second line to 'the mouse ran up the tickery', which they all thought incredibly clever.

V

The shock of recognising Marcie in the acute ward of a mental hospital through her use of the word 'knickery' reminded Judith of the happy days she had spent at Brinkley House and of her friendship with Marcie which had endured from the spring of 1952 until the summer of 1962. It was during the summer of 1962, however, that something happened that was so appalling that even now Judith could hardly bear to think about it. She groaned aloud as she thought of Marcie. Would she ever forgive herself for what she had done? Was it she who had driven Marcie mad?

Judith lay awake agonising until the alarm went off.

CHAPTER TWO

Ann, Janey & Trot

' 1990

|

H OW FUNNY TO be forty-six years old, Judith thought. She didn't feel middle-aged and yet one of her children was engaged to be married and the other had a long-term girlfriend. Ralph wasn't that far off retirement now, only another decade or two to go. As for her career, she had decided to stop working in the next few years because, although she had once found nursing tiring, teaching was utterly exhausting. Having taught full-time for a dozen years or more, Judith felt fortunate to be in a position where she could give in her notice whenever she liked, thanks to Ralph's reliable income. Mind you, she thought, as she leafed through a pile of test results, it would be a relief to chuck it in right now. She couldn't believe it: some of her pupils were still muddling facts that she had gone over with them time and time again. It was so bloody depressing.

The telephone rang. 'Yes?' Judith snapped.

'Hello, is this the right number for Judith McLeod?'

'Yes, well, I used to be Judith McLeod . . .'

'Judith! Do you remember me? It's Ann . . . from Brinkley House? Hello!'

Instantly the image of a serious, bespectacled, fair-haired girl floated in front of Judith's eyes.

'Ann? Of course I remember you. How could I ever forget you? How are you? Are you all right? Has anything happened? Is everyone all right?'

'How lovely to hear your voice, Judith. No, everyone is fine, as far as I know . . . Look, I'll tell you what this is about. Sally Griffiths has bought Brinkley House.'

'Bought Brinkley House? You mean, the school? In Aberdovey? Why on earth would Sally want to buy that old dump?'

'Honestly, she has, and don't forget she is Welsh. Anyhow, about four or five years ago she and her husband, Don Saunders, bought the school and transformed it from an almost derelict condition into a fantastic hotel. It's now the hotel it was originally meant to be before the war, only much better.'

'Good heavens!'

'Yes, I *know*. Sally contacted me just after they decided to buy Brinkley House and we've kept in touch ever since. Believe me, I have been privy to the whole saga of how they bought the old place and brought it back to life. Anyhow, the point is that Sally wants to invite some of her Brinkley House friends back there for a reunion. You, me, Marcie, Janey, Roxanne, Livia and Trot – that makes seven, and with Sally herself that makes eight of us.'

'Good gracious, that's so exciting. When is it? Hopefully it'll be in the school holidays. An old girls' reunion at Aberdovey? I *love* it!'

'We're all invited to spend the weekend at the Brinkley House Hotel, starting with a bang-up dinner on the Friday (the last Friday of September, by the way) and ending after tea on the Monday. The problem is that Sally and I are woefully out of touch. You're bound to have Marcie's telephone number, and Marcie will be able to give us Roxanne's – although rumour has it that Roxanne is living in New Zealand at the moment. Do you know anything about that?'

Judith hesitated fractionally before replying.

'Marcie and I seem to have temporarily lost touch for some reason. And as for Roxanne, I haven't a clue, I'm afraid.'

'Never mind. I recently got back in touch with Janey, so I'll ring her next. She'll probably have information about Marcie and Roxanne. I'll get back to you in the next few days and keep you updated as we get nearer to the event.'

The two women chatted for a while, and Judith noticed how much more confident Ann seemed now that she was, as she learned, happily married with children. It was also a relief to know that Ann had assumed that she and Marcie were still friends. Judith hoped that the others would think the same. Little did they know that she and Marcie had ceased to be friends in 1962, and that in 1974 Marcie had gone stark staring mad, and had to be locked away in a mental institution. Judith didn't want to think about that right now; instead she thought about Ann. They had had so much in common when they were pupils at Brinkley House.

II

Ann Edwards (*née* Ross) hung up the telephone, tucked her long blonde hair behind her ears and, putting on her reading glasses, settled back into her deckchair to re-read the case-study of Mary Bell, the famous child murderer. Comfortably ensconced on her little balcony, book in hand, Ann gazed out over the harbour, wondering what Judith looked like after all these years. She had been such a little shrimp when she first started at Brinkley House, and yet, interestingly, she had never been teased by the other girls. Roxanne Selkirk, and 'Fat Fanny'(who had joined Brinkley a year later), had been bullied right from the start, and yet Judith had always been her own person and the other girls instinctively knew this. Ann pondered the mysteries of human nature. *No wonder Child Psychology is so fascinating*, she thought.

As she watched the tide going out and the reeds and mud-flats slowly emerging, Ann felt very contented. She loved this little harbour down on the south coast, this happy place she had known since childhood. It was here that she had first learned to sail and it was here that, as a child, she had first met Jack Edwards, the love of her life. They had married young but had eventually saved up enough money to buy a house overlooking the harbour they both loved. From then on, thanks to Jack's hard work and resourcefulness, they had gone from strength to strength, and Ann knew that she owed everything to him: Jack her best friend, Jack her passionate lover, Jack her staunch ally and soul-mate. Yet she had not always been so fortunate.

When Ann was eleven years old, her father had driven down to Brinkley House to tell her that he was divorcing her mother, who had fallen in love with a man she now planned to marry. Her father then told her that he too intended to re-marry just as soon as he was at liberty to do so. Ann was upset by this news, but failed to appreciate the long-term consequences of this two-way split.

It did not take her long to realise that things would never be the same again. There were to be no more family holidays by the sea, no more happy hours sailing with her friends. Quite quickly Ann realised that she had become a peripatetic visitor, an outsider, at the homes of both her mother and her father. All of her step-siblings (and half-siblings as they came along) went to local schools and had their own rooms, while Ann had no space of her own. By law she had to spend half of each holiday with each parent, but because she was away at boarding school most of the time, both her mother and her stepmother felt justified in putting her up in their guest-rooms for the duration of her visits. Soon Ann started to see Brinkley House as home and, regardless of the dormitory she happened to be in, the little bedside cupboard served as a repository for the few possessions she carried everywhere in her overnight case. Ann remembered how Judith, Janey and Marcie had tried to help her when, in a state of confusion, her academic work plummeted. This confusion, combined with feelings of isolation and abandonment, had remained with Ann until she was fifteen years old – at which point Janey Collins's mother had come to her rescue.

Mrs Collins lived in an imposing Victorian house in Paddington and, for Ann, there was something incredibly comforting about the old-fashioned formality of her household. Everything about Mrs Collins's house (the well-trained servants, the traditional décor and unchanging routine) leaned towards a pre-war lifestyle. Sundays were particularly enjoyable, with Janey's mother very much in charge of the itinerary. First there would be Matins, then a large formal luncheon would be laid on, after which they would take a brisk walk along the River Thames, where clusters of motley river-boats were moored. Later in the afternoon, tea was served with scones, clotted cream, and home-made jam, followed by delicious cakes. After that Mrs Collins would read aloud to them both in a clear, unaffected voice: Saki, Trollope, Forster, D. H. Lawrence, Woolf, Henry James, and many other authors whose works formed the basis for a genuine love of literature that grew and grew as time went on.

Now, sitting on her balcony, Ann tried to pinpoint exactly what it was that had made Janey's home so particularly inviting. It wasn't just the food, the walks, the stories, or the sheer bliss of having her own room, it was something else as well. What was it? Of course! After all these years she could finally put her finger on it. Mrs Collins had *mothered* her: *that* was what it was – and how badly she had needed it! But now Mrs Collins was dead, and Janey was living alone in her mother's house in Paddington. Ann closed her book. She dialled Janey's telephone number, which she knew by heart.

III

Janey Collins was stuck in the bath. She had twisted her ankle earlier that morning and now, having failed to get up from both squatting and kneeling positions, she wondered what to do next.

I know, she thought. *I'll float myself up!* Janey turned on the taps, and when the bath was nearly overflowing she tried again: it worked, and as she clambered out of the bath, chuckling, the telephone rang. She grabbed her towel and limped out on to the landing.

'Hello?' she shouted. 'Who? Ann Edwards? Good heavens! Ann – how lovely to hear your voice. How are you? . . . A reunion at Brinkley House? Who is organising it? Sally *Saunders*? Who's that? . . . Oh! You mean Sally *Griffiths*? . . . A hotel and conference centre? Good grief! And will you and Jack be there? . . . But that's incredible! Of course I can make it. I wouldn't miss it for the world . . . You need contact details for Roxanne or Marcie? Of course, if I can . . . Doesn't Judith have Marcie's number? . . . Oh, I see, but don't worry, I should have it somewhere. And Marcie is sure to have Roxanne's details . . . It'll be fantastic to see everyone again after all these years . . . *Good*! I've found Marcie's country address here but, sorry, no telephone number! Would you like it anyway? . . . Right, are you ready? . . . Okay. Marcia Stanton-Gray – now Selkirk, of course – Redcliffe, Whitstone, Worcestershire. That's all I have. The Stanton-Grays have a London house too. Marcie or Randall, or Marcie's parents, should be able to provide you with Roxanne's contact details . . . But anyhow, as I was saying . . .'

Sitting in a small armchair next to the telephone on the landing, Janey looked older than her forty-six years. Her body was rather chubby, and her 'salt and pepper' hair badly cut, and yet, as she listened to Ann's voice, her face became animated and her grey eyes danced with affection, intelligence and humour. After a long conversation, the two friends said fond farewells and set a date to meet each other in London, prior to the old girls' reunion at the end of September.

IV

Judith had mixed feelings about the old girls' reunion. She was looking forward to seeing Ann and Janey, and curious to see red-headed Sally, now the proud owner of the Brinkley House Hotel, and yet she dreaded having to face Marcie again.

Judith decided to clear her mind by going out for a long walk, but just as she was leaving the telephone rang again. She lifted the receiver and a clear voice spoke out.

'Judith? This is Trot.'

On hearing these crisply enunciated words, Judith had a vision of Alexandra Trotter staring down at her inquisitorially, hand on hip, short dark hair flopping over one eye.

'Good heavens, Trot, how are you? Where are you ringing from? I thought you were in the States.'

'Good God, no! I came back ages ago.'

'How long were you there for, and what were you doing?'

'I was a secretary there for a couple of years. Shocking to think that secretarial work was all I was fit for after nearly ten years at Brinkley House. In the States even those with only half a brain have a university degree, so without a degree I was considered the lowest of the low. I worked in a department concerned with animal husbandry at a university in the Midwest – remember "Corn Belt"? We did it with Miss Bell. Anyway, I got caught up in internal politics and the whole thing blew up in my face. The set-up was biased: I took the side of the underdog and left under a cloud.'

'What actually happened?'

'Well, some of my colleagues were concerned about a

cluster of privacy violations carried out by a senior administrator, so they asked me to mention it at the next meeting. When I raised the issue, it went down like a lead balloon, and because I was an outsider, when push came to shove, I was left holding the baby. Result? I was taken to task for speaking out when I should have kept my trap shut.'

'That seems very unfair.'

'Yes, it was. Anyhow, a special meeting was held during which I was called to account for myself. So I explained to my inquisitors that as a British subject, not only did I have the right to speak out without fear or favour, but moreover I had a duty to stand up against injustice. Then I resigned and walked out of the meeting.'

'That's so brave, Trot!'

'Well, anyhow, I left and flew back to dear old Blighty. I've been here ever since.'

'What a horrible experience. What are you doing now?'

'Horses, of course. I'm not called Trot for nothing. I run a stud farm actually, but you're not horsey so I won't bore you with it all. But I do need to get your advice about something before we all meet up at Brinkley House. It's to do with Livia . . .'

Judith immediately knew what was coming. Everybody knew that Trot and Olivia Bard had been an 'item' during their final year at Brinkley House. Grasping the nettle, she met the subject head-on.

'Yes, I remember that you and Livia were particularly attached to each other in the sixth form, and presumably the relationship carried on after you both left Brinkley House?'

'Yes, we were more than just good friends, for a short

while, but looking back it's clear that the whole thing was just puppy-love. We grew out of it. I've been completely heterosexual ever since. Unfortunately certain friends keep dwelling on the subject and so I'm hoping you could do Livia and me a big favour and tell the gossips to move on before the reunion. In another four years Livia and I will be fifty, for God's sake – we're not eighteen any more! One of the reasons I took myself off to America was to get away from the silly rumours that kept following me about. So, please, Judith, if people gossip about us, be a dear and shut them up for me? I'd much appreciate it, and so would Livia, I'm pretty sure, though I haven't seen her for ages.'

'Of course I'll do that, and I'll also ensure that Sally and Don don't put you in a double room together for the weekend! That would be most unfortunate. Leave it with me, and if you have any trouble with anyone, just let me know.'

'Thank you, Judith, I feel much better about it all now. I'm sure Livia will be fine – in fact I'd really like to see her again, but . . . on a different basis. She was always a good friend to me.'

'Of course she was, and I'm sure still is. So now, what do you think about Sally buying up Brinkley House? It will seem so weird to be back there again – Brinkley House School with en-suite bathrooms. Fancy that!'

'You do realise, Judith, that some of the staff at Brinkley House were Victorians. No wonder the school was so archaic. Do you remember foot-baths?'

'God, yes! How many grubby Juniors queued up to wash their feet and dainty *derrières* in the same bath-water? Eight? Ten?'

'God knows, but I do know that we were allowed two baths a week in the Senior School – or of course there was always the alternative of strip-washing.'

'Heavens, yes, will I ever forget *strip-washing*'

Trot laughed. 'Oh, and quickly changing the subject, do you remember the day Randall Selkirk turned up at Brinkley in his sports car?'

Hearing this last comment, Judith was relieved that Trot could not see her blush at the mention of Randall Selkirk's name. It still seemed strange to think that Marcie was married to him, and that he was Roxanne's big brother.

'Yes, of course I remember.'

Judith remembered the occasion well. It was a Sunday. A group of them had just returned from church, and were trudging across the school drive towards the Senior Common Room when a blue sports car drove in, stopped, and a young man jumped out. He was simply the most beautiful creature Judith had ever seen – and yet it wasn't just his physical beauty that thrilled her. He exuded something else. What was it? Sex-appeal? Whatever it was, Judith would never, ever forget the moment she first saw Randall Selkirk, and, later on, at his wedding, he had been so charming and funny. They had all been enthralled by his extraordinary good looks, wit, and humour. Trot's memory was running along similar tracks.

'Do you remember Marcie's wedding? Wasn't Randall hilarious? Actually, it was at Marcie's wedding that Livia and I first realised we had grown out of each other, perhaps owing to Randall's incredible charm. But, you know, there is one thing I never understood about Randall's wedding.'

'What was that?'

'Why wasn't Roxanne there? I mean, fancy not turning up to your own brother's wedding! Actually, I don't remember seeing any of the Selkirk family there either.

That strikes me as very odd. Why didn't Randall's parents attend the wedding of their only son? Do *you* know why?'

'No, I don't . . . but yes, it does seem strange when you think about it. Maybe we'll be able to find out when we all meet up at Brinkley House. Their wedding certainly was a memorable occasion.'

'Yes, and the whole event was even more wonderful for me because Marcie suggested I bring my riding clobber and when I got there she loaned me one of her horses for the whole visit. Marcie and I went out together several times, and I went out on my own too. I loved it there. Worcestershire is such a stunning county.'

The two friends chatted for a while, and then Trot decided that time was running out.

'Well, I'd better get off the line. I'm so pleased we're in touch again, and thanks for helping me out. I'll ring you again nearer the time.'

V

After putting the telephone down, Judith recalled the schoolgirl crush that had kept the whole sixth form agog with curiosity. In Trot's and Livia's case, of course, the term 'crush' was a misnomer, because it was clear to everyone that it was much more than *that*. Judith thought fondly of Trot who had always been a good friend: brave, honest and true; but Livia's personality had been more difficult to fathom. Although popular, and one of the brightest pupils of their year, Judith recalled how distressed she used to feel when Livia went on and on about the wonderful holidays she spent with her parents, while Judith's own parents were still working abroad. Later, after her own parents returned to England, her relationship with Livia improved. She clearly remembered the occasion when Livia came to her rescue after she had slipped on the ice outside the sports hut and twisted her ankle. As she had lain on the ice, clutching her ankle and rocking with pain, Livia had tenderly helped her up and kissed both her tear-stained cheeks before escorting her to Matron. Nobody could have been kinder.

As she strode along the lane to the wood, Judith mulled over her conversation with Trot, thinking how trivial Trot's love-affair seemed compared with the enormity of Marcie's mental breakdown. After all, who knew that in 1974 Marcie had gone stark staring mad and had to be shut away in a mental hospital? Well, she thought, at least Marcie had a loving husband and family to care for her. Her thoughts moved on to the enigma of Randall and Roxanne Selkirk, two siblings so similar and yet so totally different: Randall sociable, sexy and popular; Roxanne gauche, irritating and lacking *savoir faire*. Judith recalled Roxanne's social awkwardness and wondered if it was her inability to read people that had prevented her from making friends at Brinkley House. Surely, now that Randall had married into the Stanton-Gray family, Roxanne's social skills would have improved. With these thoughts in her mind, Judith forced herself to confront the events of Marcie's wedding at Redcliffe in 1962.

Redcliffe, in Worcestershire, had belonged to the Stanton-Gray family for many generations. The estate consisted of an imposing eighteenth-century manor with its original out-houses and stable blocks, surrounded by a great many acres of arable farmland. Judith remembered her amazement when, arriving for Marcie's wedding, she had entered Redcliffe through large stone gates, driven past an elegant lodge, crossed a large tract of parkland and around a lake before arriving at her destination.

Throughout her stay at Redcliffe for Marcie's wedding to Randall Selkirk, Judith had felt strangely out-of-kilter. She had had no idea that Marcie lived in such grandeur, and had wondered why her best friend had let her believe that she was just an ordinary person when all the time her family had been so rich and aristocratic. Judith recalled how disconcerted she had felt when she realised that Marcie was not the person she thought she was and, looking back, wondered if these unworthy feelings had had anything to do with the events that occurred later.

Marcie had looked very elegant in her white wedding dress. Her long dark hair had been swept back into a chignon, over which she had worn a simple, yet exquisite, veil that set off her long white wedding dress perfectly. Marcie, a talented sportswoman, was tall and broad-shouldered, yet the dress had been cut so expertly it had made her look slender, even willowy. As sole bridesmaid, Judith had followed Marcie and Randall down the aisle, taking care not to disarrange Marcie's train.

After the wedding ceremony the reception had been held at Redcliffe, and Judith remembered that the blonde-haired girl hired to look after them for the week was part of a large team serving food in the main dining-room. After a magnificent wedding breakfast, the bride and bridegroom had left to spend their wedding night at a nearby hotel while Marcie's parents had made a huge effort to entertain them all. Then, the following day, when Marcie and Randall returned, things became even more delightful. The happy couple had arranged to spend their honeymoon in Italy and were due to fly out in two days' time. During these two remaining days Randall had been witty, charming and attentive to all of Marcie's friends and Judith, who knew nothing about men, was flattered by the way he seemed to single her out for attention.

On the final night of their visit, cocktails were served. Everyone let their hair down and Randall was particularly amusing. Judith felt herself to be on excellent form. She was wearing her little black dress and she knew it suited her. It did not occur to her that she was flirting with the man who had married her best friend just three days earlier; she was enjoying herself far too much. Gradually, though, Judith had started to feel tired and rather fuzzy-headed, so she decided to go to bed.

She was just about to fall asleep when Randall appeared at her bedside holding a cocktail in each hand.

'What are you doing in here? Go away,' Judith said sleepily.

'I've come to tuck you in.'

'I don't need tucking in.'

'Of course you do. There is a special "tucking" ritual for very special bridesmaids, didn't you know?'

'Don't be silly.'

'Yes there is – and I'm duty-bound to carry out the "tucking" ritual, whether you want me to or not. So I've brought you a special "tucking" cocktail and you have to drink it as part of the ritual.'

'Just one drink, and then you must go. Promise?' Judith had laughed. 'Oh, all right then.'

She had sat up in bed, modestly raising her bedclothes to her neck. She had thought his remarks funny at the time but, looking back, Judith was appalled at her stupidity.

'*You silly, silly little girl*!' she scolded her younger self.

Randall had sat beside her on the bed, and while she drank the cocktail he had whispered sweet nothings into her ear. Then other things had started to happen and, looking back, Judith's memory was unclear. Had she drunk the other cocktail too? She couldn't remember.

Judith had never been kissed by a man before, but she had imagined what it might be like. When Randall started to kiss her, it was not at all how she had imagined it to be. She remembered feeling weightless and disassociated, and repeatedly saying, 'Please, *no*!' She was only vaguely aware of her bedclothes being rolled down and her nightdress being rolled up; only dimly aware of Randall's body on top of hers, his mouth on her breast, and then . . .

Judith had woken in the morning with an appalling hangover and, as she lay in bed, the shocking realisation of what she had done hit her. She forced herself to confront the truth of what had happened. She had lost her virginity to Marcie's husband just three days after being bridesmaid at their wedding! She writhed with mental and physical anguish. What on earth had she thought she was doing? Why had she allowed Randall do it? She must have sent out all the wrong signals. Somehow she must have asked for it. What if she was pregnant? The whole thing was so appalling, she didn't know what to do. How could she have betrayed her dearest friend like that?

She had got up, bathed, dressed, and packed. Then she had forced herself to join the others for breakfast, and left early with Janey and Ann, who gave her a lift to Oxford. She would not tell her secret to anyone. She returned to her little flat in Iffley and tried to forget it had ever happened.

VI

A few weeks after that fateful night, Marcie had telephoned Judith. She had sounded completely distraught. Had she, Judith, had sex with Randall? Had she? Had she? How could she, of all people, betray her like that – and after she and Randall had been married for only three days? And she was her best friend, and her bridesmaid, and a guest in her house! Randall had told her everything.

'He told me the way you threw yourself at him. He said you were all over him, flaunting yourself at him, touching him. He said you were *disgusting*.'

Judith felt the floor open up beneath her and thought she was going to faint. She gripped the corner of the kitchen dresser with her free hand as she replied:

'Marcie. It wasn't really like that at all. It was never meant to happen. What can I say, but that I'm so *very* sorry! I know you can never forgive me for what I did. I can't really understand what happened that night, but believe me that I am deeply ashamed.'

'I never ever want to see you again. Randall and I love each other, and just because you are jealous of what we have together doesn't give you the right to try to destroy our marriage. Randall and I have erased you from our lives. You no longer exist, as far as we are concerned. Do you understand that?'

'Yes, Marcie, of course I understand. I fully take the blame for what happened. You're both justified in your decision to cut me out of your lives. All I can say is sorry.'

'I'm putting the phone down.'

Marcie had rung off, leaving Judith trembling with remorse and distress. Marcie had been so good to her, and such a loyal friend over so many years, that the pain of what she had done made Judith shrink inside. She was such a bad person, she should remain single all her life for fear of contaminating some other decent man. Judith had collapsed into a chair and sobbed her heart out.

VII

In the months that followed, Judith had tried to pick herself up after the shameful events of Marcie's wedding and the subsequent loss of Marcie's friendship. It was all her fault. She could never forgive herself. She would have to bear the guilt and shame of her actions for the rest of her life.

At first she felt extremely sad and depressed: the days seemed long, and the nights interminable. After a while, however, she started to recover from this disgraceful episode in her life and a few months later she met a man who gradually became indispensable to her. Ralph was four years older than her and settled in his career as a lawyer. Although he was quite tall and she was quite short, they both had wavy brown hair and hazel eyes and were often taken for brother and sister. They both had Scottish fathers, so that two years later, when they married, Miss Judith McLeod became Mrs Judith McKenna, and life settled into a harmonious pattern.

Judith decided not to tell Ralph that she had had sex with Marcie's husband just three days after being bridesmaid at their wedding. There were some things that could not, should not, be shared. She had not pressed Ralph for information about his sex-life prior to their marriage and nor had he pressed her about hers.

A few years after their marriage they had bought a

house situated right on the edge of the Surrey countryside, yet with a reliable rail service to London. Judith, Ralph and their two children had quickly adjusted to their new home and it was only because they lived near a large Victorian mental hospital where a friend of hers worked, that Judith had found herself working two nights a week as an auxiliary Night Nurse.

On one particular night in 1974, Judith was working on Acacia Ward when Marcie Stanton-Gray went mad.

VIII

A middle-aged couple sat in an office surrounded by filing cabinets, typewriters and telephones. The woman was pleasant-looking, with red hair and a pale, freckled face, her straight back and upright deportment indicating a well-knit and coordinated physique. The man was tall and thin, with an anxious expression on his face. Sally and Don Saunders, the proud owners of the Brinkley House Hotel at Aberdovey, were going over their plans for the old girls' reunion for the umpteenth time.

'Sally, darling, are you are *quite* sure that Jack Edwards is happy to put Ralph and me up on his yacht over the weekend?'

'Yes, everything's sorted. I've ordered plenty of food and drink for you three, and arranged for Ifor to drop it off at the quay, ready to be rowed over to *Manatee*. Judith and Ralph McKenna are driving Janey Collins down with them, and the plan is that Judith drops off Ralph and picks up Ann Edwards close to where the yacht is anchored at Point A on our map of the area.' Sally stabbed her forefinger against a large map pinned on to a noticeboard.

'Yes, I understand that bit,' said Don.

'Then Judith will drive Janey and Ann over here to Brinkley House, while Jack rows you, Ralph and the food and drink, out to the yacht. Jack says there are three bunks on his yacht and that you'll all be very comfortable. Apparently *Manatee* has recently been overhauled and updated, and everything is in working order. Jack assures me that, although *Manatee*'s mooring is at Chichester, he knows Cardigan Bay like the back of his hand.'

'Good! That means that all seven of your school friends have accepted your invitation. So if nobody drops out there'll be eight of you for dinner that evening?'

'Yes, there'll be Judith, Marcie, Ann, Trot, Janey and Livia – and Roxanne Selkirk, of course. Judith has asked me not to put Trot in with Livia – apparently their lesbian affair fizzled out shortly after leaving Brinkley. Which reminds me, don't forget what we decided about giving the staff the weekend off – all apart from Annie and Ifor.

'Yes, I've told them all that, but Janet will still have to come in on the Monday to help out in the office.'

'Yes, we'll need her to take bookings for us.'

'I have to admit that I'm feeling a bit anxious', said Sally. 'It's a massive problem we have got to sort out this weekend. We must be strong and use this reunion to remove this great weight hanging over our heads, but don't forget, we're not alone. There'll be other victims who'll want to tackle this with us.'

'Yes, I know, it's just that so much could go wrong.'

'Look, Don, several of us have been affected by this issue so don't worry, I'm sure that if we all put our heads together we'll come up with a solution.'

'Yes, of course. I wonder what they'll think of the Brinkley House Hotel?'

'They'll love it,' said Sally.

CHAPTER THREE

The Brinkley House Reunion

1990

I

O N THE LAST FRIDAY of September 1990, Judith and Ralph picked up Janey Collins at a prearranged spot near London, and set off on the long journey across England and Wales to Aberdovey on the Welsh coast. While Ralph drove, the two school friends chatted happily, catching up on gossip and asking each other questions about their lives, from their careers to their hobbies. Judith already knew that Janey's mother had died a few years earlier, and that Janey was now living alone at the Collins family home at Paddington. Judith was curious to find out what she was doing with her life but, rather surprisingly, all she was able to find out about Janey's life revolved around church, charity work and the occasional tea-party. Judith started to wonder why her witty, outspoken and talented school friend had become so staid and conventional.

When they eventually arrived at Aberdovey, having made several stops on the way, Ralph parked the car at the prearranged rendezvous spot close to where Ann and Jack Edwards' yacht, *Manatee*, was lying at anchor. Judith was curious to see Ann after so many years, and was relieved to find that she was still the tall, serious-looking, bespectacled blonde she had known and liked so much at school. Then, after Judith, Janey and Ann had greeted one another with hugs and kisses, Judith introduced Ralph to Ann.

'Ann, this is my husband, Ralph,' she said proudly. 'Ralph, this is Ann.'

Ralph and Ann shook hands.

'How do you do?' Ralph spoke formally. 'I've heard that you have children of ages similar to ours?'

'Yes, though I think they are a year or two younger.'

Ralph smiled, turning to Jack.

'I gather you are kindly putting me up on your yacht over the weekend. I hope you are braced for the task! By the way, I don't think you've met Judith and Janey.'

'Hello, Judith and Janey. Yes, Ralph, you are to be my guest – but don't worry, *Manatee* is very safe and snug.'

While Ralph was introducing himself, Judith had a brief chance to study Ann's husband at close range. Jack was a stocky man, shorter than Ann, with a suntanned face, a thatch of untidy brown hair, piercing blue eyes and an engaging, slightly toothy, smile. Wearing a red *marinière*, scruffy trousers and plimsolls, Judith felt that here was a man who was completely at ease with himself. She noticed that Ann and Jack often smiled at each other, reinforcing the feeling of joy that exuded from them both.

Jack turned to a tall, thin, shy-looking man with dark hair standing slightly outside the circle of friends.

'Hello, you must be Don Saunders. I gather that you're the owner of Brinkley House.' Don nodded. 'Ah, I thought so! I'm Jack and this is Ralph. Can I speak for us all and say thank you for putting on this get-together.'

Don, whose downcast eyes held all the discomfort of the true introvert, smiled shyly.

'Thanks.'

Ralph introduced himself.

'I'm Ralph, Judith's husband. I'm afraid I'm a landlubber of the worst variety, so you and Jack will have to look after me tonight.'

'And me too,' said Don. 'I've never been on a yacht before, let alone slept on one.'

'Don't worry, you two, I'll look after you.'

Don smiled anxiously at Jack and Ralph, but a few minutes later he found himself striding along to the Dyfi Arms, comfortably wedged between his new friends. He was starting to enjoy himself. The plan was to have a drink or two before Jack rowed them (and their dinner) over to *Manatee*. The three men were to rejoin their wives at the hotel after breakfast the following day.

II

It was nearly dark when Judith turned her car off the coast road and headed up the winding lane she knew so well. Janey and Ann, who had been talking non-stop, were suddenly silenced when a large sign saying BRINKLEY HOUSE HOTEL AND CONFERENCE CENTRE loomed up in front of them.

'Heavens, look at *that*!' Ann exclaimed.

It was incredible to think that this imposing building had ever been the shabby place where they had spent the larger part of their childhoods. Today, in the fading afternoon light, the Brinkley House Hotel stood out majestically against the darkening hillside, the whole building epitomising good taste, elegance and style. Judith, Janey and Ann were amazed by what they were seeing.

Judith drove up to the main entrance and stopped to drop off Janey and Ann, who quickly disappeared from view when two vast automatic doors opened, sesame-wise, and closed behind them. Judith drove on around to the back of the hotel and parked her car.

As Judith was walking back towards the hotel, another car drove into the car park. A tall woman with short dark-brown hair got out on the driver's side and walked around to the passenger door to help an old woman out of her seat. After being handed two walking sticks, the disabled passenger struggled to get out of the car. Then, agonisingly slowly, the two women made their way towards where Judith was standing and, as they approached, Judith started to recognise the tall woman as Roxanne Selkirk. Roxanne called to out her.

'Judith! How lovely to see you. Have you travelled down on your own? Where are the others?'

'*Roxanne*, how are you? Janey and Ann are here already, I dropped them off with our stuff. Would you like me to help you with your suitcases?'

'No, I can manage, thanks,' Roxanne replied.

Judith looked at the invalid with the sticks.

Who could she be? she wondered. *Oh my God, oh my God! It couldn't be Marcie, could it?* Judith tried not to show the shock-horror she felt.

'Hello, Judith.'

'Hello, Marcie. I'm afraid it's a bit of a hike round to the front.'

'I'll be fine in a minute. I get a bit stiff when I've been sitting for a while. If you could take one of my sticks, Judith? Thanks. I think I'll manage better if you let me hang on to your arm.'

'Of course.' Judith suddenly felt afraid she was going to burst into tears. *Oh my dear Marcie*, she thought, *what on earth has happened to you?*

Marcie took her arm and the three of them slowly made their way round to the main entrance. As they walked along, Roxanne's banter about Sally's brilliant conversion-job saved Judith from having to talk to Marcie. Instead she thought: *Dear God, she's only forty-six*. Yet, despite everything, Judith felt happy to be close to Marcie again.

Soon they were inside the unrecognisable, yet strangely familiar, hotel reception area, where Sally stood waiting to greet them. There was a lot of noise and excitement as Marcie, Judith, Ann, Janey, Roxanne and Sally met each other again after so many years. Soon they were being served tea in what had once been the Senior Common Room but was now a luxurious hotel drawing-room, and everyone was talking at once when Sally entered the room with Trot.

Sally made an announcement.

'I've just had a call from Livia. She is going to be late. She says she's sorry.'

The rest of the group responded to this news with remarks such as *'Typical!'*, *'Wouldn't you know!'*, and *'What a nuisance!'*

After the general excitement had died down slightly, Trot spoke for the rest of the group when she asked Sally if they could have a look around the hotel.

'Would you mind if we explored a bit, if we promise not to break anything?' Trot asked.

'Of course I wouldn't. In fact I'll come with you,' said Sally. 'I can explain everything as we go along.'

'Will you be all right, Marcie? Would you like me to

stay with you?' asked Roxanne.

'Judith's here. I'll be fine!' Marcie replied graciously.

So, with much squawking and giggling, Sally, Trot, Janey, Ann and Roxanne went off to look around the hotel.

Judith heard Janey's clear voice announce to the group: 'This was the gym where we used to practise our skipping, remember?'

'*Knickers!*' someone exclaimed. There was a coarse guffaw.

Marcie and Judith were left alone together.

III

Sitting side by side on the sofa, Judith and Marcie sat in silence for a short, awkward moment.

'I fell off my horse and it rolled on top of me,' Marcie explained.

'Are you going to be like this permanently?'

'Apparently not. I've just got to take things easy for a while to let my body recover. I was luckier than my horse, Crichton. He had to be shot.'

'Poor horse! But thank goodness you are going to recover fully in due course.'

'Yes, and I have to say to you in particular, Judith, how pleased I am to be here. I've missed our friendship so much. I gather you're married to a lawyer called Ralph McKenna and that you have two grown-up children.'

'Yes, but I've never forgiven myself for what I did to you all those years ago. I've never mentioned what happened to anyone, but I still bear the burden of it, the guilt, all the time. I'll never be able to erase that stain on my character. *Never.*'

'If I had known then what I know now I would never have reacted the way I did. Poor Judith! Look, now that so much water has passed under the bridge, why don't you tell me exactly what happened.'

'What? You want me to tell you about that night?'

'Yes. As the whole thing seems so out of character – especially for a respectable little person like you!'

'I'll give you a brief summary if you want me to, but if the others come back I'll stop. Nobody but you must know what happened.'

'All right.'

'Well, that last evening we drank cocktails for the first time. We were eighteen then, and I doubt if any of us had ever had a cocktail before. We all flirted with Randall who was very attentive, and I remember feeling . . . *special* – if that's the right expression. After a while I started to feel tight so I went to bed. When I was nearly asleep, Randall appeared beside my bed with a cocktail in each hand and I told him to go away, but he didn't go. He said he would only go if I drank one of the two cocktails he had brought with him. I do remember drinking one of the cocktails. Actually, I may have drunk both of them. Randall was so charming and persuasive. Then he started to pull down my bedclothes. I asked him not to, and remember repeating *"Please, no"*. By then he was having sex with me and, to be honest, I can't really remember anything about it. I woke in the morning with an appalling hangover! But I *knew* what had happened. I bathed, packed and left Redcliffe after breakfast. That's it!'

'Thank you for telling me. It is just as I thought. In my heart I knew the whole beastly business was totally out of character for a moral person like you. So let me put you straight right away. Here are the facts. Randall entered your bedroom without being invited. You told him to leave, but he didn't. He knew that you had already imbibed more than you should have, and yet he brought two more cocktails with him and encouraged you to drink them. He waited until the alcohol took effect, and had sex with you even after you made it clear you didn't want him to. So, my dear Judith, all these years you've taken the blame for something that wasn't your fault. You are innocent of what happened that night. *You were raped*! At the time I didn't understand, but I soon found out that you were the first in a long succession of Randall's conquests. It pleased him to rape my best friend and it pleased him to lie about it and destroy our friendship. He is a dreadful man and was a lousy, *lousy* husband. He wrecked my whole life.'

As Judith listened to Marcie's words she tried to reply, but words failed her. For so long she had kept her guilty secret, and now, at last, she was free. Her eyes filled with tears and she felt an enormous surge of relief now that she was able to piece together facts that had previously eluded her. She realised that if Randall had purposely set about seducing Marcie's friends, then Randall was indeed a dreadful man. Marcie must have felt so isolated and betrayed: no wonder she had had a mental breakdown.

'Thank you, Marcie. Yes, I see it now. Are you and Randall still together?'

'No, I divorced him in 1972, but you know, Judith, what he did to you and me in 1962 was just the tip of the iceberg. You'll find out more about him over the weekend. You see, he did things that drove me stark staring mad. Literally! Eventually, after my mother died, I had a total breakdown while I was staying with my cousins in Surrey, and they were obliged to put me into a psychiatric hospital near where they lived. After spending several weeks there

I was allowed to leave, but I've had to have years of therapy since then.'

'Randall is a psychopath, isn't he?'

'Yes. He destroys everything and everybody who has the misfortune to cross his path. But you know, Judith, it's so strange to be talking to you again because I had a really strange experience that first night I was incarcerated in that awful mental hospital. I really was completely out of my mind and while in this state I had a terrible nightmare. I was running, running to save my life, but I couldn't escape this evil person pursuing me. As I ran I could hear his footsteps gaining on me, and just as I was about to be caught and killed, I had an amazing vision! *You* appeared in front of me wearing robes of blue and white and illuminated by a shaft of golden light that shone all around you. Then the footsteps stopped and I felt safe. It was so strange. I've never had that hallucination again . . . but don't you think that was weird?'

Judith quickly decided not to tell Marcie that it really had been her that night at the mental hospital – at least, she decided not to tell her right now.

'It sounds as if you've been to hell and back again. What a terrible experience. But now what we have to remember is that we are friends again, and things *will* get better. But you know, you said something just now that I don't understand.'

'What was that?'

'You said that I'd find out more about Randall over the weekend.'

'Yes. Sally, Don and I have an ulterior motive for inviting everyone here. Basically we have decided that it is in all our best interests that we try to understand what makes Randall tick and the sort of crimes he commits. If we can join forces and decide on a course of action as a group, we hope to be better placed to cope with his unwanted attentions in the future. All eight of us here this weekend know Randall to some extent, though obviously Roxanne and I know him best. If we pool our experiences and agree on a communication network we should be better placed to deal with him, especially those of us who have been, and still are, his victims.'

'Will I have to tell everyone about what happened after your wedding?'

'Of course not, it's not an inquisition! I think Sally plans to explain exactly why she has invited us here after Livia arrives. Perhaps after dinner.'

'What about our husbands? I gather they won't be joining us today.'

'No, it's just the eight of us today, the men will be joining us tomorrow and Sunday.'

'Why are they joining us?'

'To crack this particular nut, we all need to contribute our ideas and experience. We are a pretty impressive bunch when you think about it. We have Sally and Don who own and run this hotel, but before that Don was a highly successful Chartered Accountant working for a large City firm. Then we have you, an experienced history teacher, and Ralph, a top-ranking Family Lawyer. Ann is a qualified doctor and specialist in Child Psychology and Jack owns and directs a large furniture business. Trot breeds racehorses and her stud farm is fast making a name for itself. Roxanne has a PhD in Agriculture and has helped me enormously now that I am running Redcliffe on my own. As for Livia, she is a Director of a well-known City bank and doing very well indeed. So the eleven of us have quite a lot of different experiences to contribute to the

"What to do about Randall?" issue.'

'What about Janey? You didn't mention her.'

'Oh, yes, well, that's a mystery. Nobody knows what she does. Isn't it ridiculous! Do *you* know?'

'No, she's very involved in church matters, I know *that*. Her mother is dead, so maybe she doesn't need to work.'

Now that Judith understood that this was going to be an old girls' reunion *with a difference*, she was curious to find out about some of the things Randall had done to other members of the group, especially to Sally and Don. She would have to wait for answers but, as she sat next to Marcie in the elegant drawing-room that had once been their dusty old Common Room, she felt supremely happy.

A growing swell of chatter reached her ears. The door swung open as the rest of the group returned from their guided tour of the hotel. They were full of praise for Sally's brilliance in turning their crumbling old school into a modern, yet charming, hotel. With smiles on their faces, Judith and Marcie sat on the sofa and listened to their friends' excited comments. Then they all went up to their rooms to unpack.

IV

Sally had given Marcie and Judith adjacent double rooms on the third floor while Roxanne had been given a single room on the second floor. Roxanne was concerned about Marcie.

'Are you going to be able to manage on your own?'

'Don't worry, I'm sure Judith will help me if I get stuck,' Marcie replied.

'Of course,' said Judith, 'but if I can't, can I ask you

for help, Roxanne? Look, why don't you come up with us so you know where we are.'

'Certainly.' Roxanne smiled at Judith. 'I can help with the unpacking.'

'Yes. Good idea.'

Roxanne helped Marcie into the lift, and the three friends went up together. With Roxanne's help, Judith and Marcie quickly found their airy and modern en-suite bedrooms overlooking the front of the hotel with views out towards the shoreline and sea beyond. It was hard to believe that these spacious rooms had once been their stuffy, damp and overcrowded dormitories. After Roxanne and Judith had unpacked Marcie's suitcase, and Roxanne had left to change for dinner, Judith went to her room, quickly washed, and put on her favourite dark-green dress ready for the special dinner that Sally had organised for them all. She then knocked on Marcie's door to see if she needed any help. Marcie was relieved to see her. She had managed well, but was stuck trying to get her trouser-suit on; her left knee simply would not bend enough for her to put her foot into the trousers. With Judith's help the problem was quickly resolved and soon they were able to join the rest of the group in the drawing-room where champagne was being served.

The drawing-room buzzed with excitement and a large open fire added to the general feeling of comfort and conviviality as the school friends caught up with each other's lives. Judith glanced out over the front drive, which seemed strangely unchanged even after all this time, and felt unexpectedly happy to be back at Brinkley House. After about an hour the old school gong announced dinner and they strolled through to the dining-room. As they sat down to eat, Sally announced that Livia had just arrived and would soon be joining them. True to her word, Olivia Bard came straight in and greeted them all.

'Hello, everyone! Sorry I'm late. I'm afraid I couldn't get away on time and the traffic has been grim. Where am I sitting? Between Ann and Janey? Fantastic! Ah, there you are, my naughty children.' Livia quickly crossed over to where Ann and Janey were sitting, and sat down to a crescendo of noisy greetings and applause.

Seated diagonally opposite Livia, Judith was able to scrutinise her at close quarters. At first she thought that she had not changed since she had last seen her at Marcie's wedding; her dark, shoulder-length hair and well-cut light-blue suit gave an impression of youthful confidence. And yet, upon closer scrutiny, Livia's face did not live up to this positive assessment. Watching Livia as she chatted to Ann, Judith noticed that despite eyeliner, rouge and lipstick, she looked tired, even haggard, but considering that Livia had a very demanding job in the City and had been delayed from leaving London on time, this was only to be expected. The Welsh coast was a very long way from London, especially when driving alone and in failing light.

Judith wasn't able to examine Livia for long because Roxanne, who was sitting next to her, wanted to know everything about her life: her family, her teaching career, her children's education, Ralph's career and family background . . . After Roxanne had found out everything she wanted to know about Judith's family, she leaned forward to tell Judith all about her career in agriculture, stressing the importance of agronomy and organic farming. Roxanne talked with her mouth full, occasionally spraying spittle on Judith's pristine dress and Judith, who was nothing if not fastidious, desperately wanted to dab at her dress with her napkin but courtesy disallowed this action.

The bony face that swam so close to hers was handsome in a way, the eyes a striking shade of dark violet, and yet Judith found herself wondering how Marcie really felt about having the sister of her ex-husband, the man who had ruined her life, as her friend. Despite her concerns, Judith respected Roxanne's academic accomplishments and even felt rather sorry for her. After all, who'd want Randall for a brother?

Dinner was excellent, and afterwards, as the group drank their coffee, Sally stood up and announced that she wanted to make a speech. Predictably, this was greeted with a few unladylike comments, and shouts of '*Speech, speech!*'

'I'm so glad you've all been able to come,' said Sally. 'I hope you are comfortable in your rooms, but don't hesitate to tell me if you're not. I feel so relieved to learn that you seem to like what Don and I have done to Brinkley House and, before I forget to say it, do please use the gym and swimming pool if you want to. You can go anywhere you like – you're not at school now, so you won't get a detention. Incidentally, you probably already know that Ann's husband, Jack, has sailed his yacht over here and anchored it further down the coast. Judith's husband Ralph, and my husband Don, are both staying on the boat overnight with Jack, but they are all coming to join us tomorrow morning. So now I'm going to ask Roxanne to draw your attention to a more personal reason for my asking you all to join Don and me for this reunion. Roxanne?'

There was much applause as Roxanne stood up to speak. Judith pushed her chair away from Roxanne's to give herself a bit more room.

Roxanne spoke.

'We are all very grateful to you, Sally, for organising

this reunion, but there is an ulterior motive for holding it which some of us already appreciate. Certainly Sally and Don, Marcie and I know that we've reached a point where something has to be done about a potentially dangerous situation that has dogged our lives for years and now seems to be getting worse. It is even possible that others of you at this reunion know what we are talking about. Anyhow, Sally has brought us all here so that we can put our heads together to try to solve a problem that has been upsetting us for so long, and this is it: what can we do to protect ourselves from my psychopathic brother, Randall?

'As Randall's sister, I feel particularly worried by his behaviour, and feel that, in order to protect ourselves, we all need to understand what we're up against. As we all know, Ann is not only a doctor, she is also a qualified psychologist, and so we've asked her to kick off tomorrow's discussion with a brief summary of the main characteristics of Randall's psychopathy and how these manifest themselves in real-life situations. To illustrate this point, Marcie and Sally have prepared short accounts of what he has done, and is still doing, to make their lives unbearable. If, during this part of the meeting, others feel they would like to add their own experiences to our prepared statements, or provide further evidence, that would be greatly appreciated. On Sunday, the aim is to tackle the issue of what to do about Randall and to discuss ways we can protect ourselves. And finally I should say that just in case he has followed us here, please don't wander about on your own. Thank you.'

For a second or two there was silence. Then, as Roxanne resumed her seat, there was a short, awkward burst of applause, followed by another silence. The group seemed lost for words. The first person to speak was Trot.

'I can understand why those connected to Randall might want to discuss ways of dealing with him, but why have those of us *not* involved with Randall been invited here? Marcie, what do *you* think?'

'Sadly,' Marcie replied, 'it is becoming ever more evident that everyone who attended my wedding in 1962 is a potential victim. To be forewarned is to be forearmed.'

Judith listened with a certain amount of discomfort, knowing that she too had been one of Randall Selkirk's victims and she wondered what Ralph would make of the whole weekend. After all, hadn't they been invited to Brinkley House under false pretences? She felt she ought to say something, and was relieved to see that Trot had her hand up again.

'I'm sorry to go on about this,' Trot said, 'but there are things I still don't understand. I thought that I had been invited to an old girls' reunion, but now find myself taking part in some kind of tribunal against a man I met decades ago and hardly remember. Of course I feel sorry for Marcie, but shouldn't we have been told the real reason for the reunion in advance, to give us the option of declining the invitation? Also, if Randall has committed crimes against some of us, who is going to represent *his* point of view? Who is going to stand up for Randall's interests in all this? Or is this merely a witch-hunt?'

Trot sat down to cries of '*Hear, hear!*' Then Sally stood up.

'I'm sorry if any of you feel you've been deceived, but truly I haven't lied to you. You are my oldest and dearest friends which is why I've invited you here as my personal guests for this reunion. All I'm asking is that we put our heads together during the short time we are together to see if there are any ways we can protect ourselves from

Randall's evil influence: and I don't use the word "evil" lightly. This is not a tribunal, and Randall is not being accused of anything. We already know what he's done to us. All we are asking you to do is to try to help us to think up ways to protect ourselves and our loved ones now and in the future. Don and I feel so frightened and vulnerable on our own. We hope and pray that the wide range of skills and experience we represent as a group will help us to find a solution to our problem.'

There was a brief hush, followed by applause.

Then, with great difficulty, Marcie stood up again, leaning against the table. Her voice was calm, almost matter-of-fact:

'As you can see, I'm a bit of a wreck. This is because a short while ago somebody tried to kill me. There were no witnesses to the crime, but there is little doubt in my mind that it was my ex-husband, Randall, who shot my horse from under me. I'll go into more detail when we meet tomorrow, but clearly something has to be done to protect not only his victims of this generation, but also his potential victims of the next. Please, Trot – please, all of you – please support us.'

'Of course we support you – don't we, everyone?' Roxanne looked around the table aggressively, and there was a unanimous cry of '*Yes, yes!*'

Trot stood up again.

'First of all, thank you, Sally, for laying on this reunion. Now that I understand the situation better, I'll certainly do what I can to help.' Again, there were shouts of '*Hear, hear!*'

Trot sat down to a buzz of chatter and relieved laughter during which Sally turned to speak to Janey.

'Janey, I'm sure you have specific attributes that will help us with the Randall problem. I feel remiss for not knowing this, but what do you *do?*'

'Who, me? What do *I* do? Nothing much really, I'm afraid. After I left Brinkley House I took several courses and did a bit of amateur dramatics, but a lot of the time I looked after my mother. Sorry!'

Sally was disappointed, but quickly regained her optimism. Tomorrow the three husbands would be joining their group, bringing their own unique insights and experiences to bear on the 'What to do about Randall Selkirk' issue, and after that things were bound to get better.

V

It was dark now. On board *Manatee* the three husbands were drinking brandy. They had already been to the Dyfi Arms for a drink, and then consumed several glasses of an excellent red wine to accompany a delicious dinner provided for them by the Brinkley House Hotel. Now they were snugly ensconced on chairs that would soon fold out to become their bunks. Everything had been cleared up and made ship-shape, and although Jack and Ralph had never met before, the rapport between them had been immediate. At first Don felt worried about fitting in, but these anxieties were quickly dispelled by the genuine friendliness of his new acquaintances. By the time they had finished their dinner and started on the brandy, Don knew himself to be an equally valued member of the trio.

'Now *that* was a superb meal, Don. The best I've had in ages.' Ralph, somewhat inebriated, waved his brandy glass in the air.

'Yes, we're lucky to have Annie and her husband, Ifor. They are a remarkable couple – she is a superb cook and he is a competent caretaker. In fact, Ifor will be collecting us from the quay and driving us up to the hotel after breakfast tomorrow morning, so you'll meet him then.'

'Mmmm! I'm looking forward to more of Annie's excellent cooking.'

'This brandy is pretty good too,' said Jack. 'With the calm weather predicted for tonight we should sleep very well. I'm looking forward to meeting Sally and the rest of the Brinkley House group tomorrow. Mind you, apart from our wives and Janey, I don't know anyone. What are they like?'

'A formidable lot, no doubt,' said Ralph.

' I met Judith, Janey and Ann earlier, but I don't really know them yet.' There was anxiety in Don's voice.

'Don't worry, Don,' said Ralph. 'We'll look after you. We'll be like the Three Musketeers – all for one, and one for all! Or, as I'm a Scot – we'll be clansmen, *och aye*! Actually, I think I've probably had enough brandy for one night. Perhaps it's time for bed, don't you think?'

Twenty minutes later, the three men were sound asleep.

CHAPTER FOUR

Randall

I

ON SATURDAY MORNING, at 10.15 precisely, the hotel caretaker Ifor Thompson picked up Jack, Ralph and Don at the quay and drove them over to the Brinkley House Hotel. Once there, they were greeted by Sally, who lovingly kissed Don and introduced herself to Ralph and Jack. Then she ushered all three men through to the drawing-room, where coffee and biscuits had been set out for them. Soon Ralph, Jack and Don were joined by Judith and Ann, and a few minutes after that, Janey joined the group. Then, while Janey was talking to the men, Trot and Livia came in. Then Marcie arrived, assisted by Roxanne, and soon all eleven of them were happily laughing and chatting to one another as a single, cohesive group.

After a while Judith and Ann took Ralph and Jack aside to try to explain to them the serious threat posed by Marcie's husband, Randall. Although Jack knew that there was a problem with Randall, neither he nor Ralph had ever met him. For this reason, Ann and Judith took this opportunity to explain how Marcie and several other guests at her wedding had had their lives blighted by him.

'Marcie stayed married to him for ten nightmarish years during which she completely lost her health,' said Judith. 'Not long ago Randall tried to shoot her, and the worrying fact is that he is still very much at large. He could even be here at Brinkley House right now, for all we know.'

The two men needed little persuading. They both agreed that something had to be done. Each couple had children and, potentially, grandchildren to protect, and they certainly didn't want this man going anywhere near their families. Ann then explained that she was shortly going to open the discussion with a brief summary of Randall's psychopathology. The group was to reassemble in the smallest of the hotel's three Conference Rooms in ten minutes.

II

The eight school friends and the three husbands seated themselves around the table set out for them in the Conference Room.

'Just like King Arthur and the Round Table,' whispered Janey.

'Except that this table isn't round!' quipped Trot.

Pushing her blonde hair behind her ears and readjusting her glasses, Ann stood up to speak.

'Sally and Marcie have asked me to speak first because, although I specialise in Child Psychology, I am also a qualified doctor. So, bearing Randall Selkirk in mind, here are the main facts.'

'Most psychopathic behaviour starts early in life. Lying, stealing, and misdemeanours of various kinds usually lead to exclusion or expulsion from school. Later, as psychopaths approach adulthood, a history of antisocial behaviour, deceitfulness, poor relationships at home, and lack of sustained effort at work form a pattern characterised by the projection of an unrealistic self-image. Some psychopaths lie merely to get praise and adulation, others lie, cheat and steal for material gain and power. Some psychopaths, like Randall Selkirk, lie to get praise and admiration and to manipulate and defraud other people.

'Randall is highly successful at targeting people he can manipulate into giving him what he wants, and what he wants is wealth, high social status, and power. After meeting Marcie, and in order to attain these three objectives, Randall used his charm, intelligence and charisma to insert himself into the Stanton-Gray family and, like a parasite entering the body of its host, once he had established himself within Marcie's family unit, he was able to start destroying it from the inside.

'When psychopaths reach a point where their hosts cease to satisfy their needs, there is no knowing what they will do or how far they will go. In a minute Roxanne, Marcie, Don and Sally will describe some of the ways Randall tried to wreck their lives, but first here is a very short "check-list" of the personality traits that seem most applicable to Randall: early behavioural problems; pathological lying; lack of empathy; a parasitic lifestyle; and, relationships usually short-lived and destructive.'

Ann paused for a moment, and looked around the table.

'So, Roxanne, in your view, how does Randall's behaviour tally with this list?' Ann sat down as Roxanne got to her feet and scanned the notes she had made.

'Thank you, Ann. Yes, Randall exhibits all the

characteristics you mention. He is definitely a pathological liar who finds it easy to charm his way out of trouble – or into it. And . . . yes, he is very, very manipulative. He doesn't care whom he upsets as long as he gets his own way, and yes, he targets people he instinctively knows he can put pressure on to give him the things he wants. As his little sister? Yes, he was an awful big brother. He upset me so much I had to be sent away to live with my grandparents when I was four and later to board at Brinkley House, where, as you know, I was bullied – at least, to start with. Randall was home-taught because of his antisocial behaviour, and on the rare occasions we were together he was horrible to me. Apart from breaking my toys and teasing me, Randall made me steal and lie for him, and although I was bigger than him when we were children, I was always afraid that if I didn't obey him he would do something horrible to me. Once he made a harness out of rope and hauled me up a large tree in our garden. Then he left me dangling for what seemed like ages. It was some time before my mother heard my screams, and even longer before she managed to find him and get him to lower me down. So yes, Ann, your summary of his behaviour is, unfortunately, spot-on. Thank you.'

Roxanne sat down to gentle applause.

The next person to stand up was Marcie, but it was so difficult for her to stand, everyone told her to sit down again. Roxanne helped her back into her seat, and poured her a glass of water from the jug on the table.

'Thank you,' said Marcie. 'As you can see, I'm in bad shape, but this is temporary, I'm told. As I mentioned earlier, a few months ago while I was exercising my horse, he was shot; and as he died he rolled over on top of me, pinning me down. It was a long time before I was found.

When it happened, I tried to see who had attacked me but my view was obstructed. The police just assumed it was an accident – some poacher firing off his gun, but there is no doubt in my mind that it was Randall who shot Crichton. In answer to the question *why* all these years after our divorce, the answer has to be that despite umpteen restraining orders, Randall has continually turned up on my doorstep to threaten and harass me. In 1976 he was found actually living in one of my out-houses. He had literally done the place up with a fitted kitchen, bathroom, bedroom and sitting-room – the lot. The police had great difficulty removing him and I had to pay a lawyer to fight his contention that he had a legal right to remain on my property. Apart from these and countless other offences, Randall has sent me a great many abusive letters, made telephone calls and demands for money. As for the shooting incident, it happened just after I'd won a couple of prizes at a local horse-show and received local media attention, so yes, I think envy may have played a part in that particular attack.'

Marcie paused for a moment, but calmly went on.

'The death of my beloved horse and all the other dreadful incidents that have punctuated the eighteen years since my divorce, pale into insignificance when compared with the damage Randall did to me, my parents and my friends during the ten years following our marriage in 1962. So please excuse me if I rattle on through the worst bits of my marriage as quickly as possible. Some of them are too painful to dwell upon.'

Marcie looked up and smiled bravely as the group sat there in stunned silence.

Judith felt her heart pounding as she took in the horror of what Marcie was telling them, and looked at Ralph with raised eyebrows. Unconsciously their hands met. Judith had told Ralph about Marcie's mental breakdown at the time, but it was hard to equate this calm woman with the lunatic of Acacia Ward.

'Everything is always easier with hindsight,' Marcie continued. 'When I married Randall I thought he loved me, but I was wrong. It took me an unconscionably long time to realise that what he really loved was my house and the profitable farmland surrounding it, not to mention my possessions, my family name listed in *Burke's Peerage*, and, of course, the fact that, as an only child, everything my parents owned would eventually pass to me. Even then, despite being so young and naïve, I wondered what a handsome and charming man like Randall saw in a big "jolly-hockey-sticks" girl like me . . . but love is blind and I was madly in love with him. My mother was suspicious of his motives right from the start but, I'm sorry to say, I ignored her warnings. Now I'm older and wiser, having learned the hard way what happens to a girl when she marries a psychopath.

'He was unfaithful to me almost from the moment we were married and to begin with I believed him when he told me that several of my closest friends had thrown themselves at him – "and what was a man to do?" I was so ignorant and stupid in those days . . . I accused my friends of seducing *him* –' Marcie shot a glance at Judith – 'and subsequently lost their friendship. It took me a while to realise that, in actual fact, the opposite was true: he had even raped some of my closest friends, who were too shocked and ashamed to tell anybody what had happened. Over time I became more and more paranoid and isolated, unable to trust anyone or make sense of my life. I wanted to escape and run away, but as Redcliffe was my whole world, I had nowhere to go.

'When I first married Randall, I felt so blessed, but all too soon I realised that Redcliffe was what he wanted, not me. Once he had squandered my money and stolen my possessions, I was now surplus to requirements. Before our wedding he had been so attentive and charming, but now that I'd swallowed his lies hook, line and sinker, he felt free to reveal his true self – his cruelty, his lying, his unfaithfulness, his dishonesty, his abusiveness, his thieving, his idleness – knowing that he was safely installed and there was nothing I could do about it.

'Gradually I even lost faith in my father, who had always been my hero, because he took Randall's side against me. He thought that Randall was wonderful, the son he had always wanted, and so he fired his loyal estate manager of many years' standing and allowed Randall to take control of Redcliffe. By the time my father realised his error, it was too late, and it didn't take long for Randall to reduce both my family and the estate to near-bankruptcy. In addition, though we only realised this after the event, he made off with a large number of my family's possessions – small items of furniture, china, paintings, glassware, and even antique farming equipment – before pocketing as much cash as he could and flying off to pastures new. Oh, and before he left, he burned down the guest annexe and shovelled manure into our swimming pool. He also verbally abused, threatened and *terrified* my parents, who were rather courteous, old-fashioned people. Aptly, this morning I found this torn remnant of a note in the pocket of my macintosh. It typifies the kind of stuff he was sending me all the time . . .'.

Marcie unfolded a crumpled slip of paper.

> *. . . you are such a stupid woman. I could have done everything if you and your pathetic father hadn't blocked me at every turn. You can't organise anything, any of you, and now you blame me just because you are so lacking in vision. As for you, all you are good for is clumping around on that damned lump of horse-meat, showing off when you should have been supporting my agenda for Redcliffe . . .*

'After my father realised that his own personal lack of judgement had brought us to our knees, he tried to repair the damage, but by then he was exhausted. He lost his health and died in 1974. Then, just four weeks later, my mother died too, and I fell to pieces. After my mother's funeral I went to stay with my cousins in Surrey and while I was there I had a major breakdown and had to be hospitalised. Since then I've been struggling to come to terms with what happened to my family, but this has been hard because Randall has continued to harass and torment me. At night I'm alone at Redcliffe and, although the house is fully alarmed, I am often too afraid to sleep. Since my divorce and the death of my parents I have been working hard – with Roxanne's help – to try to build up Redcliffe to its former state, but the going is very hard. My father let down a lot of people who depended upon him, so now I am trying to help them get back on their feet. There have been several sightings of Randall on the estate and in the village and each time the police have been informed. Yet the shooting of my horse shows just how vulnerable we all are. That's all I have to say, you'll be glad to know.'

There was a stunned silence, then broken applause. In

semi-silence they all filed out of the Conference Room to a side-room where tea and coffee were being served. Gradually they resumed their normal behaviour, but each of them had been deeply shocked by Marcie's story. As they looked at her limping out of the room on Judith's arm, it was as if they were seeing her properly for the first time. She was smiling bravely, but looked utterly exhausted.

Jack brought his tea over to join Ralph: 'There are some people who don't deserve to live, don't you think? That man should be put down like a rabid dog.'

'Dear God, poor Marcie!' Ralph said in reply. 'What an appalling thing to happen to such a decent and honourable person. She was such a good friend to Judith and I know she took her under her wing when they were small. I'd certainly like to meet that awful man face to face in a proper court of law. The trouble with psychopaths is that they can lie so convincingly even lawyers can't always see through them.'

Shaking and close to tears, Trot strode up to Livia, who was drinking coffee on her own.

'How could that vile person shoot a harmless animal? How could he kill Marcie's beloved horse? Crichton never did him any harm. *Randall* is the one who should be shot. That monster took away that beautiful creature's life just to upset Marcie. What a horrible, *horrible* man. God, how I hate him. How could Marcie have had anything to do with a creep like that? Poor Marcie!'

'You are *so* right, my tender-hearted friend,' said Livia. 'Anyone who kills a defenceless animal just to make a point is a total monster. Marcie fell for his sex-appeal and is now paying for it, poor thing.'

'I'm sorry. It's just that it's all so tragic. Poor Marcie – and poor Crichton! Look, I think we'd better go back now.

Who's talking next?'

Trot and Livia walked back to the Conference Room and sat together.

III

Don and Sally Saunders stood side by side next to the oval table, but slightly set back to save everyone from getting stiff necks from looking up at them at close quarters. Sally started without preamble.

'Don has asked me to do the talking, which I'm happy to do. Some people aren't cut out for public speaking and Don is one of them. I want to start by saying that we have two daughters. Esther, our older daughter, is in her final year at London University, and Cathie has just started her training at Barts. They share a flat with some other girls in South London and recently Esther saw a man skulking around in the entrance hall of their block. She thought it was Randall, but he skipped out so quickly she couldn't be sure. I thought I'd just drop that one in as a starter.

'In 1962, when I first met Randall at Marcie's wedding, I found him quite amusing, but that's all. I've known Don since childhood and, in 1966, we got married and Esther and Cathie arrived a few years later. At that time Don was working for a well-known City firm. He had been promoted several times and was progressing very well indeed. Anyhow, in 1977, Don bumped into a man who said he knew me. His name was Randall and he said that, like Don, he worked as an accountant for a well-respected and profitable City company. Randall wined and dined Don, introducing him to a select group of his business colleagues and because Randall was married to my illustrious school friend Marcia Stanton-Gray, Don trusted him implicitly. Don and Randall became friends, and now and then Randall would pop over to Don's office to pick him up for lunch or to discuss business. They telephoned and wrote notes to each other on a regular basis.

'Well, a few months after their first meeting, Don lost his job. Apparently his signature had been found on cheques transferring money to a false account. A professional document examiner stated there were indications that the signatures on the cheques could be Don's, and even though this conclusion was weak – since only copies were available for examination – suspicion fell on Don because the cheques came from a chequebook for which he was responsible. The case was never taken to court, but a short while later an excuse was found to have Don replaced and, subsequently, Don found himself unable to get a similar position in the City. While all this was going on, Randall stood by Don, who felt blessed to have such a loyal friend.

'While Don was trying to find a new job, I sold our house and rented a flat so that we could keep our daughters in their schools. Time went by, but still Don hadn't been able to get another accountancy job and so I started to work full-time as a secretary. It was a difficult period, but we managed to keep our heads above water. Randall kept in touch and, just as we were getting back into our stride, he came up with news of a "fail-safe" investment plan. Apparently Don and I could make up some of the money we had lost by investing in a kind of company scheme from which, he said, he had recently made a killing. Because of the recent circumstances, Randall had explained, it might be better if Don didn't use his own name, but not to worry – he'd look after everything and it was a sure winner. So, as we were both thrilled to find we were expecting a baby, we went to my parents and borrowed a lump sum which Randall invested on our behalf. Randall took it and we never saw the money again.

'By the time we realised that Randall had stolen a large amount of money from our family, it was too late. We tried to find him, but the company that Randall told Don he worked for had never heard of him. So I telephoned Marcie and, when she told me the truth about Randall, I was appalled. I asked her where we could find him. She said she didn't know. Marcie had sold her London house, so he wouldn't be there. Then Marcie suggested that, as Roxanne was working in Wales at the time, Randall might be holed up in her flat in North London.'

Sally looked at Roxanne, and smiled.

'So, having failed to get an answer to my telephone calls, I went to Roxanne's flat and climbed the long flight of stone stairs leading up to her door. When I rang the doorbell Randall opened the door. He didn't invite me in, even though he knew – and could see – that my pregnancy was close to full term, so I stood in the doorway and accused him of stealing my parents' pension pot. He tried to bluff his way out of it, but his charm didn't work on me. Eventually he told me to get out of *his* house – what cheek, Roxanne! – but I stood my ground. "Not until you give back the money you stole from us," I told him.

'At this point Randall's charm totally disappeared and I saw him for the murderous beast he really is. Suddenly, without warning, he stuck his fist into my stomach as hard as he could and shoved me backwards down the entire flight of steps on to the street. Someone called an ambulance, but our little boy was still-born a few minutes later.

'After Don and I lost our only son, that was it: there were to be no more babies. So now that we realised the truth about Randall, Don and I put our heads together to try to find out more about the false cheques that had caused Don to lose his job. We contacted the colleagues that Don had been introduced to by Randall and they admitted that they hadn't actually had business dealings with him. Slowly it dawned on us that we had unwittingly provided Randall with all the information he needed to cheat Don's employers, damage Don's reputation, and cause Don to lose his job. In addition, we now know that Randall purposely cheated our parents out of their savings and, of course, it was Randall who brought about the death of our only son.

'So that's our story about Randall, but there is just a bit more information you might be interested in. My aged aunt learned about the terrible tragedies that had befallen us and left us enough money in her will to buy Brinkley House, which we did in 1984. Both Don and I have put everything into this project and it is beginning to pay off. Just a few months ago, however, in the early hours of the morning, a fire broke out in a ground-floor reception area. The alarm went off and the fire was quickly controlled. Our caretaker, Ifor Thompson, saw a man driving away in a sports car, but sadly it was too dark to read the number plate. Anyhow, that's it! Thank you so much for listening to our tale of woe! Please help us to find a way to protect all those of us who attended Marcie's wedding in 1962 and our families.

'Now, may I suggest that you all take yourselves off to the drawing-room and have a drink? I think we could all do with something strong after all the terrible facts that Roxanne, Marcie, and Don and I have thrown at you this morning. Lunch will be served at one o'clock and Livia has asked me if she can briefly add a bit more information after lunch. So shall we say we meet at two thirty? After that, the day is your own. Dinner will be served at eight.'

Lunch was a quiet affair; the nine guests at the Brinkley House Hotel and their two hosts were in sombre mood. Judith mentally totted up the number of people she reckoned Randall had harmed in some way: – Marcie, Marcie's father, Marcie's mother, the Stanton-Grays' estate manager who lost his job, Roxanne, Don, Sally, their unborn son, and Judith herself. Now it looked as if Livia might be another victim. So many lives blighted by the behaviour of one man whose psychopathy had led him to believe that he could swan through life grabbing everything he wanted for himself without regard for anyone else!

As she ate her soup, Judith looked at her friends sitting around the table and noticed that Livia was looking very pale. Only the night before, Judith had ascribed Livia's worn-out appearance to the long drive to Wales, but today she looked even more exhausted. Judith wondered what Randall had done to her.

After lunch, Judith and Ralph escorted Marcie up to her room. She was tired, and wanted to lie down for a few minutes. Judith checked that she was comfortable before she and Ralph went quietly back to their room to review the incredible events of the morning.

Ralph reclined on the double bed.

'It seems extraordinary that Randall was able to take in so many people with his lies,' he said, 'but *come on*! Surely you and I would have seen through him, don't you think?'

'Well . . . no, actually', said Judith, sitting up beside him on the bed. 'Or rather, it all depends on the circumstances.'

'What do you mean?'

'Well, the young people he raped – you know, Marcie's friends . . . *they* didn't see through him, did they? At least, not until it was too late.'

'No, I suppose not. Do you happen to know any of these friends?'

'Yes, I know one.'

'Where did it happen?'

'At Redcliffe just three days after Marcie and Randall's wedding. Can you believe it? That evening Randall was on particularly brilliant form: funny, witty, charming. We all felt relaxed with him, now that he was a happily married man. We knew that Marcie and he were due to fly off to Italy the following day, so this was to be our last evening all together. To celebrate this great occasion we all imbibed cocktails, which none of us had ever done before. After drinking one glass of the stuff, this particular wedding guest started to feel woozy and went up to bed. She was just falling asleep when she saw Randall standing beside her bed. She politely asked him to go away, but he said he would only go if she drank one of the two cocktails he had brought for her. She drank one – or maybe both – cocktails, and then started to feel very intoxicated indeed. She was almost blotto when he started to have sex with her, and yet she remembered pleading with him to leave her alone: but he had sex with her anyhow. In the morning she woke up with a dreadful hangover and recalled what had happened. She was horrified, but told nobody about it.

'A few weeks later, Marcie telephoned her, saying that Randall had told her all about what she had done that night. She had literally *thrown* herself at him! What was a man to do in that situation? He thought her behaviour *disgusting*. Marcie then told her that she was no longer her friend and that she never, ever, wanted to see her again.

That's it.'

'Good grief! That's a terrible story. And, yes, that was definitely rape. So who was Randall's victim? And how old would she have been in 1962 – eighteen? Nineteen? What a dreadful thing to happen to a young guest at a wedding party. To be raped by the bridegroom just three days after his wedding . . . So, who was it?'

Judith turned away from Ralph with shame.

'It was me,' she said, bursting into tears.

Ralph sat bolt upright on the bed and twisted his torso so that he could look at her properly. His face was suffused with love and pity.

'Judie! My wee Judie!' He spoke gently, cradling her in his arms as she buried her head into his shoulder and wept.

'I'm so sorry I didn't tell you earlier,' she mumbled, 'but it all happened before you and I ever met, otherwise I would have told you. I wouldn't have mentioned it at all if it hadn't been for this reunion . . . but you do see, don't you, that it isn't just Marcie and Sally, it's me too, *and* Roxanne – who, incidentally, didn't attend the wedding, and now we know why. So that's four victims out of the seven Brinkley House old girls who attended Marcie's wedding, and five out of the eleven of us here this weekend. And there's Don and Sally Saunders' baby, whose chance of life was snatched away from him.

'Do you think I should come clean about the rape?' Judith added. 'I mean, tell the group? Marcie and I have talked about it this weekend and, as you know, we are good friends again. She is so sorry that she reacted the way she did, but that was before she knew what Randall was really like. Perhaps I should tell everyone the truth about what happened that night. What do you think?'

Ralph held Judith close, kissing the tears from her eyes.

'It's up to you, my wee Judith. I'll not stand in your way. Mind you, I always think it's best to get things out into the open.'

They embraced and, after calling on Marcie, the three friends linked arms and headed for the lift.

'I've told Ralph about what Randall did to me,' Judith told Marcie as they waited for the lift to arrive. 'So . . . do you think I should come clean with the others?'

'As long as you feel up to it, yes, I think it would be a good idea to clear the air, and it all adds weight to our argument.'

The happy trio descended to the ground floor and headed for the Conference Room to find out what Livia wanted to tell them about Randall.

IV

Ralph, Judith and Marcie greeted their friends warmly and sat down in their usual places around the table. As Livia stood up to speak, Judith observed that her dark, shoulder-length hair had been carefully re-curled since the previous evening, and that her face had been carefully made-up once more. Livia was wearing a pale-grey skirt, a blue, long-sleeved blouse and low-heeled shoes. A well-worn tweed jacket lay over the back of her chair. Judith reckoned this to be the perfect outfit for the occasion.

Livia was a natural speaker.

'There isn't much you lot don't know about me, but for the sake of the men here I'll try to describe how I used to be at Brinkley House because I know I've changed a lot since then.'

Judith wondered at Livia's comment, realising that she didn't really know much about her either.

'Well, I think "sociable and confident" sums it up. I was the only child of doting parents who were always one hundred per cent supportive of everything I did. Unfortunately, as some of you know, my father was killed in a car crash in 1961 – some young idiot driving too fast – and two years later my mother died of cancer. After these tragic deaths, I combated my depression and loneliness by channelling my energies into becoming what you might call a financial whizz-kid and gradually became sufficiently proficient at the "money game" to buy into the City life-style.'

Livia smiled, made eye contact with her audience, and spoke clearly without raising her voice. Judith wondered if she had always been like this. She certainly did not remember her as being a particularly good communicator, although she did recall thinking her a highly motivated and ambitious sixth-former. Judith drew her attention back to Livia's words.

'I bought a house in central London, and a few years later I bought another house in Hampshire. I was doing a lot of entertaining, and so in 1986 I employed a cook-housekeeper to help me. Her name was Katie Gilbert and from the very day she started work for me my life started to pick up. Katie looked after everything. Catering, cooking, cleaning, house maintenance and gardening – there was nothing she couldn't manage, and over the next year or two she became my prop and stay.

'Last spring I was chatting to Katie on the telephone – she was at my Hampshire house and I was at my office – when she just happened to recall something she had read in the papers some while back. She knew I had been to

Brinkley House and wondered if I remembered hearing about the divorce of another old girl, "someone called Marcia". It had all happened a while ago, she said, but the divorce had caused quite a splash at the time. Naturally when she told me that Marcie's marriage had broken down I was shocked, and told her that I had attended Marcie's wedding in 1962.

'So then she told me that she had heard that Marcie's ex-husband had refused to accept the divorce and, in a bid to get back at Marcie, had taken to venting his rage on her closest school friends. For that reason, Katie suggested, I should take steps to make sure that all my assets were made secure and accessible only to me. I was able to reassure Katie on that point, telling her that everything to do with my finances and my two houses had been locked up as tight as a drum – bricks, mortar, contents, salary, investments, the lot. She seemed relieved to learn this, but I decided to warn my bank and my solicitor about Randall, just to be on the safe side. So that was that. Randall could not steal anything of mine, but he did something else instead. I'll be brief . . .'

'A few weeks later I received a letter from Katie telling me that she wanted to give in her notice. I was appalled, and immediately telephoned her to ask her why she wanted to leave me, and offered her a generous pay increase. But it was no good – she just kept saying that she felt it was time to move on. I was sorry to lose her as I couldn't run my two houses properly without her. But she insisted that she needed a change and so she left, and within weeks my complicated lifestyle had become too much for me. I found a replacement, but sadly the girl wasn't up to the job so I had to dismiss her.

A short while later, I decided to drive down to my

country house for the weekend. I left on the Friday afternoon and made quick work of the journey. I drove into the small lane leading to my drive and parked in my usual spot. Then I walked round to the front door and let myself in. As I walked in I was shocked to hear laughter coming from upstairs. With trepidation I tiptoed upstairs, following the sounds coming from my bedroom. Silently I opened the door and the sight that met my eyes shocked me beyond belief.'

Livia looked around the table at her friends, all of whom were sitting forward in their chairs, staring at her with anticipation.

'There, lying together in *my* bed, stark naked, were my former housekeeper Katie and . . . Randall Selkirk. When they saw me standing in the doorway, Randall sat up and shouted, "*Hello, Livia! Welcome aboard!*" Then he laughed, pulling back the bedclothes to expose himself to me, saying, "*Come on in, old girl, let's make it a three-some!*" He made several more obscene comments, but I'll spare you the details.

'I was shocked to the core. I ran downstairs, past the kitchen, where I saw the remains of their meal still on my kitchen table, and out to my car. I drove off, parked in a lay-by and sat there deciding what to do. When I returned to my house they had gone, leaving their dirty dishes, dirty bed-linen and general mess for me to clear up. Since then I've been very busy. I've sold my country house and I've also made sure that my London house is fully alarmed and locked up as tight as a drum . . . I now refer to it as Fort Knox! I've also made doubly sure that nobody can access my finances, and I've warned my accountants to be on the alert. I've tried to make contact with Katie, but she seems to have vanished into thin air. That's it. End of story. Over to you, Marcie.'

Livia sat down and poured herself a glass of water.

V

Marcie looked down at her hands. She seemed utterly appalled.

'God! My poor Livia! I could kick myself for not telling you, not telling everyone, about my divorce, ages ago. If I hadn't been so proud and felt so sorry for myself, I could have spared you this pain and distress. What a shocking experience! I am so very sorry. I really appreciate your courage in telling us what happened, because now we all have an even better understanding of Randall's warped mindset. Incidentally,' she continued, 'I've brought along a couple of photographs of Randall to pass around. One taken at our wedding in 1962, and the other more recently. I really think that in the circumstances we should all familiarise ourselves with Randall's appearance, especially you – Jack and Ralph – as you've never met him. I'll hand them out in a moment, but before I do, I'd better check that there aren't any more of Randall's victims sitting around this table. If there are, would they be prepared to share their experience with us?'

Judith knew that Marcie was providing her with an opportunity to speak, so she grasped the nettle. Heart pounding, she put her hand up.

'Yes,' she said, slowly rising to her feet. 'I'm afraid I can add another crime to Randall's list. You see, Randall raped me in 1962 while we were staying at Redcliffe for Marcie's wedding.

'He *what*?' said Ann. 'Dear grief, that man is utterly appalling.'

'Yes, you're quite right Ann. Anyhow, Marcie knows all about it, but it's taken me a while to face up to it. Of course, as we now know, Randall raped several of Marcie's friends over the years, and it pleased him to make out that it was *they* who had seduced *him*. Anyhow, the important fact is that out of the seven of us at Marcie's wedding, four of us have since been victimised by Randall. I would have added you to this list Roxanne, to bring the number up to five, but you didn't attend the wedding which isn't surprising considering what a rotten big brother he was to you. Anyhow, Ralph and I just thought you ought to hear my story. Sorry it's a bit late.'

Judith's heart was still racing from the stress of telling her friends facts she had bottled up for so long, and yet she was aware of a great sense of relief now that everyone knew the truth. Ralph squeezed her hand, and the shocked gasps coming from her friends around the table added to her feeling of relief.

'Good God! That man really is a horrible creature.' Janey was outraged.

Trot was also upset by Judith's account.

'Someone ought to rape *him*,' she said, 'and see how he likes *that*, the cowardly little shit.'

Marcie spoke again.

'Poor Judith, I'm so sorry; but what you've told us makes it even more imperative that Randall is brought under control before he does any more harm.'

'Hear, hear!' said Trot.

'Here are the photographs,' Marcie added, leaning across the table and doling out two photographs for each member of the group. She sat silently while her friends scrutinised Randall's face.

Judith gazed at the more recent colour photograph of

Randall first, immediately recollecting the impact that his charm and good looks had had on her all those years ago. He was smiling confidently at the camera, his dark violet eyes dancing and his wicked smile revealing perfectly even, white teeth. Yes, he was older – but still devastatingly attractive. She observed that although the two Selkirk siblings looked alike, the very features she had found so alluring and harmonious in Randall seemed ungainly and awkward in Roxanne.

'Who's the girl?' asked Trot. 'She looks familiar, but I can't place her.'

Reluctantly Judith drew her eyes away from the recent photograph of Randall and focused on the other one.

'Oh, don't you remember our housekeeper, Cathie Brook?' said Marcie. 'She was employed to look after our house at Chelsea, but she came to Redcliffe to help out at our wedding for the week you stayed with us.'

The girl standing beside Randall in the black-and-white photograph looked vaguely familiar. Judith recalled the wavy, fair hair and small, neatly folded mouth . . . And, yes, this was the Randall she remembered from 1962, stunningly beautiful and oozing sex-appeal.

Suddenly Judith jumped as a hoarse cry cut through the general buzz of conversation . . .

'*I know that face! I know that Cathie person! She used to live in the village where Randall and I lived as children. But her name isn't Cathie . . . It's Cheryl.*'

CHAPTER FIVE

Who is Cheryl?

I

R OXANNE WAS HOLDING up her photograph of Randall Selkirk and Cathie Brook.

'Her name isn't Cathie Brook, it's *Cheryl*,' she said again, more quietly now. 'I knew her when I was little, but I can't recall her surname. Randall knew her better than I did because he was home-taught. I *do* remember her coming round to our house though, and my aunt may remember her. Would you like me to contact my aunt? Right now? . . . Yes? Of course, please excuse me.'

Roxanne's hurried departure was greeted with a buzz of excitement. Then Marcie struggled to her feet, and everyone stopped talking.

'The girl in the photo is definitely Cathie Brook,' she said. 'A short while before I met Randall, my father took on Cathie to help look after our house in Chelsea, and sometimes she used to drive over to Redcliffe to help out when we had house parties. She was an excellent employee and totally dependable, and yet, now that I come to think about it . . . Good heavens!'

'What is it?' said Trot.

'I've just had an extraordinary thought,' said Marcie. 'You remember I told you some of the ways Randall carried out his "hate campaign" against me after our divorce? Remember? I told you that Randall secretly moved into one of the out-houses at Redcliffe and lived there for some time before I became aware of it? Well, I always felt that someone must have helped him. Someone who knew the set-up at Redcliffe and how to get the out-house up-and-running without causing suspicion. Yes, Cathie Brook definitely had the know-how and the opportunity to get the job done, and if Roxanne is right, and if Randall really was her childhood friend, then there would have been a strong bond between the two of them. The question is, who is – Cathie, and what is her real relationship with Randall?'

As Marcie sat down, Sally spoke, her freckles standing out against her pallid complexion.

'You know, if you're right, there is something very odd about Cathie's behaviour. Something doesn't fit. It just doesn't make sense!' She frowned and looked up at the ceiling, struggling to express her thoughts cogently.

'What do you mean?' Janey asked.

'I mean, assuming you're right, there's something very odd about Cathie's behaviour. but I can't quite find the right words to express what I instinctively feel.' Sally looked at her friends for inspiration. 'So assuming you *are* right, how does a dutiful, reliable and trusted housekeeper morph into the sort of person who would go behind the back of her employer in such a deceitful way? Think about it. Organising a house-conversion on the Redcliffe estate must have cost a pretty penny and you can bet your bottom dollar that Cathie didn't pay for it, and neither did Randall. After your divorce, Marcie, if Cathie really did set up

Randall on your property at your expense and without your permission, then she is guilty of theft and gross disloyalty, both to you and to your family. So how do these actions square with the hard-working and decent Cathie that you describe? That's the question.'

As Sally sat down, Roxanne rushed back into the Conference Room, her bony face flushed with excitement.

'Her name *isn't* Cathie Brook – it's Cheryl Gibson. I've just spoken to my aunt. Cheryl and Randall were inseparable, even when they were toddlers. That's all my aunt can remember, I'm afraid.'

Ann sat up straight, a puzzled expression on her face.

'Hang on! So that means that at your wedding, Marcie, your housekeeper Cathie Brook wasn't really Cathie Brook at all but a young woman called Cheryl Gibson who just happened to grow up in the same village as Randall, your bridegroom. If that's the case, why did Cheryl Gibson change her name to Cathie Brook, and what was her real relationship with Randall Selkirk?'

'I can't make any sense of this,' said Marcie. 'I always knew her as Cathie Brook, and my family always considered her an excellent employee. I'm in a muddle. Everything seems to contradict what I believed to be the truth. Can anyone help me on this?'

It was Ralph who put his hand up.

'Please excuse me if what I'm about to say offends anyone,' he said politely, 'but there are clear parallels between the two different scenarios we've learned about today. Marcie and Livia have both praised the loyalty, industry and efficiency of their housekeepers, Cathie Brook and Katie Gilbert. Subsequently, each has expressed shock and distress upon being betrayed by her housekeeper in hurtful and uncharacteristic ways. It seems that, as Sally says, each housekeeper has suddenly "morphed" from a trustworthy and hard-working employee into a callous cheat and liar. The question is this: what is the common denominator between these two housekeepers? Answer: – Randall Selkirk, of course. So now, comparing the behaviour of both Marcie's and Livia's housekeepers, would you not agree with me that it seems possible that "Cathie" and "Katie" are one and the same person – Cheryl Gibson?'

There was a brief silence while everyone absorbed this new possibility, and then Janey spoke.

'You know, Ralph, what you say makes a lot of sense . . . but Livia, wouldn't you have recognised Katie when she came to work for you? I mean, if Cathie and Katie *are* the same person, wouldn't you have recognised Cathie as the housekeeper who looked after us all at Marcie's wedding?'

'Well, I didn't!' Livia shot back. 'I mean, had they been alike, surely I would have looked at the photograph you gave us just now and thought, *Oh look, here is a photograph of Katie!* But I didn't. I do, vaguely, remember Cathie, of course, but I just don't think that Cathie Brook and Katie Gilbert can be the same person. Sorry, Ralph, I think you've got hold of the wrong end of the stick. This Cheryl idea doesn't hold water.'

'Well, there is one sure way to find out,' said Janey. 'I have an old friend called John Green who is a police officer at the Met. John may be able to find out who Cheryl Gibson really is. Unfortunately there isn't much of today left, but I reckon we might be lucky if we ring him right now. I'm sure he will help if he can.'

'Brilliant idea!' said Marcie, a smile lighting up her face.

'Right,' said Janey. 'Roxanne, I need to know the name

and location of the village you grew up in, plus any other information about Cheryl that might be useful. In fact, why don't you escort me to a telephone and I'll ring him right now?'

But as Janey and Roxanne stood up to leave, Ann spoke again. There was a touch of urgency in her voice.

'A quick thought, Janey. We don't want to broadcast the fact that our old girls' reunion is happening at Brinkley House this very weekend, do we? If Randall finds out that we're all here together right now, he might be tempted to do something nasty to us out of spite.'

Livia looked at Ann with a concerned look on her face.

'But Ann, you *do* realise that Randall already knows that we're all here at Brinkley House this weekend, don't you? Katie was still working for me when Sally's invitation arrived. Had I known about her liaison with Randall, I'd have made damn sure she didn't find out about it, but at the time I didn't even know that Marcie had divorced Randall. Sorry!'

There was a pregnant pause before Ann spoke again.

'Right then. We'd better decide what to do, now that we have a better idea of the risks involved in staying here. Quick question before you go, Roxanne. Is Randall able to sail?'

There was a hush, and all eyes turned to Roxanne.

'I'm afraid to say that Randall is an excellent sailor, and so that raises the question: is *Manatee* safe?'

Ann looked at Jack, who stood up.

'You make a very good point, Roxanne,' he said. 'Ann, don't bother to come with me. I'll soon be able to see if all's well. Back soon.'

'Actually,' said Sally, 'I need to show Annie and Ifor Thompson that photo of Randall and Cheryl before you check up on *Manatee*, so I'll come with you, Jack.'

Janey, Roxanne, Jack and Sally hurriedly left the Conference Room.

II

After they had gone, the remaining members of the group were left to digest the worrying fact that Randall knew that they were all staying at the Brinkley House Hotel this particular weekend. Ann felt particularly anxious at the prospect of Jack spending another night on *Manatee* and annoyed that after months of listening to Sally prattling on about the pros and cons of buying Brinkley House, Randall's name had not once been mentioned. Now, thought Ann, not only was her home at risk, her beloved husband and children were now potential targets for Randall's psychopathic behaviour.

A few minutes later, while Janey and Roxanne were telephoning John Green, Sally returned to the Conference Room.

'Now, first of all let me reassure you that Ifor and Annie Thompson haven't seen Randall or Cheryl in, or near, Brinkley House, so that's good news. Tonight Ifor is going to show the photos to our local policeman when he calls on his rounds, and, by the way, both Jack and Ifor have gone to check on *Manatee* together. They should be back soon. Now then, why don't we all have tea and then do our own thing for a while? Dinner will be served at eight, so you'll have plenty of time after tea to sit and mull things over, have a swim or use the gym. Personally, I could kill for a cuppa!'

Just as the group was about to leave the room, Janey

and Roxanne returned. Everyone looked at them expectantly.

'I've spoken to my friend, John,' said Janey, 'and he says he's happy to start looking for a Cheryl Gibson right away. He has promised to telephone us tomorrow if he's able to find out anything about her.'

'Excellent news!' said Ann. 'But may I add that if Randall knows we're here this weekend, then Jack, Don, and Ralph could be sitting-ducks if they spend the night on *Manatee*. Secondly, the coast and shoreline should be off-limits for all of us, don't you think? Finally, as most of us have left our homes empty this weekend, I don't think we'd be overreacting if we made telephone contact with our friends and neighbours and asked them to keep an eye on them over the weekend? Personally, I'm going to ring my neighbour right now and ask her to check on my house regularly until I get back.'

'Good idea, Ann,' said Trot. 'I'm going to ring my manager right away. Randall better not mess about with my horses – well, not if he wants to live!'

'Absolutely, Trot,' agreed Marcie,.'And actually I think Ann's right. We should *all* take measures to make sure our homes are safe over the weekend.'

Everyone went off in different directions; some to the drawing-room to have tea, some to their rooms to make telephone calls, and some to the swimming pool or gym to get some exercise. Meanwhile Jack was checking over his yacht.

III

Once on board *Manatee*, Jack was relieved to find that everything was just as he had left it. He prowled around to make sure nothing had been tampered with, closely followed by Ifor Thompson, who showed great interest in the fittings, especially in the wooden cupboards designed to house the boat's supplies and equipment. In the cabin, Jack, noticing Ifor's interest, opened up a cupboard to reveal a pile of blankets.

'There you are! You can't go far on a yacht without blankets, especially when friends drop in for the night.'

'You've certainly got enough space in here,' said Ifor.

'Well, when you're on a boat, you never quite know what you're going to need or when you are going to need it.'

By the time Jack had made them both a cup of tea and they had worked their way through a packet of chocolate biscuits, they were on first-name terms. Ifor, sitting back in a comfortable chair, was thoroughly enjoying himself.

'You know, Jack, I could take to this life in a big way.'

'Well, I'm afraid I'm an addict. I'm always as happy as a grig when I'm sailing.'

'What's a grig?'

'Haven't a clue!'

They both laughed.

'The wooden fittings are beautifully crafted. You've clearly found yourself a first-rate carpenter!'

'No, I did it all myself. That's what I do. I'm a carpenter. That's what I trained as before I went into the furniture business. Sailing and carpentry – my two favourite activities. How about you, Ifor? Do you have any interests outside work?'

'Well, yes, I do in a way. I breed pointers, but only as a hobby. We don't get many puppies each year, but I always manage to find good homes for them. They're quite popular around here, both as pets and working dogs.'

The two men carried on chatting for a while, and then, after Jack had decided to sail *Manatee* southwards to the safety of the harbour at Aberystwyth, Ifor rowed himself back to the quay, and a few minutes later he was driving up the hill to the hotel. Once there, he dropped in at the office to pass on Jack's message to Sally; Sally, in turn, passed on Jack's message to Ann.

'Jack thinks *Manatee* is too vulnerable to remain moored here at Aberdovey, so he's decided to sail her to Aberystwyth. The journey shouldn't take too long and Ifor is going to drive over to pick him up in the car. They'll be back in time for dinner.'

Ann was pleased with this arrangement, and so too were Don and Ralph when they were told about it. They greatly preferred the idea of sleeping snuggled up to their wives on dry land than bobbing about like corks in Cardigan Bay.

IV

An experienced yachtsman, Jack made short work of the journey down the coast to Aberystwyth harbour. He moored *Manatee* and walked over to the pub which was only a short distance from the quay. Once there, Jack telephoned the hotel to let them know that he was ready for Ifor to collect him and was informed by Sally that Ifor was already on his way. With time to kill, Jack bought himself a pint of beer and sat down to await Ifor's arrival.

While he was waiting it occurred to him that, should Randall Selkirk want to make a surprise visit to Brinkley House from the sea, this might be where he would choose to anchor his yacht. Jack finished his drink, gathered up his gear, and went outside to wait for Ifor in the fresh, autumnal air.

Jack was standing next to the pub wall, looking down the lane, when he heard a voice behind him.

'Excuse me. You wouldn't be waiting for a lift by any chance, would you?'

Jack swung round and found himself looking straight into the dark violet eyes of Randall Selkirk.

V

Staring calmly into Randall's eyes, Jack responded in his usual friendly manner.

'Hello . . . Yes, I'm waiting for my friends to pick me up. They should be here any minute now.'

Casually looking along the road, Jack could see no sign of Ifor's car. He had purposely referred to being met by friends, rather than a friend, so that Randall would think himself outnumbered should there be any trouble.

'I watched you sail into the harbour just now,' said Randall.

'Really? Well, actually I come here quite often. It's a good spot, although this weekend is proving to be a bit complicated, one way or another.'

Smiling, Jack looked Randall full in the face, and watched the dark eyes shift fractionally.

'Actually, I sailed past your yacht at Aberdovey last night,' said Randall. 'You were moored near that new hotel

– the Binsey House Hotel, isn't it? Then I saw *Manatee* again today and wondered if you had actually stayed there. If so, what's it like? If it's any good, perhaps you and your friends could drop me off there.'

'Well, that's the trouble,' said Jack, his face crinkling up with false bonhomie. 'We thought the same as you, but as luck would have it, the hotel is closed to the public this weekend. There's some private function going on, so we spent the night on board *Manatee*, and then this morning the other two went off to visit friends for lunch. They should be coming to pick me up any minute now.'

Jack was used to thinking on his feet, so when he saw Ifor's car heading towards the pub he was ready with his story.

'By the way, it's called the *Brinkley* House Hotel. Oh, and another thing. When we went there, the hotel was crawling with policemen. Well, three of them actually! They were handing out photographs of a man wanted for questioning.'

'Oh . . . Did you happen to see what he looked like?'

'No. I wasn't wearing my glasses, I'm afraid, but my friends did. Actually I think that's them coming along now. I can't quite see . . . Yes, it is! One of them's bound to have the photo on him if you'd like to check him out for your own safety. Anyhow, if you still want to be dropped off at Brinkley House, be our guest – though it's quite a distance by car. We're going the other way, but I'm sure we'd all be happy to make a detour, should you still want to go there. Excuse me, won't you . . . Hello there, hello!'

Jack walked briskly towards the car, waving his arms so that Ifor was forced to pull up about twenty yards from where Randall was standing. Although there was only one man in the vehicle, this was not apparent from where

Randall was standing in the fading light. With Ifor leaning over to open the passenger door, and Jack leaning into the car, his view was blocked. A brief dialogue ensued, and then Jack turned back to call towards Randall.

'Come on, then,' he shouted. 'Everyone says it's okay. There's room for you in the back, and we'll get you there if you still want to go. Come on over and I'll introduce you to everyone.'

Jack and Ifor noticed that Randall seemed quite unconcerned as he called over to them from outside the pub.

'You know what?' he said. 'I don't think I'll put you to the trouble, now that I know that the hotel's closed to the public. But thank you for your advice. You've saved me a wasted journey. Good talking to you. Let's hope we bump into each other again sometime. Goodbye.'

Turning on his heel, Randall walked briskly into the pub and out of sight.

Jack and Ifor sat in the car, briefly weighing up the situation, and then Ifor drove into the pub car park and, leaving Jack in the passenger seat, entered the pub from its rear entrance. Inside, Ifor saw Randall ordering himself a drink at the bar, his place at a table cluttered by his kit: a duffel coat, oilskins, and a bag with a large tartan Thermos flask sticking out of it. Then, crossing over to the telephone booth, Ifor telephoned the hotel to update Don on recent events before rejoining Jack in the car. The two men drove back to Aberdovey in high spirits.

VII

As the afternoon wore on, Sally decided to join Trot and Ann for a swim, but she had only done a few lengths when Don beckoned her from the side of the pool. She swam over to him and listened attentively. Then, after swimming a few more lengths, she dressed and joined Don in the office. A while later, the hotel car arrived and Jack and Ifor were given a warm welcome before they all went their different ways – Ifor to help Annie in the kitchen, Jack to join Ann in her room overlooking the sea, and Don and Sally to light the fire and set out the drinks and glasses in the drawing-room.

Half an hour later, Jack, still wearing his red *marinière*, was regaling an admiring audience about his encounter with Randall.

'You see, the harbour at Aberystwyth is the largest in the vicinity and so I reckoned that if Randall was sniffing around this particular part of the coastline this is where he'd be most likely to show up – and I was right. Mind you, I had to think on my feet when he asked me for a lift to Brinkley House, so I told him that it was closed to the public this weekend. Of course he knew that, but he didn't know that I knew that he knew. Then I decided to bend the truth a bit to stop him thinking he could just sneak into Brinkley House whenever he liked. So I told him that the hotel was swarming with policemen on the trail of some criminal and that umpteen mugshots of this person had been circulated in and around the hotel. Randall asked me if I had seen this photo and I said that I had, but that I couldn't see it properly as I wasn't wearing my glasses at the time – he wasn't to know that I don't wear glasses. Anyhow, he suddenly decided that he didn't want a lift to

Brinkley House after all. He's a cool customer, though.' Jack smiled at everyone and took another hearty swig of his whisky.

There was a clamour of voices asking Jack for more details, but the evening was drawing in and it was time for dinner.

Sally took charge.

'Just before we go in to dinner,' she announced after the gong had sounded, 'on behalf of us all, I'd like to thank you for your quick thinking, Jack. You've made it almost impossible for Randall to turn up here, and I'm sure that everyone feels safer now. Thank you very much. So now . . . dinner is served.'

'I'd like to add my heartfelt thanks too, Jack.' Marcie smiled at him as she struggled to stand up. Jack immediately went over to help her up, and he and Ann escorted her to dinner.

They all filed into the dining-room and sat where Sally had set out name-places for them. The conversation was lively, aided by an excellent dinner and plenty of wine. There was a general feeling of relief, only slightly clouded by the thought that although Randall was unlikely to turn up at the hotel that night, he was nevertheless at large in the area.

Just as they were finishing their meal, Annie Thompson entered the dining-room and spoke to Sally, before beginning to clear the table for the last course. Then Sally had a quick word with Janey, and the two of them left the dining-room, returning a short while later.

Janey, standing next to the table, now spoke to the assembled group.

'That was my friend – John Green. I told him about Jack's surprise meeting with Randall today and he was highly entertained. He told me that he's been trying to find out about Cheryl Gibson's background and is waiting for a call, but if this doesn't materialise tonight we may have to wait until Monday morning. What John *has* been able to do, however, is check lists of agencies that supply domestic staff to house owners in the London area. The remit was to find a housekeeper of "Cheryl Gibson's" approximate age, with the possible initials C.G., K.G., C.B or K.B., who applied for a job shortly after Katie left Livia's employ and – guess what! The agency found a K.B. who fits the bill!

'She is called Kathryn Booker and is currently employed as housekeeper to a Mr and Mrs Parry-Jones who live in Paddington. What is particularly interesting about the Parry-Joneses is the fact that they own another property – a house called Llancoed, near Aberystwyth – and spend long weekends there especially during the summer months. If we find that the Parry-Joneses' housekeeper is called Kathryn Booker and that she looks like the "Cathie Brook" in Marcie's photograph – and possibly the "Katie Gilbert" who worked for Livia – then we've caught Cheryl Gibson red-handed. We now know that Randall Selkirk's yacht is anchored at Aberystwyth, just a few miles from the Parry-Joneses' house so . . . bingo! In fact, it's possible that Randall free-loads at the Parry-Joneses' house when they're not around and sleeps on his yacht when they are. We'll need to check all this by paying a visit to the Parry-Joneses, but I'm not sure how we set about doing it. However, it's just possible that, with a very big dollop of luck, they'll be here over the weekend.'

'Thank you, Janey,' said Sally. 'If K.B. is the person we think she is, then your friend John has done us proud, and in remarkably short time. We need to make plans, so let's do it in the drawing-room over a cup of coffee.'

There was a buzz of excitement as everyone crossed the reception area and entered the drawing-room. Annie came in to serve them coffee and then retired, leaving them alone.

Once more, Sally addressed the group.

'To my mind, the obvious person to drive over to the Parry-Joneses' house tomorrow is Ifor. In fact, both Ifor and Annie together would be even better because they are locals and because both Annie and Cheryl – assuming she *is* Cheryl, that is – hold similar positions as housekeepers. Both Ifor and Annie have seen the photograph, so all they need is a good excuse for dropping in unannounced. What do you think?'

'I like the idea of Ifor and Annie driving over on our behalf,' said Marcie. 'What do you all feel about it. Any ideas?'

Janey spoke languidly from her armchair by the fire.

'Perhaps I should tell you that my mother knew a man called "Parry-Jones" who lived in Paddington and I seem to recall that he had a house in Wales. It must be the same man. He was a well-known "shot", if that's the right expression for someone who likes shooting things. What birds get shot at this time of year? Pheasants? Grouse?'

Jack chipped in excitedly.

'Now that's brilliant news, Janey, because Ifor breeds pointers . . . you know, gun-dogs? He sells them all around this area. So if Ifor and Annie drive over to ask Mr Parry-Jones if he would be interested in buying a pointer puppy, what could be more natural?'

'Now that's a marvellous idea', said Sally. 'What do you think, everyone? Ann? Trot?'

'Excellent idea!' said Marcie, backed by murmurs of approval from the others.

Sally and Don went off to talk to Ifor and Annie, while the rest of the group sat down in the drawing-room to discuss the situation over cups of coffee.

CHAPTER SIX

Home Truths

I

SUNDAY MORNING PROMISED fair for Ifor and Annie, who had driven off to Llancoed to do a bit of sleuthing on behalf of Sally and Don Saunders. Sally wished the couple good luck and waved them off before busying herself with the job of cooking breakfast for her friends. Later, while the group was enjoying fried eggs, bacon, sausages, tomatoes, and mushrooms on toast, Don came in to call Janey to the telephone.

As Janey left the dining-room, Trot's comment was characteristically blunt.

'Even if a certain Cheryl Gibson *is* working at Llancoed, so what! That tells us absolutely nothing about who she really is. What's the betting we don't find out anything important until after tomorrow when we've all gone home.'

But Trot's prediction was wrong.

When Janey returned to the dining-room she spoke to them all with quiet urgency.

'If we are correct in believing Cheryl Gibson and Kathryn Booker to be one and the same person, then I have to tell you something important about Cheryl that John Green has just found out. Apparently, in 1950, she killed a little boy. She was just ten years old.'

There was a moment's incredulous silence, quickly broken by Roxanne.

'When was this? I don't remember anything about a *murder*.'

'John says it happened during a period when Cheryl's parents' marriage was going through a bad patch. Apparently Cheryl's mother had moved out of the Gibson family home and taken up with a local man whose house had previously belonged to US Air Force personnel. Unfortunately the property hadn't been properly cleared and a large American-style refrigerator had been dumped in the garden. Cheryl shut her mother's boyfriend's five-year-old son in it and left him to suffocate.'

'Good God!' exclaimed Ann. 'They should never have left the refrigerator in the garden.'

'Absolutely!' said Janey. 'But anyhow Cheryl was deemed old enough to know what she was doing and was found guilty of manslaughter. Can you believe it? The poor little girl was sent off to a special school, a kind of reformatory, for nearly eight years and during this time her family washed their hands of her. So no wonder Randall was able to get his hooks into her. I bet you wish you'd known about all this before she came to work for you, Marcie and Livia, and let's hope all goes well with Ifor and Annie at Llancoed today – again, assuming that their Kathryn Booker really is Cheryl Gibson.'

Janey sat down to a general buzz of excitement.

'You know,' said Ann, 'so much has been written about Mary Bell, the famous child murderer, I'm surprised I've never heard of Cheryl Gibson, the child murderer.

Fortunately there are relatively few recorded case histories relating to child murderers, so the details should be easy enough to access today. I wonder what the press made of it at the time. They probably came up with some offensive nickname for her such as "Cheryl the Chiller-Killer". Anyhow, I'd certainly like to contact a couple of my colleagues to check the details of the case, so may I use your office, Sally? Would that be all right with everyone?'

After Ann had left the Conference Room, Livia made an important point.

'You know, this raises all sorts of issues and possibilities. I mean, did Cheryl really kill that little boy? Were there other children playing in the garden at the time? Did the back garden have a separate entrance? Was Randall anywhere in the vicinity? Did anyone witness the murder? Roxanne, do you have any memories or clues as to what happened that September?'

'Well,' said Roxanne in a quiet, shocked voice, 'I've kept a diary on and off ever since I could write, so I could telephone home and ask my neighbour to check that date if you like. Mrs Reed comes in every day and should be there now. It's weird, though, because although it happened during the school holidays, I have no recollection of it. Surely I would have remembered something as dreadful as *that*!'

Sally stood up with an anxious expression on her face.

'We must remember that we are here to deal with Randall, not Cheryl Gibson. We mustn't allow ourselves to get diverted. After all, Cheryl's crime is *history*, whereas Randall is a dangerous psychopath who presents a very real threat to us and our families *right now*, in the *present*. Today is the only whole day we have left as a group to decide what to do about Randall, so may I suggest that

Janey, Ann and Roxanne spend the next forty minutes trying to find out as much as possible about the little boy's murder and then report back to us in the Conference Room? After that, please can we get on with the Randall issue? Agreed? Good! See you all in forty minutes – that's eleven o'clock sharp.'

Sally hurried out of the dining-room, accompanied by Don. They both had a lot of work to do now that Annie and Ifor Thomson had gone to Llancoed to try to find out about Cheryl Gibson.

II

Earlier that morning, just as Annie and Ifor Thompson were about to drive to Llancoed, Ifor had a brainwave. Surely, he thought, they would look much more authentic if they brought Braid, their pointer bitch, with them. So he went back to collect her and soon she was settled on her blanket in the back seat of the car. As they set off, Sally and Don waved goodbye from the kitchen window.

As Ifor drove the car towards Machynlleth, Braid kept jumping about with excitement, but she quickly settled down and the couple drove on in silence – Ifor in a mood of relaxed contemplation. Something was clearly on Annie's mind though, as she sat staring ahead.

After a while she broke the silence.

'Ifor, before we get to Llancoed there's something I think I ought to tell you. I would have mentioned it earlier – years earlier – but there didn't seem to be much point until now.'

She hesitated.

'Go on, Annie. Spit it out!'

'Well . . . you know the photo we were shown yesterday? The one of that man and the fair-haired girl with him? Well, you see, I recognised her. In fact I used to know her really well, only she had a different name then. Sorry! I should have said.'

'What! You knew her and never said? Why? What a dopey thing to do! Come on, Annie, you'd better come clean before we get to Llancoed. So what's this all about? And make it quick as we haven't got that much farther to go.'

'She was at school with me. Well, not school really – a special place for . . . for child criminals. All of us there had been in serious trouble in one way or another. I was sent there because I attacked my mother's boyfriend with a spade.'

'You did *what*?'

'I attacked my mother's boyfriend with a spade. Well, it was more like a shovel actually.'

'For goodness sake, why did you do that?'

'Well, you see, this man I called Uncle lived with us. He was my mam's boyfriend. But he was a dirty old man who used to sneak into my bedroom at night and do things to me. I didn't dare tell my mam. Then, when I was ten, Uncle took the whole thing a stage further and I simply couldn't bear it any more. So I decided to take action. It was Christmas and as usual we had friends over and a great big bonfire down the end of the garden. While Uncle was pouring drinks and chatting to our guests, I stuck the shovel into the back of the bonfire to get the metal really hot. Then when Uncle came over to check the fire, I whacked him with it. He toppled over, and I pressed the shovel against his face before anyone could stop me. He had to have plastic surgery, eventually. The police came, but my mam swore me to secrecy about what Uncle had been doing to me over the years and so the police said my attack was "unprovoked". They were never told the truth and I realised that my mam had known what Uncle was doing to me all along—'

'Hang on a minute.' Ifor could hardly believe what he was hearing. 'Your mam knew that her boyfriend had been sexually abusing you for years and yet did nothing about it? Or rather, she let the police think you had whacked him with a shovel *for no reason?*'

'That's right. Anyhow, I was sent to this school where I met Cheryl. We were all given different names starting with the same letter as our real names. So I became Amy, and she became Cora, and we were all trained in cookery, housework, book-keeping and general household and staff management. Cora and I became good friends, and even though she was in there for murder I loved her to bits! So now, you see, we . . . we're in a bit of a pickle, aren't we?'

'Good God! *Murder?* Why didn't you tell me all this before? Who did she murder?'

'A little boy, I gather, though she said she had no recollection of doing it.'

'It gets worse and worse! By the way, is that "Uncle" person still alive? If he is, where can I find him? He needs *castrating!*'

'Don't know and don't care! It's ancient history now. But I do know that Cora was a good friend to me and I'm really looking forward to seeing her today. Whatever the two of us did or didn't do, we've paid for it many times over, and today both of us are highly qualified and experienced cook-housekeepers.'

'Well, my dearest girl, I don't blame you for anything. I only wish you could have told me about it sooner. When we get back to Brinkley House we'll have to keep quiet about your past. If she is Cora, we don't need to tell anyone that you know her and . . .' Ifor paused for a moment, struggling with his emotions. 'And d'you know, I'm very, very proud of you. You've been through so much, yet never a snivel or a whine. I just wish I'd been there to protect you while you were growing up.'

They drove on in silence for a while, and then something else struck him.

'Another thought, though,' he said. 'I don't think we should let on to Cora that we work at Brinkley House – and don't forget that she is that man Randall's lover; he may well be lurking about Llancoed while we're there. Anyhow – *mam's the word.*'

'Okay. So we're just there to ask if Mr Parry-Jones wants to buy one of Braid's puppies. That's it. But what if she asks us where we're working. Then what?'

'Well, I suggest that we only say what is true. That we live near the coast and that we breed pointers – let's stick with that.'

Ifor and Annie continued their journey southwards on the main road and then turned eastwards towards the Cambrian Mountains. An undulating road running along the south side of the Nant-y-Moch Reservoir, followed by a right-hand turning to Ponterwyd, brought them to a T-junction where Ifor decided to turn left into a narrow lane running alongside a large forest. Gradually the forest gave way to pastureland and, after a mile or two, another T-junction. Then, after a couple of false turns, Ifor found himself driving down yet another narrow lane which terminated in a cul-de-sac consisting of six farm cottages. There was no way forward, apart from a muddy farm track, so Ifor turned the car around and went back along the lane, driving slowly and looking out for Llancoed.

'There it is!' cried Annie. 'There on the left. That must be it.'

Ifor's eyes followed Annie's finger which was pointing towards a narrow lane partly concealed by an oakwood. Ifor slowed down, and taking a left turn drove straight down the lane to the far end of the wood, where a gate bearing the sign *Llancoed* stood open. Ifor entered the drive, steered the car around to the back of a large stone house, and parked. Then Braid woke up and started jumping around so Annie put her on her lead and, together, the couple walked over to the back door, knocked on it, and listened.

Silence.

They knocked again.

'Hello? Is anybody there?' Ifor called.

'Hang on! Won't be a minute,' came a muffled reply from behind them.

Almost immediately a slender woman carrying a coal scuttle emerged from one of the sheds directly behind them. She came over to where they were standing and put the scuttle down.

'Yes? How can I help you?'

'Good morning. My name is Ifor Thompson, and this is my wife, Annie. We just wondered if Mr Parry-Jones would be interested in buying a puppy next time our Braid here has a litter. We've heard that Mr Parry-Jones is a highly rated shot in these parts and Braid has a pedigree a mile long. I've got all the details in the car. So I wondered if he is at home, because if he is, he might be interested in seeing us.'

The woman bent down to stroke Braid's head. Ifor noticed that her long dark-brown hair was drawn back into a loose bun that sat in the nape of her neck.

'Hello, Braid,' she said, 'aren't you *lovely*! But look, I'm sorry, my employers are out and won't be back until later.'

The woman's eyes moved to Annie's face, and Ifor was able to watch her expression change from uncertainty to surprise and then to excitement as she slowly recognised her old friend from the reformatory.

'Hello, Cora,' said Annie.

'Hello, Amy,' said Cheryl, smiling, and the two friends embraced.

'Oh, I'm so happy to see you. I never thought I'd see you again!' said Annie, her voice shaking with joy.

'I never thought I'd ever see you again either. I can't believe it. Both of you, come into the kitchen and I'll put a kettle on. Braid, you can come in too, you good little girlie! Amy, I can't believe it! Are you real? I want to hear everything about your life since we last met, and this time *please* let's keep in touch.' She looked into Annie's eyes, and added, 'My secret is safe with you, isn't it?'

'And mine with you?' said Annie. They both looked at Ifor, who beamed at them.

'Well, I'm keeping Annie's secret safe, so whatever your secret is, you can count on me to keep it too. Whatever you did, you've paid for it. I'll respect that and not say a word.'

They drank tea and chatted and promised to keep in touch. There was only one awkward moment and that was when 'Cora' asked for Annie's address and telephone number, but Ifor was quick in his response.

'I'm afraid we are temporarily homeless right now, but we'll never move away from Wales, Cora, so Annie – or should I say Amy! – will never be far away. Another thing, about Braid's puppies: you know, I'm not sure that the

Parry-Joneses are the right people for one of our puppies if, as you say, they live in London most of the time. Our puppies need lots of love, exercise and training, so may I suggest that you don't bother to tell them about our visit? There are people literally queuing up for Braid's pups, so we'll not lose out. And it goes without saying that we'll honour your secret, as you'll honour ours. If anyone finds out about it, it won't be from us.'

They chatted for a while and then pencilled in a date for Amy and Cora to meet for lunch in Aberystwyth in a few weeks' time. As they took their leave, Ifor asked if he could use the cloakroom before driving back to the coast. Then, with kisses all round, they took their leave.

Cheryl waved Annie and Ifor goodbye, picked up the coal scuttle, and made her way to the scullery where she put it down. Then, back in the kitchen, she collected the cups and saucers, the teapot, and the dish of water she had put down for Braid, washed up, and deftly set the kitchen straight.

Standing at the kitchen sink, Cheryl did not turn around when a man came up behind her.

'Who were those people?'

'Nobody important. Just a local couple who breed dogs wondering if the Parry-Joneses would be interested in buying one of their puppies. That's all. They didn't know that Geraint works in London and isn't in a position to take on a puppy. Anyway, they were very nice, so I made them a pot of tea.'

III

As the Thompsons drove away from Llancoed, Ifor could not keep the excitement out his voice.

'He was there. *He was there.*'

'*Who* was *what?*' said Annie.

'Randall Selkirk was there *all the time – at Llancoed.*'

'What! You mean that all the time we were there, Cora knew he was in the house and said nothing?'

'That's exactly what I mean. Although I didn't actually see him, I know he was there because when I went to the cloakroom just now I recognised his sailing equipment stacked up in a corner. I know it's Randall Selkirk's stuff because I saw him with exactly the same things at the pub only yesterday – even down to the tartan Thermos flask. D'you know, it's possible he overheard everything we said. God, I do hope he didn't recognise the hotel car from when I picked up Jack in Aberystwyth yesterday. Come on, let's get the hell out of here, we could give Braid a run on the way home and still be back at Brinkley House in time to help Mrs Saunders with Sunday lunch. We can get our story straight on the way back.'

IV

Punctually at eleven o'clock on that same Sunday morning, the Brinkley House contingent assembled in the Conference Room to find out what Roxanne, Ann and Janey had learned about the murder of Peter Sims by Cheryl Gibson.

Roxanne was the first to speak.

'My neighbour has found my diary entries for the summer of 1950. I was living with my grandparents in

99

Hereford and going to a day-school there. Randall had made it too dangerous for me to live at home. According to my diary, around the time the little boy was killed, what was bugging me was the fact that I was being made to have piano lessons with a dreadful woman called Miss Spence who used to shout at me. That Christmas I visited our new house in Hampshire for the first time. That's all. Over to you, Ann.'

Ann obligingly stood up, characteristically hooking her blonde hair behind her ears.

'I've made some enquiries,' she said, 'and, yes, it's all here. The death of the little boy, Peter Sims, didn't cause a great stir at the time, perhaps because it happened just prior to the school holidays, or perhaps because it happened in such a tiny village. Anyhow, it received hardly any press coverage, and none of my colleagues could recall the murder at all.' Ann eyed Janey, who was trying to interrupt her.

'What is it, Janey?' said Ann.

'The lack of media coverage seems very unusual. Usually the press can't resist a nice juicy murder, especially one like that – a child murderer and child victim.'

Ann carried on, ignoring Janey's comment.

'Another possible reason for the general lack of interest in the trial relating to the little boy's death could have been due to a certain squeamishness on the part of the public about pinning the term "manslaughter" on to a ten-year-old child. Today Peter Sims's death would have most certainly been seen as an unfortunate accident, not manslaughter. In the 1950s very few people had heard of Piaget, and his publication on the development of logic in young children wasn't published until 1958. Today we appreciate the fact that although ten-year-old children know that we need to breathe air in order to live, they might not necessarily consider the consequences of playing a silly game which involves shutting one another inside a refrigerator. Apparently Cheryl had herself been shut in that fridge by Peter while playing this same deadly game. In my view, the true criminals here were Cheryl's mother and Peter Sims's father for leaving the refrigerator in the garden. Apparently Cheryl's mother could actually see Cheryl and Peter messing around with the fridge from her kitchen window, and yet did nothing about it. Oh, and there's no record of any suspicion falling on Randall. His name wasn't mentioned at all.'

Janey briefly concluded the group's research.

'In short, John says that Cheryl herself was adamant that she was the only person playing with Peter at the time of his death. She confessed to shutting Peter into the refrigerator saying, and I quote: "*I don't remember doing it, but it must have been me because there was nobody else.*"'

Sally stood up again.

'Poor Cheryl, and poor little Peter Sims! Thank you for all this. There's a lot to take in, so perhaps now would be a good time for a short break. I know it's still early, but if by some miracle Ifor and Annie Thompson have already returned from Llancoed, I'll get them in to tell us about Kathryn – Cheryl – or whatever she calls herself, and then *please* can we concentrate on the Randall issue and try to come up with some answers today?'

V

Just as Judith was settling down into a large armchair with a cup of tea, Sally returned from the office.

'Is everything all right, Sally?' she asked.

'Yes, I suppose so, though I'm getting rather frustrated by all this time-wasting. We need protection from *Randall*, not Cheryl. Anyhow, Ifor and Annie may have good news for us. They got back a few minutes ago and Don is going to bring them in for us when they've had a cup of tea.'

Sally sat down with the rest of the group, and a few minutes later Don ushered Ifor and Annie into the drawing-room. Everyone was quiet as Ifor stepped forward respectfully.

'Mrs Thompson and I have just got back from Llancoed. The owner of the house was out, so we talked to the housekeeper. She was definitely the lady in the photograph and she turned out to be very friendly. She liked Braid and asked us in for a cup of tea. We discussed the possibility of Mr Parry-Jones buying one of Braid's puppies next time round but, to be honest, he's not right for raising a puppy because he spends most of the time working in London. I told the housekeeper so and she agreed. So that was that. As we left to go home I asked if I could use the toilet, and there, in the corner of the cloakroom, was the exact same stuff I saw Randall Selkirk with at the pub yesterday. Same duffel coat, same old oilskins and same bag of sailing stuff with a tartan Thermos-flask sticking out of it – exactly the same.'

Standing next to Ifor, Sally thanked him on behalf of the group.

'We owe you an enormous debt of gratitude for going to Llancoed for us,' she said. 'Thanks to you both, we now know that the Cathie Brook in the photograph is the same person as the housekeeper you saw today, and now, thanks to you, we also have evidence that Randall Selkirk was probably there too. We know that Cheryl and Randall Selkirk were childhood friends, but we didn't know that they were still friends. A long time ago, when Cheryl Gibson was ten years old, she killed a little boy and spent several years in a reformatory for a crime that, today, would have been seen as a tragic accident, nothing more. And just to add to Cheryl's misery, her family completely disowned her, so that's maybe why she took up with Randall again. Of course, she may have to be nice to him because he's blackmailing her about her past – we just don't know. So now you know as much as we do. Again, thank you very much for undertaking this fact-finding mission for us. We really do appreciate what you've done.'

Ifor and Annie listened to Sally's words politely before leaving the room together.

'Please excuse me a moment,' Janey called as she followed Ifor and Annie out into the hall. 'Sorry, but would you mind if I asked you another quick question?'

'No, not at all,' said Ifor, looking surprised.

'In the photograph, Cheryl's hair is short, blonde and wavy, so what is it like now?'

'Quite different', said Annie. 'It is long, dark brown and pulled back in a bun.'

'Thank you', said Janey.

VI

Annie was busy cooking Sunday lunch, and even though she was cooking for eleven people, she found it pleasantly relaxing. Normally there would be fifty or more mouths to feed, and she would have to coordinate her activities with a motley team of mostly untrained kitchen staff. Cooking for a small group on her own was much more satisfying, and it also gave her a chance to mull over what Sally had said just now. She wondered how Cora would feel if she knew that she was innocent of causing the death of that little boy. *She really ought to be told*, she thought, and, on the spur of the moment, she decided to squeeze in a quick call to Cora just before serving coffee. Having made her decision, she turned her attention to a large plum and apple pie, effortlessly kneading the pastry with powerful fingers.

After lunch, while Ifor was taking Braid for a walk, Annie dialled Cheryl's number on the kitchen telephone.

'Hello? Cora? It's me, Amy. Can you listen a mo? . . . Look I haven't got much time so I'll keep it short. Ifor and I told you a fib this morning. Sorry! Ifor and I work at the Brinkley House Hotel at Aberdovey. We were sent to Llancoed to see if a "Cheryl Gibson" worked there. They had a photo, so I knew it was you we were going to see even before we left the hotel. I told them *nothing*, honest, you've got to believe me. I hope you're not cross with me.'

'For goodness sake don't worry, Annie. It was such a lovely surprise to see you again and to meet Ifor – and Braid.'

'Thank you for being so understanding. In actual fact it wasn't you they were worried about. It was someone called Randall.'

'Randall?'

'Yes, I think that was the name. Well, anyway, after I got back to the hotel I was told that one of the weekend guests had found out about your past. She said that you should never have been blamed for that little boy's death because you were too young to know what you were doing. Today it would have been considered a tragic accident, and not your fault. You can't be blamed for what happened when you were such a little girl. That's really why I'm ringing you now. You are innocent.'

There was a pause on the other end of the line. Then: 'Are you sure? I'm . . . innocent? Good heavens! . . . I can't believe it. Thank you so much for saying that, Amy. I've always blamed myself for little Peter's death, but now I feel so relieved. Thank you so much for telling me. You are an angel.'

'Look, Cora, I've got to go and serve coffee . . . but please don't be cross with me, I never told them, honest. Bye-bye, Cora. *Love you.*'

Annie replaced the receiver and, smiling, returned to the dining-room. She felt very pleased with herself.

VII

Cheryl put down the telephone and stood looking out of the kitchen window. She thought of that skinny little boy, Peter Sims, and how much she had resented the attention her mother had given him. She remembered how badly she had wanted him to just go away, to disappear for ever, and how vibrantly alive and happy she had felt when teaching him the 'fridge game'. The result of her actions? Nearly eight years at a reformatory and total rejection by everyone, including Mum. Only Randall had stayed loyal. She picked up the telephone and dialled his number.

'Hello, Randy, it's me.'

'What gives?'

'The Brinkley House lot have located me here at Llancoed. They sent those people who came here this morning to spy on me. The woman was Annie, their housekeeper.'

'Good God!'

'Yes, but what they didn't know was that Annie – or Amy as she was called then – was at the reformatory with me. We were good friends there.'

'I love it! What did Annie do to get sent there?'

'She attacked her mother's lover with a red-hot spade and pushed him on to a bonfire. He had been sexually abusing her for years, but her mother gave evidence against her, and that was that.'

'Nasty! So where does this leave me?'

'Well, I don't know yet, which is why I'm calling you.'

'We could use this information to our advantage, but at the moment I can't quite see how.'

'Well, I do think we've got to think of something, because Annie has just rung me to say that it wasn't just me that they had been sent to Llancoed to find out about – it was you as well. That means we've been rumbled . . . !'

'Ah, now that puts a completely different complexion on the whole thing. If they've cottoned on to what we've been up to together, things could start getting serious.'

'Yes, so we need to come up with something quickly. I've still got *the letter* and so tonight when we meet at Aberdovey we'll need to use the current situation as the springboard for another rewarding enterprise now that the Brinkley lot know that we're an item.'

'You're a clever old sausage, aren't you! Yes, we'll think up something when we meet up at the Black Stallion tonight.'

'Can't wait – but, look, I've got to go. See you later.'

'See you tonight.'

CHAPTER SEVEN

Puppet or Puppeteer?

I

A AFTER LUNCH JUDITH and Ralph slipped out for a short walk. They badly needed the exercise as they had been sitting too long and eating too much ever since they arrived at Aberdovey. Keeping their eyes on the time, they headed down to the shore and were soon striding along a sunless beach enjoying the sharp sea air.

'You know,' said Judith, 'Sally has played a really dirty trick on us by not warning us of the risks involved in coming here. I've had no contact with Randall for nearly thirty years yet now, thanks to Sally, we are sitting-ducks should he decide to pop over tonight. I really think we should consider leaving Brinkley House right now.'

'Yes, I think we should, too,' said Ralph. 'And yes, Sally and Don should have provided us with the relevant information before inviting us to stay. A brief summary of Randall's treatment of Marcie attached to our invitations would have warned us of the risks involved in coming here and, had Janey been pre-warned, she could have asked her policeman friend to find out about Randall's antics in advance. That way we wouldn't be sitting here on a Sunday afternoon full of fear and trepidation having accomplished nothing and with time running out.'

Judith, her dark hair flying in the wind, looked lovingly up at Ralph.

'It's funny to be back on this beach again. When I was a little girl I could never have imagined that one day I'd be walking along here with my beautiful, wonderful husband, the father of my two lovely children. I'm so lucky!'

'I'm the lucky one,' said Ralph, laughing as he picked Judith up in his arms and effortlessly swung her around. 'You are everything to me, my little spinning-top!' He kissed her tenderly as he gently put her down on the sand. Soon they were walking back to the hotel.

'What do you really think of my school friends?' asked Judith.

'Well, I think Marcie is the best of the bunch. It's just a shame she and her parents failed to see through Randall's charm in time to save themselves from him. That's the trouble with thoroughly decent people; they tend not to recognise deficiencies in others. Ann is a charming woman too, intelligent and kind, and I really like Jack. Now, Janey is an interesting character – because I bet she hasn't spent the last thirty years just looking after her mother. There has to be more to her than that . . . so I wonder what she's really been up to and why she's keeping it to herself. And what's her relationship with this policeman, John Green, she keeps going on about?'

'Yes, I'm surprised about Janey, because she was a strong character at school, a brilliant mimic and extremely funny at times. She had lots of interests and hobbies too. I can't imagine her sitting at home doing nothing. So anyway, apart from Don and Sally, what about Livia, Trot and Roxanne?'

'Well, all three women are high achievers. Each one of them is a top-ranking career woman in her own field. I like Trot best. She's straightforward and honest, and, in my estimation, the most attractive of the three. Livia and Roxanne are in a different category, as far as I'm concerned.'

'How interesting!' Judith was fascinated by Ralph's comments.

'Well, here's one fact that I think we need to bear in mind this afternoon, though I'm not sure if anyone else picked up on this when Livia was talking.'

'What's that?'

'That she was madly in love with Cheryl Gibson – Katie Gilbert – or whatever she calls herself. Yes, I think so: *madly* in love.'

'No! Poor Livia!'

'Don't worry, she's a tough businesswoman. I expect she soon got over it.'

Hand in hand, Judith and Ralph walked back to the hotel where they joined the rest of the group.

II

Sally looked at the clock on the Conference Room wall. It was already past two o'clock and they hadn't even started to answer the key question: *what to do about Randall?* Only one more night and then everyone would be leaving the hotel and she, Don and the girls would be left all alone and vulnerable again. She was about to open the afternoon's discussion when Janey stood up.

'Before we get started, Sally, I wonder if I could ask Ifor and Annie to come back in, because I've got a funny feeling that they haven't told us everything about their visit to Llancoed this morning.'

'Yes, of course.' Sally tried not to show her frustration.

'Thank you. I just want to make sure that we haven't missed anything. Any objections?'

Sally briskly left the Conference Room and returned with a decidedly flustered Annie in tow.

Janey addressed Annie firmly, but kindly.

'Mrs Thompson, please excuse us for calling you in again, but we wonder if we might ask you another question about your visit to Llancoed this morning? You see, we just wonder if there is anything else you know that might shed a bit of light on Cheryl's past . . . Something you may have forgotten to tell us, perhaps?'

Annie looked at Janey, and then at Sally. She started to speak, defensively at first, but then with resolve.

'Ifor is out walking Braid, but he'd back me up if he was here. I'm going to tell you everything, but please remember that we were only little at the time. Cheryl and I know each other. We were at school together for more than seven years. It wasn't an ordinary school . . . It was a special school for child criminals. As you know, when Cheryl was ten she was found guilty of manslaughter and sentenced to eight years there as her punishment. That's where we met. I was about the same age. My mam's boyfriend had been sexually abusing me for years, but it got worse. When I couldn't bear it any more, I hit him over the head with a shovel while he was bending over a bonfire. His face was badly burned. My mam swore me to silence about what he'd been doing to me, and I realised that she must have known about it all along but kept quiet. As a result the police found me guilty of what they called an "unprovoked attack". After that I was sent away to that school, where I met Cheryl – or Cora, as she was called there. When we met this morning, we were really happy to see each other, and when you said that she was too young to be guilty of killing that little boy, I rang Cora and told her what you'd said. Ifor knows nothing – he only found out about my guilty past today on the drive to Llancoed – but I know he stands right beside me. Cheryl and I have had to keep our guilty secrets to ourselves. Cook-housekeeper is what we're trained for, and we don't want to lose our jobs. So now you all know. And Mr and Mrs Saunders –' Annie stood there, her eyes cast downwards – 'I realise that you may not want me here any more. If you want us to leave, please just say.'

Sally immediately walked over and put her arms around Annie.

'My dear Annie,' she said. 'Don and I couldn't exist without you. You are everything to us! You poor little person, having to carry that dreadful burden all your life. You weren't to blame, *you* were the *victim*! Well, you are free of it now, but what an appalling thing to happen to a little girl – and to be betrayed by your own mother like that! You are completely innocent, Annie. And have no fear: you and Ifor are safe with us and always will be.'

Annie took a handkerchief from her pocket and dabbed at her eyes as she left the room, lovingly escorted by Sally and Don.

III

Ann exchanged a wifely glance with Jack, then looked around the table.

'Now *that* was interesting, don't you think? After all those years at a reformatory, Annie and Cheryl are still loyal to one another. If Cheryl is capable of retaining Annie's love and devotion all these years, then perhaps she is capable of inspiring a long-term relationship with Randall.'

'Yes,' agreed Trot, 'and if Randall has been blackmailing Cheryl about Peter Sims's untimely death all these years, now that she knows she's innocent in the eyes of the law she can tell him to jump in the lake! So now, with Cheryl out of the picture, surely everything hinges on finding a way to curb Randall's antisocial behaviour?'

Trot smiled at Sally and Don, who were quietly slipping back into their places around the table.

'Yes, but how *can* we curb his behaviour?' Ann replied. 'That's the problem. You see, Randall goes around hurting people in various ways, and yet when they respond negatively to his behaviour he is vengeful towards *them*, the very people he has abused. So we *can't* persuade him to reform because he can't reform. And we can't punish him, because that would make his behaviour even worse. And we can't get angry with him for fear of retribution. And we can't have him locked up, because unless he was shut away for life, he'd get out and probably come looking for us. So we appear to be stuck!'

'So what you're saying is that Randall is as much a victim of his own behaviour as the people he abuses,' said Sally.

'Well, yes, it's a very cruel condition,' said Ann. 'By a quirk of nature he has been dealt a faulty set of instructions relating to specific parts of the brain that control behaviour. As a consequence, he lacks some of the built-in checks and balances we all need to live in harmony with our fellow man or woman. It's a congenital condition and there's no cure for it.' She glanced at Ralph, who was politely holding up his hand to speak.

Ralph's voice was as pleasing to the ear as were his good looks to the eye.

'I notice that we have moved our position from seeking answers from Cheryl and Randall as a couple to focusing our attention on Randall alone. Personally I consider this a retrograde step because it's highly likely that Cheryl has had a profound influence on Randall's behaviour throughout his life. If we are to stop Randall from persecuting Marcie and her close friends, we cannot afford to ignore Cheryl's power over him. After all, what do we really know about Cheryl? For instance, do we know what she was doing after Marcie sold her Chelsea house in 1975?'

There was no reply, so Ralph continued.

'We can be fairly certain that Cheryl and Randall were in close contact around 1976 and 1977, the period during which we assume Cheryl helped Randall to move into your out-house at Redcliffe, Marcie. But where was Cheryl living at that time? And what was she doing?'

Again, nobody answered.

'We can also assume that Randall was living in London during the years he befriended you, Don; and we also know that during that period Randall's criminal behaviour escalated, culminating in that murderous attack on you and your unborn baby, Sally. So what was Cheryl doing between 1978 and 1983, and where was she living?'

Ralph paused and looked around the table at blank faces.

Then Ann leaned across the table excitedly.

'I think I get your drift now, Ralph. Are you suggesting that Cheryl has some way of controlling Randall's behaviour?'

'Yes, exactly that, Ann. Cheryl and Randall were playmates when they were hardly more than babies, so perhaps "baby Cheryl" learned how to manipulate "baby Randall's" behaviour during a critical period in his development. Perhaps she found that she could control him by withdrawing her friendship, bullying him, or taking his toys away from him if he didn't do what she wanted. Anyhow, if we can find a pattern linking Randall's worst criminal behaviour to specific periods when Cheryl was actively present in his life, then we may have found a clue to ways we can control his behaviour in the future. What do you think, Roxanne?'

'I like the way you're thinking, Ralph, but I just don't know enough about his psychopathy to comment on the matter.'

'Maybe Cheryl conditioned Randall, like training a horse,' said Trot.

'Yes, Trot, but here comes an even weirder thought, so bear with me. You see,' said Ralph, 'as a lawyer, when I think of Cheryl and Randall I am reminded of Bonnie and Clyde. They too were friends who became lovers and partners in crime. They too—'

'Come *on*!' Livia interrupted. 'Aren't you going just a bit too far, Ralph? I mean, you couldn't find a more diligent and trustworthy housekeeper *anywhere*.'

'How can you call Cheryl trustworthy when she lied to your face?'

'When did she do that?'

'Well, wasn't Cheryl lying to you when she asked you if you had been to Brinkley House School with a girl called Marcie? After all, she knew damn well that you'd been at school with Marcie, because in 1962 she waited on you all for the entire week of Marcie's wedding!'

'Well, yes, I suppose so . . .'

'Yes, indeed she did, and so she *lied* to you – and then

what did she do? She told you that she had heard on the grapevine that Marcie's ex-husband, "a man called Randall", had refused to accept their divorce and was venting his rage on Marcie and her old school chums. Isn't that what you said she said? And didn't you also tell us that Cheryl warned you to make sure your finances were safe from Randall's thieving propensities?'

'Well, yes, but she was always a hard-working and diligent housekeeper, as far as I am concerned.'

'Well, she may be a diligent housekeeper, but she certainly isn't trustworthy. A trustworthy housekeeper doesn't have aliases, and a trustworthy housekeeper doesn't invite her lover into her employer's home without permission. Take the Parry-Joneses, for instance. What do you think they'd do if they found out that their "Kathryn Booker" was letting her psychopathic lover live in their house while they were in Paddington? She would be dismissed immediately, and in the light of the Peter Sims murder she might even find herself before the courts again and even receive a prison sentence.'

The room had fallen silent at the logic of Ralph's account.

'Now I've probably got this totally wrong,' he went on, 'but bear with me. So, just *suppose* we are dealing with *two* criminals here. *Two* lifelong friends working together as a team. You could say that Randall works "front-of-house", selling his charm and sex-appeal like a shopkeeper displaying his wares, while Cheryl works "back-stage", plotting and planning and using her unique skills to make herself indispensable to her wealth-creating employers. Together, by pooling their criminal talents as thieves and confidence-tricksters, they are effectively able to suck money from their unwitting hosts. Think about it, Livia: it was only *after* Cheryl realised that she and Randall would not be able to access your money that she gave in her notice.'

Ralph looked around the table.

'So perhaps it's Cheryl who is running the show. After all, it is Cheryl who finds accommodation for Randall within her employers' houses, and it is Cheryl who lies for Randall and, presumably, gives him the "all-clear" when it is safe to access her employers' homes behind their backs. And another thing. Marcie, can you remember where and when you first met Randall?'

'Yes, I met him at a party I held at our Chelsea house. As your brother, Roxanne, it seemed natural that he should be there, although now that I come to think about it, you weren't actually there yourself. Silly me! Cheryl probably organised the whole thing.'

'Don't judge yourself by Randall's warped standards, Marcie. No normal person could ever imagine such devious behaviour. We know that Randall stole from you, Marcie – and from you, Sally and Don – but was it his idea, or did Cheryl put him up to it?'

There was a tense silence, and then Janey spoke.

'I'm very interested in your argument, Ralph, because for the first time we have actually put two and two together and come up with a number that adds up. Up until now, we've allowed our anxiety about Randall to obscure our view of Cheryl.'

Janey turned to Ann.

'Quick question, Ann. We know that Cheryl likes to work alone, and is highly competent at her job. We also know that she is capable of carrying out a wide range of domestic roles, as well as being extremely charming, helpful and efficient. On the other hand, we now know

that she murdered Peter Sims – whether accidentally or not
– and that she can be extremely manipulative, as well as
being an accomplished liar. Putting these facts together, it
looks as if Cheryl isn't a very nice person . . . in fact, she
now appears to be a very nasty person. So, Ann, do
Cheryl's characteristics fit any particular psychological
profile that you recognise?'

'Strangely enough,' Ann replied, 'just now, as you and
Ralph were talking, your assessment of Cheryl's
personality struck me as exemplifying one particular
personality type to a tee. I've made a few "off-the-cuff"
jottings, and I'm afraid they don't make for comfortable
reading . . .'

She cleared her throat and began reading her notes.

'*Obsessive personality, orderly, meticulous, fussy about
details. Constantly checking and double-checking. Seeks
isolation and has strong need for control. When young,
learned to manipulate others to carry out own wishes.
Enjoys holding power over others and is capable of sadistic
and cruel acts which may excite her sexually* . . . Actually,
if I'm correct in all this, the term "sadomasochist" comes
to mind, but remember, this is just an informal opinion. If,
however, my gut feeling accurately describes Cheryl's
psyche, then I'm afraid she was perfectly capable of making
Randall do her bidding when they were toddlers together,
and perfectly capable of killing Peter Sims in cold blood
when she was just ten years old – especially if he was
demanding of her mother's affections. Sadomasochists are
capable of doing very bad things, and the thought that
Cheryl might be manipulating Randall's psychopathic
personality to feed her own sadistic tendencies is not a
pretty one. If our worst fears are realised, I really think we
might need outside help on this one, but what kind of help,

and from whom, I really don't know.'

Janey broke into the anxious silence that followed Ann's statement, speaking calmly but with determination.

'Now that the situation seems to be worse than we originally thought, I think I'd better take you all into my confidence. I could kick myself for being so slow on the uptake, and for not having done so earlier. Well, anyhow, here goes.'

Janey stood up to speak, casting her cool grey eyes around the table.

IV

Janey Collins looked the epitome of conventionality as she stood there in front of her friends. Her podgy feet laced up in sensible shoes, her plump body buttoned into its drab Sunday suit, and her greying hair, all combined to make her look older than her forty-six years; and yet, retrospectively, Janey's contribution was seen as a critical break-through in the weekend's proceedings.

She spoke in a clear, authoritative voice.

'As we now suspect, Randall's behaviour was particularly criminal and violent during the late seventies, as tragically witnessed by you, Sally and Don. And Ralph, you asked what Cheryl might have been doing between then and 1983, and where she might have been living. Well, I think I can answer that question. In the early 1980s I was living at Paddington with my mother and it was during the summer of 1982 that I realised that she needed full-time nursing care. So I dismissed the part-time carers that had been looking after my mother, contacted a well-respected agency, and took on the live-in carer they recommended.'

The eyes of the more astute members of the group widened as they heard Janey's words, and all too soon their worst imaginings were realised.

'Her name was Kelly Graham, and she was meticulously kitted out in a navy-blue uniform and beret, the latter worn over short, dark-brown hair. She was a most attentive employee, fully justifying the agency's faith in her. Kelly was clean, tidy, organised and efficient, and I was particularly pleased, because not only did my mother like her, the rest of our staff liked her too. I was delighted that Kelly fitted in so well because it gave me a chance to get out and about a bit. I knew I could trust Kelly to take good care of my mother, and felt that she liked being with us.'

Janey momentarily faltered, but quickly regained her composure.

'Later that summer, after Kelly had been with us for a few weeks, I went to Italy with a group of friends knowing that my mother was in capable hands. During the first two days I telephoned her frequently, and she seemed happy, but later on it was Kelly who picked up the phone. Yes, my mother was fine, she would reassure me, but was asleep, or having a meal, or entertaining a friend for tea. Any fears I had were swiftly allayed, and as I started to unwind I failed to ring home as often as I should have. During the final days of my holiday, when I did ring, nobody picked up the phone, so I just assumed that everyone was busy, or that Kelly was bathing my mother. Something like that. However,' she continued, 'when I returned, London was in the grip of a heatwave. I went straight home, and the first thing that hit me when I entered the house was a terrible smell. I ran upstairs to my mother's room and found my mother's putrefying corpse lying on the bed.'

There was a shocked intake of breath from Janey's friends, but Janey ignored it and continued to set out the details of her mother's death.

'The autopsy showed that she had been dead for some time, but finding no evidence of foul play, they ascribed her death to old age. Reeling from the shock of finding my mother not only dead but almost unrecognisable, I was also distressed to find the house completely empty. It transpired that Kelly had dismissed my domestic staff on full pay after the first week of my holiday, apparently on my say-so. Then, when the agency tried to contact Kelly, they found that she had disappeared. They were unable to locate her. Later I found that several of my mother's personal possessions had gone missing.'

'But that's outrageous!' Ann was appalled. 'She got rid of your mother's household staff so that she could murder your mother and then steal from her?'

'I know. It's totally outrageous. Anyhow, the local police tried very hard to find Kelly, but because there was no physical evidence that my mother had actually been murdered – because the decaying process was at such an advanced stage – and because the stolen items were of value only to my mother (things like family photograph albums, paintings by friends, tapestries and a cushion) – they were forced admit defeat. The fact that a paid carer had run off leaving her client lying dead on her bed was seen as grossly negligent and unprofessional, but they assumed that when Kelly had found her employer dead she had panicked and run away. As there was no evidence of foul play, and as my mother was so old and frail, the police saw no reason to follow it up further.'

Janey looked at the shocked faces of her friends.

'This afternoon everything finally slotted into place. Of

course – Kelly was Cheryl! I was an idiot not to recognise her from the photograph you showed me, Marcie, but I gain comfort from you, Livia, as you didn't recognise her either. A lot of water has passed under the bridge since Marcie's wedding, and in my defence I had been looking for a uniformed nurse/carer, not a housekeeper. It was only today, when Annie Thompson described Cheryl as a brunette with long hair pulled back into a bun, that I started to appreciate the level of sophistication we're up against here. You see, right up until a few minutes ago I hadn't fully appreciated the fact that in order to play the role of "Kelly Graham", Cheryl would have had to be a highly talented actress. Yet it wasn't simply her outward appearance and manner she had had to alter to fit her newly acquired employment profile. In order to get the job of caring for my mother, Cheryl must have provided the agency with references so convincing that they were believed to be genuine by experts in the field. "Authentic" lists of exams passed . . . "authentic" records of previous experience . . . and even "authentic" letters of recommendation from grateful clients. According to the agency, everything had checked out, so how did Cheryl acquire these apparently authentic references? The answer has to be that someone helped her. So who was it? Did Cheryl and Randall plan the whole thing together, or are the two of them simply part of a larger enterprise? And why go to all that trouble? My mother didn't even know Cheryl, so what was the motive for taking her life?'

There was subdued fury in Janey's voice, but she had not yet finished what she had to say.

'A great many of us have been victimised or injured by Randall in one way or another but if, as Ralph suggests, Randall is just the puppet, and Cheryl is the puppet-master pulling his strings, then in order to control him we must first control her. Thanks to your swiftness in recognising Cheryl Gibson as Randall's childhood playmate, Roxanne, and thanks also to my friend John Green for finding out that Cheryl killed Peter Sims, a tiny clue presents itself regarding a possible motive for Cheryl's murder of my mother. And so, looking back to Cheryl's childhood, we can see that her mother, Mrs Gibson, was negligent and cruel. Not only did she fail to safeguard both Cheryl and Peter when they were playing "the fridge game" right under her nose, but also, after Peter's death, she totally disowned Cheryl. So is Cheryl's mother still alive, or did *she die* in suspicious circumstances too? I've asked John Green to find out if Mrs Gibson is dead and, if so, the circumstances of her death. Secondly, in terms of my mother's death, is it possible that Cheryl murdered other mothers belonging to our group? Trot and Livia, we know that your mothers died before 1962, so that means that only five of us who attended your wedding, Marcie, had mothers still living. Therefore the question is this: apart from my mother, have any other of our mothers died under suspicious circumstances?'

Janey's grey eyes moved around the table and stopped at Roxanne.

'Roxanne, I know that apart from Randall, your family did not attend Marcie's wedding but, nevertheless, was there anything suspicious about *your* mother's death?'

Roxanne replied calmly.

'She died at home about five years ago. She was quite old, but in excellent health for her age. After she'd finished gardening, she had gone into the kitchen to make herself a cup of tea. Her dead body was later found lying on the floor, and it was assumed that she had over-tired herself gardening. She was still in her gardening clothes, and I can't help wondering why, if she felt ill, she hadn't telephoned for help. It just seems a bit odd to me.'

Marcie leaned towards Roxanne.

'I remember you telling me about it at the time, and Randall didn't attend the funeral, as I recall.'

'No, but he knew she had died.' Roxanne turned her attention back to Janey. 'You know, Janey, there is something you mentioned just now that might be important. A long shot, I admit, so I apologise for raising this painful subject.'

'What's that?' asked Janey.

'You say that one of the items that you found missing after your mother's death was a cushion. So my question is this: did the police ever consider the possibility that the cushion had been used to, well . . . to smother Mrs Collins?'

'You mean . . . ? Oh, you mean that Kelly may have removed it because it had traces of Mummy's saliva on it?'

'Yes, precisely that! So tell us more about it. You say it was one of a pair?'

'Yes, I've still got its matching partner at home.'

'What's it like?'

'Well, it's very old and – come to think of it – probably very valuable. It was made in France and has my family's coat-of-arms embroidered on it in gold thread. Of course, this raises the question: if Mummy was not smothered to death by one of her French cushions, why didn't Kelly steal both of them? One on its own is far less valuable than a matching pair. So the fact that only one is missing suggests that Mummy's murderer knew that it was an important piece of evidence, since it may have had her saliva on it.'

'Yes, and you know,' said Roxanne, 'at some point it

might be a good idea if we cast an eye around Cheryl's rooms at Llancoed to see if the missing cushion is there.'

'Excellent idea, Roxanne!' said Janey. She began to say something else, but Marcie interrupted her.

'Look, while we're on the subject, I just think I ought to say that it's quite conceivable that Cheryl killed my mother too. Her body was found soon after the death of my father in 1974 and her death was put down to grief and physical and mental exhaustion. Now I'm not so sure. As you all know, there was nothing to stop Cheryl driving over to Redcliffe any time she liked. She was probably living in the converted out-house with Randall most of the time anyhow, so she had easy access to my mother and could easily have smothered her too. My mother's death was the last straw: it broke me, body, mind and spirit – it literally drove me mad. Maybe that's exactly what Cheryl wanted.'

'Of course!' said Janey. 'So if we can prove that Cheryl murdered not only her own mother but also my mother, and possibly Roxanne's and Marcie's mothers as well, she'd be locked up for life. Perhaps Cheryl developed a sadistic compulsion to kill mothers after her own mother betrayed her so cruelly . . . If so, I wonder if any more of our mothers are at risk?'

'My parents live in Scotland,' said Judith. 'Hopefully the distance alone will keep my mother safe.'

'Good! Anyone else? I know that your mothers are no longer alive, Livia and Trot, so what about you, Sally?'

'My mother died in 1983, soon after Randall stole her life savings and killed our baby,' said Sally. 'She was very frail, and we all assumed that the events of that year had been too much for her. She just died of old age – or rather, that's what we thought. Now I doubt we'll ever know.'

Trot put into words what everyone was thinking but didn't like to say.

'If our worst fears are realised, then Cheryl has murdered five mothers – Janey's, Roxanne's, Marcie's, and Sally's, as well as her own mother. Add little Peter Sims to the list of victims, and the whole thing is quite horrific!'

As this information was absorbed, silence descended – a silence cut short by Ralph.

'I'm sorry to say this, Trot, but don't you think you are rather jumping the gun? So far there is not one iota of real evidence to support the idea that any of your mothers were murdered at all, let alone by Cheryl. As you yourself say, Janey, Cheryl had no apparent motive for killing your mother, and this lack of motive applies to your mother too, Roxanne. After all, why on earth would Cheryl want to bump off her lover's mother? *If*, however, your missing cushion is found in Cheryl's possession, and *if* a subsequent forensic examination revealed traces of saliva on it, and if a DNA test proved the saliva to be Mrs Collins's saliva, then this *might* indicate that Mrs Collins had been murdered, *possibly* by Cheryl.'

'You're right, Ralph, we mustn't jump to conclusions,' said Janey, 'but if Cheryl has hidden the cushion at Llancoed we need to find it as soon as possible – preferably today. So, if nobody objects, I'd like to telephone the Parry-Joneses to ask them if we can search Cheryl's quarters. We can't do that without their permission, and we certainly can't do it if Cheryl is there. Ideally the Parry-Joneses should accompany us while we're in their house so that we can't be accused of anything at a later date. We also need to make sure that neither Annie at this end, nor Cheryl at the other end, can overhear our telephone conversation and contact one another.'

'Yes, and if we don't get on with it, we might find we're too late anyhow,' Ralph chipped in crisply. '*If* the Parry-Joneses spent the weekend here, they're probably well on their way to Paddington by now.'

As Janey and Sally made their way to the office, the rest of the group took advantage of the short break to have a cup of tea and some excellent fruit cake while mulling over the shocking details of Janey's mother's death.

V

A few minutes later Janey and Sally returned to the Conference Room.

'I had no trouble getting through to Llancoed,' said Janey. 'Apparently Geraint Parry-Jones – and his wife Fion – were just about to drive off to London, so we were very lucky to catch them. We owe you thanks for that, Ralph.

'The first thing I found out was that their housekeeper, "Kathryn Booker" – alias Cheryl Gibson – has a separate line, and so couldn't listen in to our conversation.'

'Thank goodness for that,' said Trot, her mouth full. Janey ignored her.

'Then I told Geraint about your wedding to Randall Selkirk in 1962, Marcie, and how your parents had employed a "Cathie Brook" to look after six of your school friends for the week of your wedding celebrations. Then I told him about my mother's death and of our suspicions that her carer may have been involved, especially as certain items went missing from the house at that time. Then I told him that we think it possible that this same person now works for him at Llancoed under an assumed name.'

Janey's friends murmured their appreciation of her thoroughness.

'Finally, I asked Geraint if he would join us for a quick look around his housekeeper's private apartment in Llancoed on the off-chance that valuable objects stolen from Mrs Collins at the time of her tragic death might be amongst her possessions. He was totally supportive, and told me that his wife, Fion, was suffering from a tummy-bug and that it would be easy to tell "Kathryn" that they wanted to postpone the trip to Paddington until tomorrow morning. Apparently Kathryn likes to go out on Sunday evenings, and Geraint feels sure that she will stick to her routine. In the unlikely event that she decides to stay in, he promised to ring us straight back.'

Janey looked at her watch and spoke with urgency.

'What we have to decide now is who is going to join Geraint and me when we search "Kathryn's" rooms. Obviously I haven't told them about the French cushion, but clearly I need to be there to identify it, if it's there. You need to be there too, Marcie, because Randall and Cheryl have consistently robbed your family – so that makes two of us. Roxanne, can I ask you to be the third member of our little group? After all, Randall is Cheryl's lover, and if there is something fishy about your mother's death, we may find out more when we search Cheryl's premises.'

'Of course I'd like to come with you. I'll drive.'

Ralph nodded his head in agreement.

'Yes, Janey, that all makes sense,' he said. 'But I think Trot should go with you too.'

Trot sat up and looked daggers at Ralph.

'Why me? Cheryl hasn't stolen anything from *me*!'

'That's the reason why we need you to go along as an unbiased witness,' said Ralph. 'I'm a lawyer, don't forget. If the whole thing ends up in court, your version of events could be crucial.'

'I'm sorry, but I really don't see why I should have to go,' Trot replied testily. 'After all, all this Cheryl business has nothing to do with me. Surely you're not going to try to *make* me go.'

'Of course not,' said Ralph. 'The last thing we'd want to do is coerce you. So would anyone else be happy to accompany Janey, Marcie and Roxanne to Llancoed?'

'I'd like to volunteer,' said Judith. 'I'd be happy to go along as an unbiased witness.'

'Are you sure?' Ralph looked decidedly peeved.

'Yes,' Judith replied. 'It will be an outing *with a difference.*'

'Thank you, Judith. With you coming too, it'll be perfect!' said Marcie.

'Hear, hear!' said Roxanne and Janey in unison, and friendly glances were exchanged.

'So now,' said Sally, 'we need to plan what the rest of us are going to do. Trot, what about you?'

'Eat, read, watch TV, sleep? How does that sound to you?' A characteristic element of rebellion tinged Trot's comment.

'Well, actually, I'm glad that you and Livia will be here overnight, Trot,' Sally replied. 'You can help Don and me keep a look-out just in case Randall decides to drop in uninvited.'

'Of course.' Livia spoke sympathetically, eyeing Trot with disapproval; but Trot ignored her and so Sally returned to the subject at hand.

'Jack, I assume that at some point during the evening you and Ann will want Ifor to drive you to Aberystwyth harbour so that you can check that *Manatee* is ready for your trip home tomorrow. So while there, you can keep tabs on Randall's yacht. Is that a good idea?'

'Of course it is,' Jack replied. 'If there are any signs that *Valkyrie* is about to leave her mooring, we'll contact you immediately and follow at a safe distance.'

'Don't forget, Ann, it's just possible that Randall might recognise you even after thirty years, and he'll certainly recognise you, Jack, from yesterday's surprise encounter. As for Ifor, if he drives you there, don't forget that Randall was lurking at Llancoed this morning when he and Annie dropped in on Cheryl. Do be careful.'

'Don't worry,' said Ann. 'Jack and I are masters of disguise! So, come on, let's get cracking! Janey, Marcie, Roxanne and Judith – time for you to get going before you lose the light, so I'll say au revoir.'

'Yes, and God bless you all,' said Sally.

'Thanks.'

Roxanne and Marcie, helped along by Judith and Janey, left the room, and soon all four of them were winging their way to Llancoed in Roxanne's car.

VI

Cheryl Gibson was making a quick telephone call to her friend, Randall Selkirk.

'Randy, is that you? . . . Have you moored *Valkyrie* at our secret place as planned? . . . Good work, sexy boy! I'll be over a bit later than planned, I'm afraid. There are one or two jobs I've got to do here before I can get away . . . No, nothing exciting, just routine stuff, and it won't take long. Fion's not well, so they're staying at Llancoed overnight, that's all . . . They'll probably head off at first light tomorrow . . . So yes, I'll be setting off in under an hour and I'll park at the Black Stallion . . . We can work out details when we meet . . . Yes they're all there, the whole bunch . . . At the Brinkley House Hotel . . . Yes . . . Meet you soon . . . At the pub . . . I'll treat you . . . Okay then? Take care. See you soon. Bye.'

CHAPTER EIGHT

The Ring

I

IT WAS LATE AFTERNOON when Roxanne, Janey, Marcie and Judith set off for Llancoed. Although there were four of them in the car, there was plenty of room and, because Roxanne was a highly competent driver, they knew they could relax and enjoy the journey. Soon they had left Aberdovey and Machynlleth behind them, and were heading south towards Aberystwyth.

At Talybont they turned off the main road and headed inland, following the road leading to the Nant-y-Moch Reservoir and Cambrian Mountains. Chattering away to one another as they drove along the south bank of the reservoir, the four friends were suddenly silenced when the sun broke through dark purple clouds and flooded the wild and watery landscape with rays of pure gold. A short while later, Roxanne asked Marcie to pull out the small, hand-drawn map given to them by Ifor Thompson just before they left the hotel. This map would guide them over the last part of the journey and, sure enough, following Ifor's instructions, Roxanne swiftly located the turning off the Ponterwyd road and the country lane leading to the cul-de-sac. Carefully steering her car down the lane, Roxanne soon located the narrow cut-through bisecting the oakwood, and drove down to the end where gates and the sign Llancoed marked the front of an imposing stone house.

They were about to get out of the car when they were hailed by a middle-aged man who emerged from the front door.

'Hello! I'm Geraint' he yelled. 'You need to park round the back.' He stuck out his thumb to his left'

'Thank you,' shouted Roxanne, quickly restarting the engine. She speedily steered the car around to the back of the house and parked it, just as Geraint came out through the kitchen to greet them. He made a bee-line for Janey.

'My name is Geraint – and *you* are Janey Collins. I recognise you from Paddington, when I knew your mother. So please do the honours and introduce me to your friends.'

After being introduced to everyone, Geraint ushered them into a small sitting-room beyond the kitchen, where tea and biscuits had been set out for them. Geraint poured the tea and handed out the cups.

'Make yourselves at home,' he said, 'but don't take long. We need to get started before the evening draws in.'

'Is Mrs Parry-Jones here? We'd very much like to meet her.'

'Fion is still getting over her tummy-bug and doesn't want you lot to catch it off her,' Geraint replied.

'I'm so sorry to hear that,' said Janey. 'Please give her my best wishes. I hope she feels better very soon.'

As Judith waited for her tea to cool, she had a moment to study Geraint at close quarters, and she was not impressed by what she saw. He was a short, swarthy man with dark curly hair and a powerful, hot-tempered demeanour. Judith wondered what it would be like to be married to him. Not nice, she thought, and wondered what Fion was like.

She took her tea over to a small window overlooking the side of the house and strangely, as if on cue, she saw a woman threading her way carefully along the side of what Judith took to be a coal shed. Everything about the woman's body-language – the way she hugged the wall and the furtive way she crept along it – told Judith that here was someone who most definitely did not want to be seen. She looked so wrinkled and bent, she might have been Geraint's mother, not his wife; but if she was indeed Fion, the diagnosis of a tummy-upset was wrong. This woman looked terminally ill. Judith instinctively diagnosed cancer. Brought quickly back to earth, Judith heard Geraint speaking to Marcie.

'I see you've been in the wars, Marcia. I hope you're recovering well.'

'Yes,' replied Marcie. 'I'll soon be back to my normal self.'

'What caused your accident?'

'I was out riding when someone shot my horse dead. It fell on top of me and I was pinned underneath it for a long time. I couldn't see who shot me . . . but it is most likely to have been my ex-husband, Randall Selkirk.'

Roxanne broke in.

'I can vouch for the verity of that, I'm afraid, because Marcie's ex-husband happens to be my brother. I expect you've met him when he comes to visit.'

'Randall Selkirk has never been invited to this house, I can vouch for *that*. Right then,' Geraint went on, quickly changing the subject. 'Now that we've had some tea, let's get on with it, shall we? But first, may I make an important point? If we do find any stolen goods here, we'll need to call out the police.'

'On a Sunday evening? Aren't you being rather optimistic?' said Roxanne.

'They'll come out for me. I'm on the Police Committee, see. There'd be a big stink if they refused, I can tell you. So, if we do find anything, we'd best not remove it without informing the police, okay? Follow me.'

Geraint led them through a small hall and unlocked the door to the quarters of Kathryn Booker, Cheryl Gibson's alias. They all went inside and looked around an apartment that would have made a nun's cell seem cluttered. The sitting-room was spotlessly clean, and there were a couple of newspapers neatly folded on a footstool beside the single armchair. There were precisely two small ornaments on the mantelpiece, and the bookcase was virtually empty. In her bedroom, Cheryl's obsessive traits were even more conspicuous. Everything had been scrubbed and dusted, and the contents of every cupboard and shelf had been arranged along military lines. There was nothing under her bed or on top of her clothes cupboard. Her bathroom was so clean it looked brand new, and the airing cupboard was practically empty. Janey examined the walls, floors and ceiling for concealed trap-doors, but there was nothing to see.

Then Geraint led them through the kitchen to the utility room. This room contained a washing machine, a tumble dryer, a plastic clothes basket and a drying rack with two garments drying on it. It was spotlessly clean and there was nowhere to hide anything.

From the utility room the small group made its way over to Cheryl's garage. They knew there would be no car in it because Cheryl had left Llancoed before their arrival but, even so, they were not prepared to find it so completely empty and so completely clean. In fact, it was shiny clean, as if it had been scrubbed, and there was nothing in it except for one broom, one dustpan and brush, one scrubbing brush and one tin of car-cleaning fluid with a spotlessly cloth neatly folded on top of it.

'I think you'd better check our garage too, while you're here,' Geraint volunteered and they all followed him into a double garage outside which two cars were parked. It was just a normal garage with the normal jumble of bikes, lawnmowers, deckchairs, petrol cans, hooks with gardening implements hanging from them, and shelves with bags of fertiliser stacked upon them. Nothing else.

As they left the garage, Janey and Roxanne put their heads together.

'I think we should ask to see their attic and cellar – assuming they have them,' said Roxanne, looking up at the house thoughtfully.

'That's outrageous,' Janey whispered. 'Those are their private quarters.'

Regardless of Janey's embarrassment, Roxanne walked over towards Geraint.

'I know it's a terrible nerve to ask this, but could Kathryn have hidden anything in your attic or cellar?'

'I doubt it,' Geraint replied. 'But take a look. Hopefully it'll put your mind at rest.'

Geraint led them back to the house and they all went up to the attic while Marcie, who felt unequal to the stairs, waited for them in the little sitting-room. Up in the attic, predictably, everything was spotlessly clean. There were two trunks of clothes which Geraint opened for them to inspect, an old train set and a doll's house, and a number of cardboard boxes full of old vinyl gramophone records. There was no sign of Mrs Collins's cushion, nor any other recognisable items. Gradually they all started to feel excruciatingly embarrassed, and by the time they had descended to the cellar, they knew they wouldn't find anything, and their prediction was borne out: there was nothing there.

Finally, Geraint led them out through the front door and out on to the drive. Looking across the front lawn, they could see the oakwood and the gate leading into the lane. So that was that! They started to walk around to the car.

'Excuse me, Geraint,' said Judith, 'but you have been so kind to us, and so patient, I wonder if I could ask you just one more favour? You see, we need to tell everyone back at Brinkley House that we've looked *all round* Llancoed, so would you mind terribly if we walked back to the car around this side of the house? Would that be all right?'

'Of course,' he said.

Geraint led the way down the narrow path between the house and the oakwood, closely followed by Janey, Judith and Roxanne. Marcie trailed behind.

Suddenly there was a crash, and a cry. They turned round to see Marcie lying sprawled on the ground. Roxanne rushed back to her.

'God, Marcie! What happened? Are you all right?'

Marcie laughed as she lay there.

'Sorry. No I'm fine. I fell over my own sticks, or perhaps that little root back there. I'm just a clumsy idiot, that's all.'

The rest of the group rushed back, and Geraint was clearly worried by Marcie's fall.

'Are you all right, Marcia?' he asked. 'No bones broken, I hope?'

They pulled Marcie back on to her feet. She looked unhurt: just a little embarrassed perhaps, but otherwise unscathed.

'No, I'm fine, and I do apologise for being so clumsy.'

Janey took matters into her own hands and spoke to Geraint on behalf of them all.

'You know, it's high time we all crawled back to Brinkley House with our tails between our legs. We've prevented you from going to London, we've put you to enormous trouble, we've crawled all over your house – literally! We've been on a wild goose chase for nothing, so all we can do is apologise to you, and thank you for your superhuman courtesy and kindness.'

'Think nothing of it. I've actually quite enjoyed it and I'd be honoured if you would come back for tea and cake before you leave.'

'You are so incredibly kind and *forgiving*.' Janey emphasised the last word. 'The least we can do is leave you in peace for the rest of the evening.'

Judith and Janey carefully escorted Marcie along the path to the back of Llancoed where Roxanne's car was parked. Once more, the four friends thanked Geraint for his hospitality.

Geraint replied courteously.

'Marcia, Roxanne and Judith, it's been a pleasure to meet you. And Janey, I hope to meet up with you again in Paddington. Goodbye.'

II

They all waved goodbye, and Roxanne started to drive back along the lane; but as soon as they were out of sight of the house, Marcie suddenly cried, '*Stop the car*!' Roxanne immediately applied the brakes and brought the car to a standstill.

'What's up?' Roxanne asked tensely.

'This,' said Marcie, holding out her hand to Roxanne.

'What?' Judith leaned forward, trying to see. 'What do you mean?'

'I didn't fall over just now,' said Marcie. 'I was walking along the path and something shiny at the side of the path caught my eye. As I can't bend over properly yet, I let myself fall very gently so that I could pick it up and pocket it. The reason I asked Roxanne to stop the car just now is so that we can examine it properly. So, what do you think? Personally, it looks as if our suspicions may be justified after all. Take a close look.'

Marcie and Roxanne examined the object closely and carefully passed it back to Judith and Janey in the back seat.

Suddenly, to everyone's shock and surprise, Janey emitted an extraordinary, inhuman squeak.

'It's *Mummy's*! It's *Mummy's* ring! Granny gave it to her when she came of age. It's been in my family for generations. I can easily prove it's mine, because it's been photographed and recorded in the Gordon-Collins family archives. It's also listed as one of the items that went missing at the time of my mother's death.' Then, to everyone's horror, she burst into tears.

Marcie, kindly ignoring Janey's outburst, carried on talking.

'Another thing,' she said. 'Did you notice the stile close to where I pretended to fall?'

No. Nobody had noticed a stile.

'I found the ring lying close to this stile, and had a moment to look around before I did my collapsing act. I noticed that one side of the stile was overgrown with brambles and that the other abutted a small gate. There were lots of footprints, so clearly the stile had been in recent use. So, now, what do you think we should do?'

'Keep driving,' said Judith. 'If Geraint and Fion drive down the lane and see us here, they'll know we're up to something. So why don't we keep going, but at the same time look out for a container vehicle of some kind – a van, caravan or lorry – screened by the trees yet close to the road. That would be highly suspicious, don't you think? If we see anything, we'll have to report it immediately.'

Roxanne restarted the engine and drove along the lane. All eyes were pinned on the two sides of the wood, but no vehicles were visible there.

They were silent as they reached the T-junction at the end of the lane. A left-hand turn would take them in the direction of Ponterwyd and Devil's Bridge, and so everyone was surprised when Roxanne turned right, steering her car towards the shabby cul-de-sac that Ifor had marked on his map just before they left the hotel.

'Haven't you gone the wrong way?' asked Judith. 'Isn't this a dead end?'

Roxanne ignored her, and kept on driving along the lower margin of the oakwood. Then, noticing a gap between the trees over to her right, she crossed over and neatly parked her car in the space. She switched off the engine.

'Sorry, Judith, I've been thinking. Come on, everyone,

what does *Llancoed* mean? Tell me that!'

'Church . . . wood,' said Marcie. '*Of course!* . . . We are complete idiots! Good grief!'

'I'm not sure that I follow you,' said Judith.

'Well, several things,' said Roxanne. 'The name "Church Wood" suggests that there may actually be a *church* here in the *wood*. If there is, then originally Llancoed would have been the vicarage, and the vicar probably used the stile and footpath to access his church. His congregation, however, would have probably gained access from this road, perhaps even from this spot. What do you think? Shall we go for a little walk?'

'I'm sorry, but I'm not sure I understand,' said Judith. 'Are you saying that when Geraint Parry-Jones knew that we wanted to search Llancoed, he, Cheryl and Fion moved a whole lot of stolen stuff from their house and carried it over to the church? Surely, if that's the case, we risk bumping into them carting it all back again?'

'Good point,' Roxanne replied.

'Incidentally,' said Judith, 'I should tell you that there is no way Fion Parry-Jones could have helped Geraint move anything to the church. I caught a glimpse of her when we were having tea. She is emaciated: Methuselah on a *bad-hair* day!'

'Poor thing!' Roxanne commented. 'What we could do, though, is take a little walk in the woods. There's no law against that, is there? If caught, we can always say that we wanted to look at the church. But yes, there are risks, so is there anyone who'd rather wait in the car? Marcie?'

'Actually,' said Janey, 'in terms of Cheryl's guilt, we've already got all the proof we need now that we've found my mother's wedding ring – a ring so valuable she never took it off her finger. Wouldn't it be more sensible to check to see if there actually is a church in the wood? That would be proof enough. If they've hidden stolen goods in it, they'll have locked it anyhow. You're a speedy walker, Roxanne, so why don't you have a quick look on your own? If asked, we can simply say you've been *caught short*.'

'Okay, good idea.'

'Don't be long, though, and be very careful.'

Roxanne was out of the car and into the wood in a trice, and while the others waited in the car, they examined Janey's mother's ring again. Then Judith asked Janey how she and her mother had come to know the Parry-Joneses.

'Actually I've never met Fion, but I met Geraint in Paddington ages ago. My mother knew him because he owned an antique shop in Portobello and . . .' Janey stopped mid-sentence. 'Oh, I'm such an idiot! Good heavens! How could I be so stupid?'

'What do you mean?' asked Judith.

'Geraint is a highly successful antique dealer – that's what I mean.'

'Of course, but don't we already know that?' said Marcie.

'Yes, but Geraint isn't just an ordinary antique dealer: he's big business. In the Paddington area he's the fattest cat in a trade full of fat cats. So maybe he's a black-marketeer, and maybe he's the brains behind all the thefts and nasty things that Cheryl and Randall have done to us over the years . . . Oh dear, how could I have been so blind!'

'It's not your fault, Janey,' said Marcie. 'You thought he was your mother's friend, so naturally you trusted him.'

'I feel so stupid about my mother's ring. I reported it missing when she died, and the police asked me where I had last seen it, and I said "on my mother's finger". I expect they thought I was off my chump.'

'Well, you weren't,' said Marcie. 'It was the truth. You had been victimised by a bunch of thoroughly horrid criminals who murdered your mother out of sheer malice, and it now seems possible that your mother's friend, Geraint Parry-Jones, masterminded it all in order to steal her valuable ring and other personal items. Perhaps he's the brains behind the plundering of Redcliffe too . . . Perhaps he even orchestrated the criminal acts carried out against Don and Sally Saunders. Perhaps Cheryl and Randall are merely Geraint's henchmen . . .'

Judith was just about to reply when Roxanne appeared, strode over to the car, got in and started the engine.

'I'm going to turn the car around. Yes, there *is* a church in the wood, and yes, it *is* padlocked. So we must get to a telephone as soon as we can.' – Roxanne swung her car effortlessly around, and drove back along the narrow lane, looking out for the turning to the road to Ponterwyd.

Once on the right road, she spoke to her friends.

'The track leads to a de-consecrated church and graveyard. There are signs of trampling around the church entrance, and all along the path leading to the stile and Llancoed beyond. That means that we've got to get the police over there tonight, before Geraint removes the evidence.'

'What do you think we should do? Should we contact Brinkley House first?' said Judith.

'Yes,' said Roxanne. 'As soon as we can, we should tell Sally and Don about finding Janey's mother's stolen ring on a footpath leading directly from Llancoed to a church hidden in the wood. We should also tell them that we think that the Parry-Joneses cleared their house before we arrived, and that Geraint may be on the Aberystwyth

Police Committee. We need to ask them for advice. I'll do the talking if you like.'

'Oh, yes *please*!' There was a general sigh of relief.

'Okay. But Janey, where did you put your mother's ring?'

'It's here, on my finger. It fits perfectly.'

'Good. Remember, though, at the moment it's the only evidence we have – apart from the trampling around the church and the suspicious emptiness of Llancoed – so look after it well.'

'Don't worry, I will . . . And there's something else I need to tell you, Roxanne, something that came to light while you were in the wood.'

Janey told Roxanne how she had suddenly considered it possible that Geraint might be the brain behind all the criminal activities carried out by Randall and Cheryl over the years.

Roxanne was silent for a time, processing the theory.

'You may well be on to something here,' she said at last. 'So when we get to Ponterwyd, we must tell Sally what we suspect. To get evidence to back up our suspicions, we'll have to gain access to the church tonight. It could be empty by tomorrow morning.'

'Phew! I hope there's somewhere nice to eat at Ponterwyd,' said Marcie.

'Actually, I could do with a very strong drink,' Janey added.

'But what if there isn't anywhere to eat or drink at Ponterwyd?' said Judith. '*Then* what do we do?'

'We throw ourselves upon the mercy of the Welsh people,' said Roxanne. 'And believe me, there are no kinder folk in the whole universe. We'd be smothered by hospitality.'

Roxanne drove on into the fast-approaching night.

CHAPTER NINE

Tom Mortimer

I

ROXANNE WAS RIGHT. The George Borrow Hotel, with its well-stocked bar and welcoming atmosphere, was everything the four friends could have hoped for – and more. With a large bottle of red wine open on their table and a fish-and-chip supper for four ordered, Roxanne went off to make contact with the Brinkley House Hotel on the public telephone.

'Sally? This is Roxanne speaking.'

'Is everything all right? I've got lots to tell you, but tell me your news first.'

'Okay, I'll be brief then.'

Roxanne told Sally about Llancoed, about finding Mrs Collins's ring, about the little church in the wood and about their growing suspicions about Geraint Parry-Jones.

'Right now we are at the George Borrow Hotel at Ponterwyd,' she added. 'We are about to eat supper, after which we plan to revisit the church. We badly need help, so any ideas? Geraint says he is on the Aberystwyth Police Committee, so we don't dare call out the local police.'

'Good grief!' Sally sounded appalled. 'Well, this

evening, not long after you left Brinkley House, Janey's friend, John Green, called from London to warn Janey about a certain Geraint Parry-Jones. It turns out that John Green is a very senior policeman indeed, and when I told him where you had gone, and why, he was very concerned for your safety. Apparently he has just found out that Parry-Jones is a thief and black-marketeer who's been giving the London Metropolitan Police Force the runaround for some time. Apparently one of John Green's contacts casually mentioned the name Geraint Parry-Jones to a senior officer involved in the case and he nearly had a fit! It seems that Parry-Jones is suspected of committing a whole raft of crimes in the Paddington area, but despite the best efforts of the Met, they've been unable to pin anything on him.'

'That fits,' said Roxanne.

'Now this bit is very important,' Sally continued urgently. 'John Green has told me to give you this telephone number which you are to ring as soon as you hang up. Write this down. Ready? Here it is.'

Roxanne duly noted the telephone number Sally dictated to her and then read it back to her.

'Good,' said Sally. 'Now, you are to telephone this number *right now*. You must tell the police everything. They've promised back-up, and I'm sure they'll accompany you when you open up the church tonight. So I'll say goodbye and good luck.'

'Goodbye, Sally, and thank you for all this. I'll telephone the number right now and try to report back to you sometime later. Bye.'

'Bye.'

Roxanne hung up, and immediately dialled the number Sally had passed on to her. The ensuing conversation was short but concise and soon afterwards she went back to the pub dining-room to join Marcie, Judith and Janey.

II

After taking a swig of red wine and a few bites of piping-hot fish-and-chips, Roxanne duly passed on the information she had found out on the telephone.

'Earlier this evening, not long after we had left Aberdovey, John Green telephoned the hotel to warn us about Geraint Parry-Jones. When Sally told him that we had already left for Llancoed, he was concerned for our safety. The fact of the matter is that the police suspect Geraint of being linked to a whole raft of criminal activities, mainly in the Paddington area but in other parts of London as well. Unfortunately, each time the Met gets close to pinning anything on him he manages to slip out from their grasp. John Green gave Sally a telephone number to pass on to us with instructions to ring immediately, which I've just done. I made contact with a branch of the Aberystwyth Police Force working in conjunction with the London Met on this particular case. They have been briefed by John Green and were expecting our call. So here's the plan.'

Roxanne put down her knife and fork.

'Five policemen will be turning up at nine thirty – that's in just over twenty minutes. We must be ready to leave here before then, because a senior officer specialising in the recovery of stolen property is coming here to interview us first. Apparently he needs to find out as much as he can about specific items so that if they turn up they can be correctly identified, documented and, if needs be, forensically examined. So here's the plan.

'We're to lead a police car and van to Llancoed. The policemen in the car have orders to park in the cut-through leading to Llancoed and to keep in radio contact with the police van. If it transpires that the church is being used to hide Geraint's stolen goods, the policemen in the car are to race down the lane to Llancoed and arrest Parry-Jones. Our job is to look around the church and locate any items stolen from us or our families and see if they match the relevant police checklists. The policemen we will be dealing with have been specially trained to handle valuable artefacts so we can be confident that anything we find will be handled professionally.'

'That's impressive,' said Judith.

'Yes,' Roxanne replied, 'and *if* the police van isn't too wide for the track and *if* the padlock on the church doesn't give them too much hassle – it'll be a miracle!'

Janey leaned forward in her chair to top up her friends' wine glasses.

'Good old John, he's certainly done us proud.'

'Yes,' said Roxanne, 'and I think we'd better get ourselves washed and ready for tonight's adventure right now. I'll stay and pay the bill, and may I suggest that we are all ready in ten minutes? Our expert could be with us any minute now.'

III

A short while later, the four friends were ready to leave the hotel. Staring out at the rain-sodden road, they sat waiting for the police officer and his team to arrive.

'I hope they're armed,' said Marcie.

'The men in the police car will be,' said Janey knowledgeably.

Just as Janey said these words, they saw a police car pull up at the side of the road and, through the rain, they could just make out the figure of a tall, thin man running towards the hotel holding his raincoat, and a large bag he was carrying, tightly against his body. A moment later the man, minus raincoat, entered the dining-room..

'Hello. I think you are expecting me. May I join you?'

'Of course. Let me introduce you to everyone. I'm Janey Collins, and these are my friends Roxanne Selkirk, Marcia Stanton-Gray and Judith McKenna.'

The grey-haired policeman greeted them all.

'Hello, I'm Detective Sergeant Thomas Mortimer. Tom, *please*! Good. Now, firstly, I want to thank all of you for giving us a real opportunity to arrest Geraint Parry-Jones – and, incidentally, he's not on the Aberystwyth Police Committee. That was a lie.'

As Tom spoke, his body language and general demeanour gave the impression that here was a man truly comfortable in his own skin. Despite the late hour and stormy weather, and despite his wet collar and sodden hair, Tom radiated confidence and goodwill. Comforted by the soothing lilt of his voice, they all felt that here was a man they could depend upon.

'As you can see, I'm part of a plain-clothes unit specialising in the identification and recovery of stolen property,' Tom made eye-contact with each member of the group. 'So now, by way of introduction and to save time, I'm going to ask each of you to tell me about specific items Parry-Jones may have stolen from you, so that if the church at Llancoed is being used as a repository for stolen antiquities we can look out for them. Marcie first – if I may. Hello there! Look, you'll be pleased to learn that I've been sent a telex listing all the heirlooms and family treasures reported to us as stolen from your family since 1962. This list includes illustrations, so if we find any matches, we'll be able to restore them to you after they've been processed.'

'Oh, that's marvellous. Thank you.'

'Now Janey. Tonight you might be able to identify the valuable French cushion that went missing at the time of your mother's death. If we find it, rest assured that it will be handled professionally, checked over thoroughly by our forensic team and returned to you at a specified date.'

Tom then asked Janey to show him the ring that Marcie had found at Llancoed.

Janey held out her hand and Tom examined it with interest.

'Very fine indeed . . . And this belonged to your mother?' Janey nodded. 'Good. And I gather that some photograph albums, framed paintings and embroidered wall hangings were also stolen from your mother around the time of her death. May I briefly question you about these?'

'Yes, of course.'

'I gather that six framed paintings disappeared from Mrs Collins's house around the time of her death. Can you tell me a bit more about them?'

'Not really. All I know is that my mother kept them in her study, and that they went missing around the time she died. I know that one of them was painted in Cornwall by a friend of hers. I'm not sure about the other paintings, I'm not good at that sort of thing.'

'Fair enough, but what about the photographs? Any ideas?'

'I do know that some of them are old, and might be

considered valuable these days. As for the wall tapestries, yes, they are very old, but I don't know anything about them either.'

'Well, we'll certainly look out for them, thank you Janey.'

'Thank *you*.'

Tom turned to look at Judith and Roxanne.

'I'm not sure that I've been given any information about you two, I'm afraid. Please put me in the picture.'

'Nothing has been stolen from me,' said Judith. 'I volunteered to come along as an unbiased witness.'

'Excellent! And you, Roxanne?'

'I'm afraid that Marcie's ex-husband, my brother Randall Selkirk, has been in a life-long relationship with a woman called Cheryl Gibson. Cheryl, using the name Kathryn Booker, is currently employed as cook-housekeeper by Geraint Parry-Jones of Llancoed. Unfortunately, Marcie, Janey, and the owners of the Brinkley House Hotel in Aberdovey, Sally and Don Saunders, have been robbed, abused and victimised by both Randall and Cheryl, and we're now starting to wonder if Parry-Jones might not be behind the whole thing.'

'Thank you, Roxanne. This information is highly relevant.' Tom jotted down some quick notes.

'Oh, and I forgot to say,' added Roxanne, 'that if Janey's golden cushion fails to show up here, it might turn up at the Parry-Joneses' London house. After all, the cushion was stolen from Mrs Collins's house in Paddington.'

'Good point. I'll pass this information on to the Met.'

'Thank you,' said Roxanne, 'and if you still want us to lead you to the church, my car is ready to leave right now.

We have to get back to Aberdovey tonight, so don't you think we ought to get going?'

'Of course! You're happy to lead us there?'

'Yes, but what about you? If the police car is stopping at Llancoed, how will you get to the church?'

'Well, actually, I was slightly hoping I could scrounge a lift off you. Is that possible?'

'Of course it is,' said Roxanne. 'But how long will you want us to stay at the church? Will we have to wait while you pack up the police van?'

'No, after we've identified and docketed anything belonging to you, then, as far as I'm concerned, your job is over. After you've left, you can trust us to look after any stolen property we find and deliver it safely to a temporary police storage facility back at Aberystwyth.'

'We trust you implicitly.' Janey informed Tom, who, to her surprise, winked knowingly at her and led her out to the small reception area leading to the front entrance. From a bulky bag he produced a rectangular box wrapped in brown wrapping paper and held it out for Janey.

'Janey,' Tom whispered into Janey's ear. 'John Green wanted me to provide you with this. Don't worry, it's been officially processed. It's just in case you need it.'

Janey thanked Tom profusely, *sotto voce*. She knew immediately what was in the box.

'Isn't John brilliant?' She whispered. 'Thank you very, very much. D'you know, I think I'd better visit the cloakroom before we leave the hotel – just to be on the safe side!'

'Good idea.' Tom smiled knowingly.

IV

On his way to Roxanne's car, Tom spoke briefly to his men waiting outside in the two police vehicles, and dropped off his raincoat. Then he climbed into the front seat beside Roxanne, who was keen to get started. She switched on the engine, pulled out into the road, overtook the two police vehicles and pulled up in front of them. Then, as planned, she walked back to give brief instructions to the two police drivers before returning to her car, ready to lead her convoy to Llancoed.

As they set off, Tom decided to take advantage of having a captive audience in order to find answers to questions that were puzzling him.

'I know that Cheryl Gibson killed a little boy and was sent to a reformatory, but I gather that since then she has worked her way around your group using different aliases. So, Marcie, what was she called when your parents employed her?'

'Cathie Brook. She ran our house in Chelsea for several years. She was there when I first met Roxanne's brother, Randall Selkirk, who became my husband.'

Marcie went on to tell Tom that Cheryl Gibson (alias Cathie Brook) had looked after her school friends for the week of her wedding. Only when it was too late had Marcie learned that her marriage was part of a crazy plan to reduce the Stanton-Gray family to penury. The whole estate had eventually gone belly-up and Marcie's parents had died broken-hearted.

'I'm so sorry. Please stop me if you're finding this upsetting.'

'No, I'm fine. Actually I think it's important that you understand how badly several other members of our group have been treated by Cheryl and Randall. Would you like me to give you a quick overview?'

'Good idea. Would you mind if I jotted down a few notes to help me remember names?'

'Not at all, and I should add that it has only been during this weekend's visit to the Brinkley House Hotel which, incidentally, used to be our boarding school, that it dawned on us that Cathie Brook, Katie Gilbert, Kelly Graham and Kathryn Booker are one and the same person: Cheryl Gibson. I think you also need to know that Randall Selkirk is a psychopath who may be under Cheryl's control. She seems to be the dominant partner in their relationship.'

Trying to be concise, Marcie then told Tom how Randall had destroyed Don Saunder's promising career, cheated Sally's family out of their savings, and killed their unborn baby. Then she told them how Olivia Bard had visited her house in the country, only to find her ex-housekeeper Katie Gilbert and Randall Selkirk stark naked, having sex in her bed. At this point Janey took over from Marcie to explain to him how her beloved mother met her death.

Briefly, Janey told Tom about the carer called Kelly Graham she had employed to look after her mother. Kelly had seemed exceptionally reliable and trustworthy. Later, when Janey had returned after a short holiday, she had found her mother's corpse rotting on her bed in an empty house. Janey reminded Tom that it was at that time that the French cushion had disappeared, as well as the other personal items belonging to Mrs Collins.

Tom listened to Marcie's and Janey's accounts in silence.

'So let me get this straight,' said Tom. 'It was Randall who pushed Sally Saunders down the stairs. Cheryl wasn't there?'

'That's right,' said Judith. 'We don't know where Cheryl was living at that time, but we feel more and more certain that she controls Randall's psychopathic behaviour to satisfy her own sadistic needs. Incidentally, I was one of Randall's rape victims.'

'Good grief! I'm so sorry. How old were you at the time?'

'Eighteen.'

'But that's appalling! Thank you so much for telling me. So now, I just need to make sure I've got all Cheryl Gilbert's aliases sorted correctly. Cathie Brook worked for your family, Marcie, right? Katie Gilbert worked for Livia, right? Kelly Graham may have smothered your mother, Janey, and if the French cushion was used to smother Mrs Collins, it may turn up in Llancoed or, more likely, we'll find it in Paddington. We'll certainly look out for that. So now Cheryl works for Geraint Parry-Jones under the assumed name, Kathryn Booker . . . *Ye gods*!'

'Yes, we know that for a fact. A cook at the Brinkley House Hotel recognised Kathryn Booker at the Parry-Joneses' house. They had spent several years together at the same reformatory so there's no doubt that Kathryn Booker is Cheryl.'

'Thank you so much, you have all been incredibly helpful. There seems to be no end to Cheryl's deceit and criminality. Anyhow, while we're at Llancoed it might be interesting to visit the Parry-Joneses' house and find out what's going on there. You've been a real help, thank you, and thank you, Roxanne, for giving me a lift in your car.'

Arriving at the lane leading to Llancoed, Roxanne signalled to the police car and it peeled off the back of her little convoy and disappeared down the lane leading to Geraint Parry-Jones's house. Then, after continuing along the lower edge of the oakwood for a short distance, Roxanne slowed down, signalled to the police van and waited while it turned into the narrow track leading to the church. Then Roxanne reversed her car a short distance, halting at the entrance of the track to check that the track was accessible to the police van, before following it in her car. When they arrived at the church, Tom thanked Roxanne for giving him a lift, and then walked over to help his men, who were trying to open the large wooden church door. The four friends sat chatting away happily as the rain drummed against the windows of Roxanne's car.

The three policemen, unable to unlock the padlock with the keys they had brought with them, were now trying to cut it with a hacksaw. This was proving to be a slow job. Eventually the padlock was cut, and Tom and his two constables entered the church.

VI

What nobody noticed as Tom and his team entered the church was the tiny figure of Fion Parry-Jones watching them. Soon she was hobbling back to Llancoed to tell Geraint Parry-Jones what she had seen.

CHAPTER TEN

Llancoed

I

A FTER EATING A large dinner cooked earlier by the housekeeper and re-heated by Fion, Geraint Parry-Jones decided to relax in his special chair and watch television. He was exhausted after the events of the day. The physical effort involved in carrying all that stuff to the church, and the strain of having to be nice to all those interfering busybodies hanging around Llancoed for hours and hours, had put him in a very bad mood. Then, to cap it all, he had had to put up with a whole barrage of dopey questions from Fion – and suddenly he'd had enough. Fion was so stupid: why had he ever married her? They had had a beastly row and she had gone out into the rain crying and telling him she was never coming back.

'Go on then – *bugger off!*' He had shouted after her.

He could see that her car was still parked outside their garage so knew she hadn't gone far. He settled back in his armchair and fell fast asleep.

He woke up being shaken.

'Wake up, wake up, Geraint! Quickly. Some people are breaking into the church. Quickly – come and look! Get your boots on – it's wet – but come quickly!'

Geraint struggled to come to his senses and, still fighting exhaustion, put on his boots and jacket and ran out into the rain. He could feel his heart pounding madly as he clambered over the stile and ran along the path to the church through the oakwood, slipping and slithering as he went: but then he stopped running and stood stock-still. Fion was right. There was a large police van parked outside the church. His secret hoard had been discovered.

Geraint rushed back towards the house muttering to himself.

'*Shit!* Those effing women must have called the police. Randall's ugly sister and crippled ex-wife – they must have called the police. *Bloody hell!* Yes, and that woman, Janey, she certainly has the goods on me, *rot her guts!* So think, man, *think!* You've been found out, but you're not done for yet. The police will be here to arrest me any minute now, so I must get out fast. My emergency box, money, passports and pre-packed suitcases are already hidden in the car. I'll leave Fion behind. There's not much she can tell the police that they don't already know. Quick, quick . . . that's it. Got everything I need. Garage open, engine on, lights off and out I crawl. Wiggle, wiggle, through my secret emergency exit behind Llancoed's rear parking area – that's it. Now, a quick squeeze through the gap in the hedge and out on to the farm track behind the oakwood leading to the cul-de-sac. Good! Straight on for a moment . . . and now slow, very slow. I'm crossing the end of the cut-through leading to Llancoed and – yes, yes . . . *yes*! I can just make out the back of a police car waiting to arrest me . . . Silly buggers, you can't catch me! In a few minutes I'll be heading for Ponterwyd, and from there it's no distance to Devil's Bridge where my getaway car is waiting.

After that I'll head south. I've got my false passports and everything I need, and soon I'll be winging my way to sunny Spain. Everything will be tickety-boo. In a funny way, those boring women have done me a favour.'

Soon Geraint Parry-Jones was on his way to Cardiff Airport, singing an aria from *Rigoletto* at the top of his voice.

II

The moment Tom and his two assistants entered the church, they knew that their suspicions regarding Geraint Parry-Jones were entirely justified. They made immediate radio contact with their colleagues waiting down the lane and within seconds the police car, with sirens screaming, was speeding towards Parry-Joneses' house at Llancoed.

When the police car stopped, one of the armed policemen jumped out and rang the front doorbell while the other ran around to the rear of the house. Then, while Geraint Parry-Jones was singing opera on his way to Devil's Bridge, the front door of his house was being opened by his emaciated wife, Fion. Her thin face was pinched and an unhealthy grey colour. She looked utterly distraught.

'I'm afraid you've just missed him, but please come in and I'll tell you what I know.'

The policemen entered quickly, and one of them made a quick check of the house to make sure that she was alone while the other policeman stood around in the kitchen as Fion put on a kettle. She turned around and spoke to him, her eyes dulled by pain.

'It was me. I heard a noise and went to look. I saw the

police van and men cutting the padlock to the church so I told my husband, and he had a look too. Then he went straight to his car and drove off without me. I'll give you his car registration number but it won't do you any good because he keeps another car at Devil's Bridge and I don't know its number, I'm afraid.'

'Do you know where he's heading?'

'Yes, that I *do* know. He'll be on his way to Spain via Cardiff Airport. He owns a house just north of Madrid. I can give you the address if you like.'

'What role do you play in all this?'

'I have no role other than to present a respectable front to the world, to act as hostess and generally sit around twiddling my thumbs.' Fion's face darkened with sadness and rage as she said these words.

Armed with this information, the Welsh policemen quickly contacted their colleagues in Llancoed Church and sat outside in their car to await instructions. Fion remained in the house, alone.

III

A quick visual survey told Tom that, squeezed inside this ancient Welsh church, was a hoard that far outstripped anything he had dealt with before, but, prior to starting to concentrate on the job in hand, the three men made themselves ready for work by replacing their outer clothing with white overalls and putting on protective footwear and gloves. Janey, Marcie, Judith and Roxanne were also asked to leave their outer clothing in the porch and to put on the protective gloves and footwear provided for them.

As Tom walked around the church, his years of

academic study, his extensive police training and his wide experience of thieves, forgers and fraudsters in the antique trade, had not prepared his brain for the shock of what he was seeing right there in front of him. At first he could not take it in. Everywhere, leaning against the walls, piled on to pews and stacked into corners, lay proof that Geraint Parry-Jones was every inch the arch-criminal the Met believed him to be. Medieval musical instruments, tapestries, and embroidered wall hangings; ancient artefacts of ebony and ivory; countless objets d'art made of porcelain, jade and alabaster . . . Pew after pew loaded with antiques such as exquisite Art Nouveau glass creations by René Lalique, many of them adorned with relief figures of exceptional beauty. On the floor, neatly wrapped and stacked against the pulpit, were French Impressionist paintings, and near them, carefully housed in a corner, Tom spied two small paintings of flowers, fruit and vegetables in the style of the seventeenth-century artist, Giovanna Garzoni. They had to be copies, surely? In another corner stood a large collection of garden and farming antiquities, complete with hand-carved tables and chairs, and a carved chest full of ancient (possibly prehistoric) hand-tools. On one row of pews Tom observed a large cluster of jewellery boxes, one of them studded with diamonds. He opened it up and saw that it contained golden earrings, brooches, necklaces and tie pins studded with pearls, diamonds, sapphires, rubies and other gems. Tom had never seen anything like this before, except in books, but his reverie was broken when one of his men shouted over to him.

'Sir! Sir, they've missed him! They've missed Parry-Jones! He's got away!'

Tom came back to earth with a bump.

'What?'

'His wife heard us sawing through the padlock and told Parry-Jones, who went to see for himself. Then he drove off and left her behind. She thinks he's going to his house in Spain, flying from Cardiff Airport. He has a getaway car holed up at Devil's Bridge and we don't have its registration number, but the photograph of him has already been circulated.'

'What? Repeat that please.'

The young policeman repeated the message. 'Parry-Jones has been warned off. He's on his way to Cardiff Airport.'

'Blast and double blast! How on earth did that happen?' Tom was furious, and the four school friends looked at one another in dismay.

'You mean that Fion Parry-Jones was out here in the rain watching us?' Janey was shocked.

'Now that's something we never anticipated,' said Roxanne. 'So she tipped him off and he drove off and left her behind? Charming!'

'Yes, apparently she's been dumped,' said the younger of the two policemen.

'I don't like this at all.' Tom checked his wristwatch and gave his young constable some important orders to follow.

'In a moment I'm going to ask you to make radio contact with the police car and pass on information that must be acted upon immediately. I'd do this myself but I want to get these antiques identified before Miss Collins and her friends leave us. So, now, I want you to note down exactly what I say. Are you ready? First, tell your colleagues that this information must be passed on to the most senior policeman around – the Commissioner himself if necessary – even if it means getting him out of bed. Whatever his rank, he must be made aware of the urgency of the situation immediately.'

'What exactly do you mean, sir?'

'Get this down and tell your colleagues in the police car to make careful notes of everything you tell them. Speak slowly and clearly, so that there is no room for error. Ready?'

'Yes, sir.'

'Geraint Parry-Jones is a criminal urgently wanted by the Met – are you getting this down?'

'Yes, sir.'

'Tonight at Llancoed in Wales, Parry-Jones escaped arrest. He is now heading for Cardiff Airport, and then Spain. His photograph may have already been circulated by the Aberystwyth Police Force, but this needs to be confirmed. There are two ways Parry-Jones might try to reach the Continent – by air from Cardiff, or by sea. If Parry-Jones thinks Cardiff Airport is too risky he may decide to head for the harbour at Aberystwyth. Now this next bit is very important.'

'Yes, sir.'

'At Aberystwyth, Parry-Jones may try to make contact with a "Randall Selkirk". Selkirk keeps a yacht called *Valkyrie* – that's Victor-Alpha-Lima-Kilo-Yankee-Romeo-India-Echo – at Aberystwyth harbour. Parry-Jones may pay Selkirk to sail him to France and so the yacht must be kept under surveillance, all night if necessary, or until Geraint Parry-Jones is either seen boarding *Valkyrie* or until the yacht is seen trying to leave the harbour. Tell your colleagues to relay my name and rank, and that of Superintendent William Glyn-Jones of the Aberystwyth Police Force, as well as that of Superintendent John Green of the Met. As you know, John Green already knows who we are and why we are here so, remember, if we are successful, your parts in this operation will be fully recognised. Do you understand? Now, after your colleagues in the police car have successfully transmitted my message, tell them to return here, to the church. Now, have you got all this down?'

'Okay, sir – yes, sir, I understand. Thank you. I'll get on to it right away.'

The young policeman transmitted the radio message to his colleagues in the police car who, in turn, relayed the information to their superior officers at Aberystwyth. Then, still following Tom's orders, the two policemen left Llancoed and drove over to the church where they helped their team pack up and load the antiques into the van.

As Tom turned his attention back to the job at hand, he suddenly stopped as a new thought struck him. He turned to Roxanne.

'Roxanne, I do hope you understand the necessity of bringing Randall into all this. I hope you don't mind.'

'Of course I don't,' said Roxanne calmly.

'Thank you.' He turned to the group.

'What we're going to do now is put identification stickers on items that can be positively identified as belonging to the Stanton-Gray and Collins families. Once back at the laboratory in London, these articles will be recorded and thoroughly checked and examined. It's a pity that, so far, I can't see the French cushion belonging to you, Janey. We'll need to look out for it so that, if necessary, it can be examined forensically. Anyhow, after we've finished the job, I'll hand over copies of the relevant paperwork to you, Marcie and Janey, so that when in due course the stolen items are returned, you can check them against the lists yourself. It's a painstaking job, but it'll be worth it – especially if we can arrest Parry-Jones before he escapes to Spain. My men and I will take as much as we can back to Aberystwyth tonight and return to finish the job early tomorrow morning. Right then. We'd better get on with it.'

Tom quickly returned to the job of sorting and labelling artefacts stolen from Janey Collins's mother at the time of her death. He was amazed to note that these included signed paintings by Stanhope Forbes and other famous artists of the Newlyn School in Cornwall. Lying together on a pew were two large boxes containing photograph albums. The first album was a photographic record of a method of identifying criminals using anthropometric measurements, or 'mugshots', a technique created by the famous French police officer, Alphonse Bertillon. The second album was crammed full of rare photographs of aeroplanes constructed prior to the First World War. These albums shared a pew with some of the most beautiful and valuable medieval wall-hangings Tom had ever handled. All these priceless paintings and artefacts were duly recorded, labelled, wrapped and set aside ready to be loaded into the van.

After further assurances from Tom that John Green would be updated on the situation, and that, where possible, all the stolen articles would be returned to their rightful owners as soon as they had been properly processed in London, it was time for the police to start packing the police van. Marcie, Janey, Roxanne and Judith were tired and ready to return to the Hotel. It was time to thank Tom and his team for all their support, industry and skill, and so, wishing them good luck and showering them with thanks, the four school friends found themselves driving back down the track and heading towards

Machynlleth and Aberdovey.

Back at the church, Tom and his team worked on until the van was full. Then, after the church had been carefully re-padlocked and sealed off, they returned to Aberystwyth. On Monday morning, after an early breakfast, they would return to finish the job.

IV

It was after midnight when Roxanne and her friends left the church at Llancoed. They were exhausted and yet, despite the fact that Geraint Parry-Jones had escaped police arrest and the French cushion had failed to materialise, they felt that, overall, the day had been a success.

'It's a pity we never got to meet Fion,' said Marcie. 'I feel so sorry for her being married to Geraint. What was she like when you and your mother knew her, Janey?'

'I never met her, and I don't think my mother knew her either. It was Geraint we knew, not Fion.'

'Well, as you know,' said Judith, 'I caught a short glimpse of her walking across the side of Llancoed earlier today and it struck me that she had a whipped-dog look, as if she had been seriously maltreated over a very long period. Actually, she looked as if she was dying.'

'Poor woman. I don't suppose being married to Geraint has done her any favours,' said Marcie.

'You know, Roxanne,' said Janey, 'you were always so kind to everyone at Brinkley House, and such a good friend. It pains me to recall how unpleasant I used to be to you when we were young. You had had such a difficult upbringing with Randall as your brother; I should have been supporting you instead of being so bitchy.'

'I feel the same.' Marcie turned towards Roxanne. 'There's something bestial about children of a certain age, especially when grown-ups leave them too much to their own devices. So, yes, I'd like to say sorry too.'

'Don't worry! Water under the bridge! Anyhow, although I am not a psychopath like Randall – thank goodness – I have inherited a slight sprinkling of wonky genes that have the effect of making me a bit of a social nincompoop. So don't blame yourselves for reacting negatively towards me. I know now that I'm not good with people. I'm better off sticking to inanimate objects.'

'Well, I think you are wonderful,' said Marcie. 'How on earth could I possibly run Redcliffe without your help? I cannot thank you enough for everything you are doing, not only for me, but also for everyone on the estate.'

'Think nothing of it. It's the least I can do in the circumstances. Incidentally, Janey, what's in that box Tom gave you? I saw you rush off to the hotel lavatory with it. So what's your secret? Is it a present from John Green? Come on! Out with it!'

Well, yes, you're right,' Janey replied. 'It was John Green who organised it. He thought I should have it.'

Janey held the box up for her friends to see, and then opened it dramatically, and held it upside down. It was empty.

'I don't understand.' Roxanne sounded perplexed.

'Sorry. Let me explain. You see, when Tom passed the box to me at the hotel I immediately knew that it contained a firearm. Knowing John Green as I do, I expect he asked Tom to make sure that I was armed the moment he realised that Geraint Parry-Jones was a blackguard and that visiting Llancoed was potentially dangerous. So, before we left Ponterwyd I put the firearm into my handbag where it is now. Look, I'll show it to you. It's locked, by the way.' Janey reached into her handbag and drew out a black gun and held it up so that her friends could see it. There was a gasp from Janey's friends.

'Look, don't worry,' said Janey, putting the gun back into her handbag, 'I always carry a firearm in my handbag when I'm on duty because you never know what's lurking just around the corner.'

'But don't you have to have a special licence to carry a gun?' said Marcie anxiously.

'Yes, of course, but Tom told me that John has done all the relevant paperwork on my behalf. So the firearm is legit! So now I suppose I ought to tell you about my job as a CPO.'

'As a *what*?' Marcie exclaimed.

'I'm a CPO, a Close Protection Officer. You know, a bodyguard. It's a joke really, because the one person who I should have guarded and protected was my mother and I failed miserably.'

'That wasn't your fault,' said Judith. 'How on earth could you have possibly imagined that your mother would be murdered by her carer? There was no way you could have anticipated a crime like that.'

Judith's words were clear and, to Janey, incredibly comforting.

'Anyhow,' Roxanne persisted, 'tell us what you do as a bodyguard. Clearly we don't know anything about you, so, come on, enlighten us!'

'There's nothing to say, really. My father was in the Army, so I joined up soon after leaving Brinkley House. Unfortunately, being short, fat, and pig-headed, I wasn't much good at it, so I chucked it in and trained as a policewoman instead. I worked for the Met for a while but,

Prue Brand

after a few years, with my mother's health declining, I decided to become a bodyguard instead. Funnily enough, when I became a CPO I found that the qualities that had held me back in the Army and in the police force – if I'm honest, contributed to my success as a CPO. My ordinariness enabled me to blend into the background, and being female helped me to protect women and children after divorce or violence in the home. I liaise with lawyers, social workers – and the Met, of course, hence John Green, who worked with me when we were young. Anyhow, I think I've said enough. I haven't taken on many new cases since my mother's death, but what I *have* taken on is confidential, which is why I haven't told anyone what I do, until now. I trust you to keep all this to yourselves.'

'Of course . . . but I'm so proud of you.' Marcie beamed at Janey.

'Tell us more, *please*,' urged Roxanne.

'Yes, please tell us all about it,' Judith insisted.

After a lot of persuading, Janey grudgingly outlined the main aspects of her job as a CPO, telling them how John Green had first helped her as a colleague, and then become her friend, before becoming a high-ranking officer of the London Metropolitan Police Force. Having gained this knowledge, Janey and her friends chatted away happily, strangely warm and comfortable in Roxanne's little car. In no time, they were heading along the road to Aberdovey.

V

After an unusually frustrating journey, Geraint Parry-Jones was relieved to find himself nearing Cardiff. As he approached the airport he started to notice police cars everywhere. Yes, there was another one; *and* another. He wondered if there had been an accident, or if police cars parked by the roadside and driving down the approach roads had anything to do with him.

The number plate on his car was not known to the police, but if photographs of him had been circulated, then this would not be enough to protect him from arrest at the airport. After seeing yet another police car slowly cruising along the hard shoulder, he decided that enough was enough. Obeying his gut instincts, Geraint took the first exit and drove away from Cardiff as fast as he could. He needed to make an urgent telephone call and, a few miles later, he saw a large roadside restaurant to his left. He drove in and parked facing the exit. Then he walked into the restaurant and rang Randall Selkirk's number. No reply. He rang it again. No reply. Then he tried another number, but again nobody answered. Angrily Geraint swore and put the phone down. Randall was not on board his yacht. Now he was really stuck. Geraint stood in the telephone booth trying to remember exactly what Randall had planned for the weekend. He knew that something important had been planned – which was why that lazy tart had been so reluctant to help move everything to the church. Where were they? The two of them had planned to treat themselves to a boozy evening at their favourite hostelry in Aberdovey. Yes, Aberdovey! That's where they were. Now what was it called? The Black . . . something. The Black . . . ? The Black . . . ? The Black Stallion! Yes, that was it! Soon, with the help of the operator, Geraint found the right number. He dialled again and, finally, after a ridiculous conversation with a stupid barmaid and a long wait, he recognised Randall's voice on the line.

'Hello. Geraint here. I'm in a spot of trouble and need your help. The police are looking for me at Cardiff Airport,

so I wonder if you'd be so kind as to sail me to France –
now, tonight?'

'I'm in Aberdovey and its piddling down. Stair-rods,
I'm afraid. Not a good time to cross the Channel. Besides,
Cheryl and I have plans for tonight.'

'Look, this is very urgent. Tell Cheryl that about an
hour ago I found the police breaking into the church where
I store my antiques. They are out in force looking for me.
A police car tried to intercept me at Llancoed, and Cardiff
Airport is crawling with police cars. If they catch me I'm
facing a very long prison sentence, see. I have to get out of
the country tonight and you are the only person who can
help me. If you can get me to France I promise to reward
you very handsomely.'

'How handsomely?'

Geraint named a figure.

'All right . . . but remember, I'll hold you to that
promise. Where are you now and what is your nearest
harbour?'

'Aberystwyth. That's where I'm heading. I assume your
yacht's moored there.'

'It normally is, but actually it may be a good thing that
Valkyrie is not at Aberystwyth right now. If the police have
cottoned on to you, then they may be looking for me too.
If I'm right, then it's best if *Valkyrie* is left moored here at
Aberdovey.'

'Yes, I suppose your sister and all those damned
busybodies at Brinkley House Hotel have already told the
police everything so, yes, your yacht may well be under
surveillance. Blast! Any ideas?'

'Yes, I've got a plan formulating in my brain. This is
it. Are you listening?'

'Yes.'

'I drive down to Aberystwyth in Cheryl's car. I could be there in around an hour, between one thirty and two o'clock? I'll park the car at Harbour Creek . . . That's the road close to where the Ystwyth flows under the bridge and into the harbour. Know it?'

'Yes.'

'Good! Now, I've noticed a couple of yachts moored at the harbour that are as powerful and up-to-date as *Valkyrie*. The owners sometimes spend their weekends on board and what we need to do is borrow one of them and sail it to France. With luck the police will be none the wiser.'

'Thank you, Randall. It's *on*. You won't let me down, will you? See you at Harbour Creek in an hour or so. Drive carefully.'

'I'll be there.'

Geraint Parry-Jones drove out of the restaurant car park and set off for Aberystwyth. He started singing again.

VI

Ralph looked out of his bedroom window and then at his watch. It was past 1.30 a.m. and Judith and her friends still had not returned. He was exhausted with waiting for Judith and was starting to feel anxious for her safety. It was stormy outside and yet the long flags of light stretching across the hotel forecourt showed him that, apart from a police car discreetly parked by the car park entrance, they had not yet arrived. As Ralph stood at the window wishing that Judith had not volunteered to go to Llancoed, he saw headlights coming up the lane and recognised Roxanne's car as it swung into the car park.

'Thank God!' Ralph ran downstairs, where he joined Sally and Don who, watching from the kitchen, had seen four figures heading for the staff entrance.

Trot stuck her head into the drawing-room where Livia was reading in front of the fire.

'*Kitchen door.*'

'They must be exhausted.' Livia stood up. 'Kitchen door, you say?'

From different parts of the hotel, Livia, Trot, Don and Ralph converged in the kitchen just as Sally unlocked and opened the door for Janey, Marcie, Roxanne and Judith.

'Hello, everybody,' said Janey. 'I'm afraid we're rather mucky and dusty – sorry!'

Sally quickly took control.

'May I suggest you remove your shoes and jackets here, and then take yourselves up to your rooms and run hot baths? We'll wait for you in the drawing-room and give you a nightcap when you come down. We want to hear all about everything before we all go to bed.'

Roxanne, Janey, Marcie and Judith went up to their rooms accompanied by Ralph. Shortly afterwards, while Sally and Don were busy in the kitchen and Livia and Trot were chatting in the drawing-room, the four weary travellers were undressing and getting ready for bed.

The office telephone rang and a moment later Sally put her head around the drawing-room door.

'It's okay, you two. That was only the police car making sure it was Roxanne's car that entered the car park just now. I've told them to keep their eyes skinned from now on and to contact us immediately if they see anything in the vicinity of the hotel.'

VII

Twenty minutes later, Judith, Marcie, Janey and Roxanne entered the drawing-room escorted by Ralph. Sitting around the fire in their dressing-gowns they described the extraordinary experiences of their day to their friends.

'So what you are saying is that it seems likely that Geraint Parry-Jones orchestrated all those thefts from your family, Marcie,' said Trot.

'Yes,' said Marcie.

Sipping their hot drinks, Janey, Judith, Roxanne and Marcie felt their bodies relaxing after the exhaustion of the day, and without thinking, Marcie, who was almost asleep, blurted out Janey's secret.

'We've been able to gain the support of the Met because Janey is a CPO, a bodyguard. That's how she knows John Green. She's armed, too, which is comforting.'

There was a momentary hush, broken by Livia.

'She's a what? I don't understand.'

Everyone looked at Janey, who stared angrily at Marcie for a moment, and then shrugged.

'As Marcie says I'm a Close Protection Officer, or bodyguard. I work mainly with women and children, but not always. John Green and I met a long time ago when we were working on a case together. I like to keep a low profile out of loyalty to the people I serve. Yes, I am armed. That's it, really.'

Ralph smiled. 'I thought it might be something like that. It fits, and please don't be worried about this information getting out. Anyone who breaks your confidence will be swiftly chastised by the rest of us.'

'I promise not to say anything,' said Judith.

'Me neither,' said Trot.

'Ditto me,' said Livia.

'Ditto me,' said Don and Sally in unison.

Marcie smiled; she was so exhausted she could hardly stay awake.

'Sorry! I think I'm falling asleep, but before I go to bed, where are Jack and Ann – and have the police caught Geraint yet?'

'No, Geraint Parry-Jones is still at large, but Jack and Ann are fine,' Sally replied. 'As you know, Ifor dropped them off at Aberystwyth harbour while it was still light, but later they telephoned us to say that *Valkyrie* was not at her mooring. So then we all wondered if Randall and Cheryl had sailed up to Aberdovey to cause trouble at Brinkley tonight. The police have been looking out for *Valkyrie* but so far there's been no sign of her.'

'I see you've got a police car guarding us here too, haven't you?' said Judith.

'Yes, policemen will be guarding us all night.'

'Good!' said Marcie.

'Anyhow,' Sally continued, 'a short while ago we were informed by your policeman friend, Tom Mortimer, that Geraint Parry-Jones has so far failed to turn up at Cardiff Airport. He thinks that Parry-Jones may have cottoned on to the fact that the police were out looking for him at the airport and has bribed Randall to sail him to France. So, backing up this theory, Ann and Jack have moved *Manatee* nearer to the harbour mouth so that they can see if *Valkyrie* sails past. That's it.'

'But isn't that rather dangerous?' Roxanne asked. 'If *Valkyrie* sails past the harbour, surely Ann and Jack won't try to stop her?'

'Don't worry, they'll be fine. If they see *Manatee* they'll inform the Coastguard, so that's that. Get yourselves to bed before you keel over, and don't worry: Don and I will be taking turns to watch over Brinkley House while you sleep.'

After wishing each other goodnight, Roxanne and Judith helped Marcie into her room and made sure she was settled before going to their own rooms. Soon they were all sound asleep except for Don Saunders who, after Sally had gone up to bed, was keeping watch over them all.

CHAPTER ELEVEN

Everything at Sea

I

IN THE STORM Jack and Ann found themselves being buffeted about at their mooring at Aberystwyth harbour.

'Goodness, the wind is strong,' said Ann. 'I know we managed to get a bit of shut-eye earlier, but how much longer do you think we should stay on watch before giving up for the night?'

'Well, I'd like to keep looking out for *Valkyrie* a little bit longer,' Jack replied. 'Why don't you go down and get yourself warmed up and then we can have a snack and a hot drink before we bunk down?'

'Okay, but while we're killing time, quick question. What does *Valkyrie* mean?'

'Well, I vaguely recall that the *Valkyrie*s were female warriors who served the Teutonic god, Odin. After battle, it was their job to present the souls of dead warriors to Odin in Valhalla. Something like that.'

'Sounds decidedly worrying.'

'Well, if everything we've been told about Randall is true, *Valkyrie* is a very apt name for his yacht. Let's hope the myth remains just a myth, tonight especially.'

'*Don't!* I'm going to get us something to eat. Shout if you need me.'

'Will do.'

Ann went down the steps into the galley and put on a kettle. She noticed that there was plenty of wine left over from Jack's Friday night dinner with Ralph and Don.

'Would you rather have wine?'

'No thanks. Something hot please.'

'I'll make coffee. It'll help keep us awake.'

'Thanks.' Jack peered into the Stygian gloom.

Impenetrable mist, low cloud and driving rain had now rendered visibility to practically zero, and this and the lateness of the hour combined to discourage even the most intrepid yachtsmen from leaving the harbour. Regardless of this, Jack clung to the notion that if he caught sight of *Valkyrie* sailing across the mouth of the harbour he might be able to warn the Coastguard and help the police to make an arrest.

'Anyhow, one good thing,' he muttered to himself. 'If we can't see them, then they can't see us. It works both ways.'

Jack looked around at the yachts moored close to *Manatee* and decided that none of them were as up-to-date as she was. If push came to shove she'd give *Valkyrie* a good run for her money, he thought as he looked over *Manatee*'s port side, where he could just make out a handful of yachts with a couple of dinghies bobbing amongst them. Beyond that, darkness. On the same side, moored closer to *Manatee*, he could hear the unwelcome sound of a boozy party but could not see exactly where the music and loud laughter were coming from. To starboard there were no yachts, just the wall to which *Manatee* had been loosely hitched, ready for a quick exit if necessary.

Jack could only just see the mouth of the harbour in front of him. There were no yachts passing right now. He relaxed for a moment and closed his eyes.

Suddenly, from out of the dark, a man's voice penetrated Jack's consciousness.

'*Don't move. Keep quite still.*'

The moment Jack heard the man's voice he realised what was happening. He looked up to his right and saw a man squatting on the harbour wall close to his head. Almost simultaneously a slight juddering sensation told him that *Manatee* was being jostled astern by another vessel. He looked down and saw a second man wobbling about in a dinghy pointing a gun at him. Jack froze and glanced towards Ann, who caught his eye and quickly retreated back down to the galley.

'We're coming aboard.'

The fit-looking man on the wall dropped effortlessly down into *Manatee*'s cockpit and Jack immediately recognised him as Randall Selkirk. In the galley Ann, who had already recognised Randall, removed a small package from a box on the top shelf and put it in a pocket beneath her oilskin. Then she listened to the conversation, her heart pounding.

'We've already met, remember?' said Randall. 'How do you do! Nice to see you again.'

'Get off my yacht. Whoever you are, get off now!'

'Sorry, old bean, no can do.' Randall leaned over and hauled the fat man on board using a pre-prepared harness attached to his lifebelt.

'Don't move or I shoot,' said Geraint Parry-Jones, holding a gun up to Jack's head.

'What the hell's going on? Tell your friend to stop pointing that damn gun at my face. I'm unarmed, for God's sake!'

'It's all right, Geraint, I know this man. I recognise his yacht.'

Randall gestured to Geraint to lower his gun and grinned at Jack.

'Well, I'm sorry to say this, but I'm going to have to borrow *Manatee* for a while, so you'll have to disembark right now, pronto. Get off!'

'What do you mean – *borrow*? This is *my* yacht, *you* get off!'

'Look, we are armed and we are taking *Manatee* whether you like it or not. We're being kind allowing you to disembark alive, but if you don't want to get off that's fine by us. We can shoot you and drop your body off in Cardigan Bay.'

'All right, all right. Calm down. So what about my wife?'

'Your wife? Where is she?' Randall's violet eyes darted around. 'Come out, *now*!'

Ann climbed up the steps holding her breath. She knew that if Randall recognised her as one of Marcie's school friends, neither she nor Jack would live to see another day. Fortunately, as a precaution, Ann had previously tied up her blonde hair and put on a large, waterproof hat pulled down low over her face. She did her best to appear incompetent.

'Oh dear!' said Geraint. 'Poor little wifey-kins is going to have to get off too. Never mind, darling, *there there*! Don't fret!'

'Shall I turn off the kettle then?'

'Leave it! Don't move!' Geraint shouted, but then he stopped shouting and smirked knowingly at Randall. He whispered into his ear.

'Okay. Good idea,' said Randall, smiling broadly.

'*You're* getting off. *She* stays with us. Any trouble from you, or anyone else, and *she* gets it – understood?'

'No, I'm sorry, that is *totally unacceptable.*'

Jack suddenly felt his legs start to buckle and his head swim; he felt faint and sick. Struggling to overcome his terror, his voice sounded foreign to himself.

'She is just an ordinary housewife and she's done you no harm. Please let her go. If anything happens to her, you'll be answerable to *me.*'

'Shut up and get off or we'll shoot her right now and save ourselves a lot of trouble. You climb into the dinghy, see. It's right here.' Geraint was aiming his firearm at Ann's head as he spoke.

'For God's sake stop waving that bloody gun about.' Jack was frantic with anxiety. Ann tried to sound cheerful.

'It's all right, darling. Don't worry.'

'If anything happens to my wife, I'll find you and kill you.' Jack's voice cracked with distress.

'Goodbye, darling. I love you.'

'I love you. Good luck, my darling.'

Jack turned back to Geraint and Randall.

'If you harm my wife, I'll find you, no matter how long it takes.'

'Okay, but for now stay where we can see you. Don't move until we've left the harbour and are out of sight,' said Randall. 'One false move, and she gets shot.'

After climbing down into the dinghy Jack watched Randall make ready to leave the harbour. He felt completely impotent and time stood still. Eventually he heard *Manatee*'s inboard motor running and watched as she started to ease her way out of her mooring and away from the harbour. With his mouth dry and his heart pounding, Jack watched *Manatee* slowly disappear into the darkness of Cardigan Bay.

Struggling to overcome nausea and total misery Jack rowed the dinghy to the nearest steps, climbed up, and with legs like jelly, struggled over to the Harbour Master's office. Once there he circulated the shocking news that Ann had been taken hostage by Geraint Parry-Jones and Randall Selkirk, two criminals wanted by both the Aberystwyth and London Metropolitan Police Forces. Then Jack called the Brinkley House Hotel and told Don what had happened. Utterly appalled by his news, Don wasted no time in contacting the Met, using the contact information given to him and Sally earlier. A short while later he received confirmation that all the relevant departments had been alerted and that *Manatee* had already been located heading southwards towards Aberaeron. Don passed this news to Jack, who was shaking and shivering in abject misery, his suffering made worse by the realisation that, with Ann as hostage, vessels capable of rescuing her could not intervene without putting her life at risk. He feared that nothing could save her.

II

It took Randall very little time to get the hang of *Manatee*, and she had soon left the harbour, heading south to Aberaeron. After watching Jack disappear from view, Ann went down to the galley where she shed solitary tears of despair. Just then she heard Geraint's heavy footfall on the steps and quickly dried her eyes. He stuck his fat face into the galley. Ann pretended not to notice.

'I want something to eat and drink.'

'Oh dear. What sort of thing? What would you like?'

Ann tried to sound flustered and stupid.

'What have you got?'

'Things. You know, drink, biscuits – that sort of thing.'

'Let's see, then.' Geraint squeezed himself inside the galley, crowding Ann into the cabin doorway. 'Coffee, tea, biscuits *and* a socking great crate full of red wine!'

Geraint called up to Randall.

'There's tea, coffee and biscuits – and loads of red wine. What would you like?'

'Nothing right now, thanks.'

'I'll have a nice big glass of red wine to start with,' Geraint said to Ann as he grabbed a bottle and checked the label.

'This'll do me fine. Pour me a large glass and bring it up to me.'

'You want wine? Are you sure?'

'Good grief, we've got a proper Dilly Dewdrop here, all right. For heaven's sake, just bloody well get a wine glass, and bloody well pour red wine into it, and bloody well bring it up to me. Got that? And I want biscuits. Lots of them. Put them on a plate and bring them up too. Have you got that?'

Ann did her best to look anxious and confused. Geraint's patience ran out.

'*Pour it right now!*' Geraint briefly held his handgun right against Ann's head, and then, scowling, left the galley and went back up on deck.

With her back to the steps, Ann took two capsules from the packet inside her oilskin, opened them, and poured their contents into Geraint's wine. She stirred it briefly.

'It's ready. Shall I bring it up now?' Ann called in her best little-girl voice.

'Yes, yes. *Yes*. NOW, for God's sake!'

Ann went up and handed the glass of wine to Geraint before going back down to the galley.

'Where are my biscuits?'

'Biscuits? Sorry, I forgot. I'll go and get them.' Ann returned to the galley and re-emerged with two biscuits on a plate.

'Is that all you've got?' Geraint called out.

Ann ignored this comment and went below. She knew that by now Jack would have contacted both the Aberystwyth and Aberaeron Harbour Masters, and the Brinkley House Hotel. She knew that by now the lifeboats guarding the Welsh coast would be abuzz with the knowledge that armed criminals had not only hijacked a yacht but had also taken a female hostage. She also knew that although *Manatee* was under continuous surveillance, nobody could act against her hijackers, and for this reason she knew she would have to act quickly.

Ann weighed up the options available to her. She could see that Geraint Parry-Jones was exhausted and knew that the drugs she had put in his wine would very soon knock him out for a few hours. She knew what signs to look out for and soon, as predicted, she could see that he was fighting to stay awake. Soon he was unable to keep his eyes open.

'I need to lie down. All right with you, Randall?'

'Yes, of course, go ahead.'

Geraint clumped down to the galley.

'In there.' Ann pointed to the cabin where, earlier, she and Jack had been asleep. Geraint obligingly squeezed himself through and flopped down on the double bunk. Ann heard him yawn, and peered up to see how Randall was faring at the helm. She could see that he was a natural sailor and that riding the storm on *Manatee* gave him great satisfaction. They were speeding along and soon would be past Aberaeron and on their way to St David's Head. After that, it would be Land's End and the English Channel. She would have to act quickly.

'Can I go into the cabin?' She called up to Randall.

'Why?'

'I've got blankets for your friend. He says he's cold,' she lied.

'Go on then.'

Ann entered the cabin and quickly looked to see if Geraint was still responsive. This was a critical moment because she needed to tie him up, and to do this successfully she had to ensure that he was too drugged to realise what she was doing. Having sailed since childhood, Ann knew her knots, but now she needed some kind of twine thin enough not to show. She did not want Randall to come down and find out what she had done. She hunted around hoping to find some thin twine, or long shoe laces – without success. She then returned to the galley and searched through her medical box. Immediately she found the perfect solution to her problem: a roll of extra strong 5cm-wide stretch adhesive strapping. A few minutes later Ann had neatly tied Geraint's ankles together with adhesive tape, and repeated the same manoeuvre with his wrists, before covering him up with a thick blanket. After tucking a pillow under his head and making sure that he was lying comfortably, she quickly prepared a single bunk for Randall. On her way out of the cabin she took Geraint's firearm, checked it, removed the bullets and hid both gun and bullets in the galley.

It was even more squally and wet now, and Ann could see that Randall was having difficulty holding *Manatee* on course. Hindered by poor visibility and buffeted by cross-currents and strong winds, Ann feared that they may have already passed St David's Head and she knew that if she did not take action soon, rescue would be extremely dangerous. She heated up some milk and made herself a hot chocolate drink. Loitering at the galley entrance she sipped it with obvious relish.

'What are you drinking?' Randall enquired.

'Who, me? Oh, nothing much.'

'Listen, dumb-nut, I need a hot drink. If I get dehydrated and pass out, you are as good as dead. So I'll ask again. What are you drinking?'

'Hot chocolate,' Ann replied, trying to look stupid.

'Then make me one.'

'What? Another hot chocolate?'

'Yes, please.'

'What? Right now?'

'For God's sake, yes! Right now.'

Ann tried to hide the relief in her voice. She went below and made Randall a cup of hot chocolate, emptied the contents of two more capsules into it, stirred it, and went up on deck and handed it to Randall.

'Your drink,' she said.

'While I'm drinking, come here and take over from me. It's hard to hold a straight course. I'll tell you what to do.'

'Why don't you put *Manatee* on autopilot?'

'I will, but I want you to steer her now.'

Ann took the wheel from Randall and, after a short lesson on steering (while she bit her lip), he started to drink the hot chocolate. Sitting next to him, though she was exhausted and terrified, she was aware of a delicious warmth exuding from Randall's body. It would seem quite natural to snuggle up close to him, but Ann ignored this foolish notion.

'Aren't you going to put us on autopilot? My husband always does when I bring him drinks.'

'Not now,' he replied.

Randall made quick work of his drink and took the wheel away from Ann. She took his mug down to the galley. After a few minutes Randall called down to her.

'God, I'm tired. Did you put something in my drink?'

'No, of course not,' Ann reassured him. 'Perhaps you're just tired. You haven't even visited the head since you came aboard.'

'Good point! Yes, I think I'll go down for a moment.'

Randall soon appeared in the galley and walked through the cabin to the head. He saw Geraint lying comfortably asleep as he passed through. A minute later he came out again looking ill and worried.'

'God, I can't stay awake. What have you put in my drink? I have to stay awake.'

'Why? What's the matter? You've been drinking the same hot chocolate drink as me, and I'm all right.'

'For God's sake, I can't, I can't . . .'

Ann watched as Randall slowly collapsed on to the other bunk and started to lose consciousness. Then she quickly ran up the steps to the cockpit to make sure that *Manatee* was on autopilot and safe to leave for a few minutes. Then, after returning to the cabin, she checked that the drug had been fully absorbed before strapping up Randall's wrists and ankles just as she had done with Geraint's. Finally, she checked his pulse before covering him up with a blanket and returning to the cockpit.

III

Although visibility was still very poor it did not take Ann long to turn *Manatee* back towards the Welsh coast, at which point she made radio contact with the lifeboat that had been following them at a safe distance ever since she had been hijacked. After a few minutes the lifeboat emerged from out of the darkness and slowly closed in on *Manatee*. Even in the darkness, Ann recognised this lifeboat as an Atlantic 21-class, part of the RNLI inshore fleet that had been used to patrol the UK and Irish coastlines during the past decade or two. Slowly drawing closer to *Manatee*, the lifeboat attached itself to her using grappling hooks and, little by little, drew her alongside. Then, when the two vessels were side by side and the bouncing and jiggling had calmed down, two crew members climbed on board *Manatee* to help Ann down into the lifeboat – a vessel that Ann knew was well equipped with radio and a GPS navigation system. The coxswain welcomed her on board.

'Come aboard and relax, your ordeal is over. What can I offer you – brandy?'

As he spoke a member of his crew whispered into his ear.

'Now I've just been informed that there are two men lying unconscious on bunks on board *Manatee*. Is that correct?'

'I drugged them. So yes, they are sound asleep. They are criminals wanted by both the London Metropolitan and Aberystwyth Police Forces. Their names are Geraint Parry-Jones and Randall Selkirk. They boarded *Manatee* and held up my husband and me at gunpoint while we were moored at Aberystwyth. They then threw my husband off and took me hostage with a gun pointing at my head. I think they were trying to escape police arrest by sailing to the Continent. My name is Ann Edwards and both my husband Jack and I are the owners of *Manatee*. I am a GP, and in order to save my life I put strong sleeping draughts in both men's drinks. When they became unresponsive I put them to bed and tied them up with adhesive medical tape. The obese man, Geraint Parry-Jones, was drugged earlier than Randall Selkirk, but both men will stay under for an hour or two longer. I took Parry-Jones's gun from him and hid it behind the biscuit tin in the galley. The bullets are there too.'

'Congratulations! You have done a remarkable job, and please don't worry about *Manatee*. I've got good men looking after her and she'll be brought back to Aberystwyth a short while after we've dropped you off at a prearranged place where your husband is waiting for you.'

'Thank you,' said Ann, 'you've saved my life, and there is no adequate way to express my gratitude. By the way', she added pulling off her waterproof hat to reveal her long, blonde hair, 'I do hope Jack's all right.'

'Of course he is. He has been in contact with us ever since *Manatee* was hijacked. He knows you're safe now and he'll be waiting for you with a car and driver, ready to take you both back to Aberdovey – for a very early breakfast, no doubt.'

Upon hearing these reassuring words Ann felt so relieved, she forced herself to concentrate on facts to stop herself from bursting into tears.

'And what will you do about Parry-Jones and Randall Selkirk?'

'They'll stay on board *Manatee* under guard until she

is safely moored at Aberystwyth. Then they will be handed over to a welcoming committee at the harbour and taken to the police station where senior officers of the Aberystwyth Police Force will be wanting to make their acquaintance. It will be our pleasure to introduce them.'

Treated as royalty by both coxswain and crew, Ann gradually stopped shaking and started to look out towards the Welsh coastline. It was becoming less murky as the first streaks of dawn appeared in the sky, and after a while she was able to recognise the outline of the harbour. A few minutes later, as the lifeboat approached the shore, Ann saw Jack waiting for her and as she came nearer and nearer to where he was standing, braced against the storm, she felt such a surge of joy and relief, she could not contain her feelings any more. Tears streamed down her face, and she called out to him.

'Jack! Jack, it's all right. I'm fine! Everything's all right!'

A few minutes later Jack and Ann were in each other's arms, sobbing with exhaustion and happiness. Hugging each other and shaking with relief, the warmth of their bodies combined to calm and soothe them. Even Ifor, who had been keeping Jack company in the car for some time, embraced the pair of them with genuine emotion, before escorting them both to the car.

Soon they were on their way back to the Brinkley House Hotel where Ifor and Annie helped them off with their oilskins and wet outer clothing. Don was waiting for them and the couple thanked him profusely for his brilliance in coordinating their rescue. Then the happy couple went to bed where, covered in piles of thick blankets, they fell asleep in each other's arms while high above them a clear blue sky heralded a fine autumnal day.

CHAPTER TWELVE

The Last Day

I

LYING ON HIS bunk at Aberystwyth police station in the early hours of Monday morning, Randall Selkirk was confused. How on earth had he ended up here? One moment he was being given hot chocolate by that man's halfwit wife, and the next he was waking up in a prison cell. Maybe that woman wasn't such a fool after all. Maybe her dopiness was an act and it was they who were the idiots for not suspecting that she might drug them. They must have been picked up by a lifeboat even though he had made sure they were not being followed. Earlier, as he was coming round from being drugged, he was informed that he and Geraint Parry-Jones were being moved to Wandsworth Prison later that same day – an idea that Randall found utterly depressing. How much did the police know? How long a prison sentence would he get? *Valkyrie* was anchored at Aberdovey: would he ever sail in her again? He closed his eyes, trying to block out the depressing thoughts that crowded in on him.

II

At Llancoed, Fion Parry-Jones lay slumped on her bed, the telephone lying beside her emaciated body. She looked at her clock. It was only seven o'clock on Monday morning and already she was exhausted. Where was Geraint? He had to be home in Madrid by now, so why wasn't he answering her calls? She felt really let down and angry. It was so unfair of him to run off to Spain leaving her to face the police all on her own, and now, as things stood, he wouldn't be able to return to England for quite some time. She knew she would never see him again and decided there were three options open to her: she could lie and confess to being Geraint's accomplice and die in prison; she could struggle over to Spain and die there; or she could drive back to Paddington and die there. A fourth option would be to remain here at Llancoed because she'd soon be dead anyway.

I suppose I could shut myself in the garage with the engine running, she reflected, *that would do the trick, but why should I die all alone like that? It's not fair! I need to go somewhere where I'm not alone, somewhere I can die with friends around me.*

Fion struggled to sit up. She turned to her glass of water and the array of pills beside it.

What's the point of taking all these? I'll soon be dead anyway, with a bit of luck! She leaned back and closed her eyes, and then a new idea struck her.

If I confessed to being an accessory to Geraint's crimes, at least I'd be well cared for in prison. They'd have to look after me. Then a better idea crossed her mind.

Painfully slowly, Fion climbed out of bed and started to dress. She heard the sound of the police van returning to the oakwood to finish clearing the church, but apart from that all was quiet. It was going to be a sunny day and she knew a place in Aberdovey where she could have a late breakfast with friends. It took her a while to finish dressing, but eventually she was ready to leave Llancoed. Slowly she crept out through the kitchen, locked up, and made her way over to the garage where her car was waiting.

III

As dawn broke over the Brinkley House Hotel, Judith sat up in bed and shouted. It was a very strange shout and it woke her out of her nightmare: her dream had seemed so real. She nudged Ralph.

'What is it?' Ralph complained. 'You've woken me up!'

'I've just had an awful dream. Please, hold me tight and say something. *Anything.*'

'I'm still asleep.'

'I've just had a terrible dream. Please wake up and hold me, *please.*'

'What is it, darling?' Ralph rolled over and put his arms around Judith. He kissed her gently and went back to sleep.

IV

When Sally came downstairs she bumped into Don just as he was coming out of the office.

'Come in, come in.' Don smiled, holding the office door open.

'Why?'

'Come in and I'll tell you.'

'Well, buck up then. I'm late and I've got lots to do.'

Don pulled Sally into the office and shut the door.

'A short while ago Randall Selkirk and Geraint Parry-Jones were arrested by the police and taken to Aberystwyth police station. It's all over. Ann and Jack are asleep upstairs.'

'Randall and Geraint Parry-Jones? *Arrested?* You're not joking?' Sally sank down on to an office stool, her freckled face darkening as she burst into tears of relief.

'Oh, thank God! *Thank God!* I was beginning to think that this whole weekend was going to be a complete disaster. Tell me everything. What happened after I went to bed at . . . about one thirty, wasn't it?'

'Very briefly then . . .' Don marshalled his news into a logical sequence.

'When Parry-Jones suspected that the police were out looking for him at Cardiff Airport he persuaded Randall to sail him to the Continent because, as I think you know, the Parry-Joneses have a place in Spain. So Randall borrowed Cheryl's car and met up with Parry-Jones at Aberystwyth. Then they hijacked *Manatee*.'

'Hijacked *Manatee*! What, with Jack and Ann on board?'

'Yes, except that they threw Jack off at gunpoint and kept Ann on board as hostage.'

Sally was aghast.

'You mean that Ann was held captive by Randall Selkirk and Geraint Parry-Jones on her own yacht?'

Don told Sally everything he knew about the events of the night, stressing the point that nobody could intervene for fear of Ann being killed. Then he told her how he had contacted both the London Met and Aberystwyth Police Force, as well as everybody on the list they had been given earlier by John Green, and how they had kept in constant contact with Jack, and the lifeboat secretly tailing *Manatee* as she passed Aberaeron and approached St David's Head.

'Good God!'

'A few hours later I had Jack on the line telling me that the lifeboat crew had boarded *Manatee* and picked up Ann. Apparently they had found Randall and Parry-Jones lying drugged and tied up in the cabin. Ann was brought back to Aberystwyth harbour where Jack was waiting for her, and then Ifor drove the two of them back here. They arrived just as Annie was starting to prepare breakfast.'

'Good grief! Tell me what Ann did, all over again.'

Once more Don summarised the main facts, after which Sally put them into context.

'So let's see now . . . Apart from hijacking *Manatee* and holding Ann hostage, there are all Randall's crimes against Marcie and us – including his cruel tricks, thieving *and* murderous actions that caused the death of our little boy – as well as countless other offences to take into account. So, hopefully, he'll be put away for a very long time. I can't believe it, Don! So Ann scuppered both Randall and Parry-Jones single-handed. Isn't she brilliant? Isn't she brave? And think about it: had Randall recognised her, he would have killed her without a second thought.'

'Don't forget that Jack has been very brave and resourceful too. He's been through hell, and in a way his ordeal was even worse than Ann's. Ifor has been wonderful too: we're very lucky to have him, *and* Annie.'

'There's another hero you haven't mentioned.'

'Who's that?' Don asked.

'*You*, of course! Without you, all might have been lost. It was *you* who coordinated the rescue operation, and without your brains and efficiency Ann might now be in

France – or dead. I think you are wonderful.'

Sally stood up and put her arms around Don.

'God, I can't believe it's all over,' she said, holding him close.

But she was wrong. It was not over yet.

V

By ten o'clock the whole group was sitting around the breakfast table. Ann and Jack who, despite having had very little sleep, were enjoying coffee and hot croissants with the rest of the group and listening to Janey's summary of the previous day's events recounted for their benefit. While Janey was talking, Sally looked at her wristwatch and estimated that by now Tom Mortimer and his team would have finished the job of clearing Llancoed. She imagined the police van driving away from Llancoed laden with its second, and final, load of Geraint Parry-Jones's hoard.

'So now, Ann,' said Trot, 'for those of us who were asleep when you came in, and don't already know, what exactly happened to you and Jack last night at Aberystwyth harbour?'

'I'll keep it brief,' Ann replied. 'Last night Jack and I decided to hang around the harbour mouth so that we could warn the police and RNLI if Randall's yacht came sailing past on its way south from Aberdovey. We were being somewhat optimistic as visibility was practically nil, but anyhow, at around two in the morning a man suddenly jumped off the harbour wall on to *Manatee*'s deck. It was Randall Selkirk.'

'*What!*' Trot's exclamation conveyed the shock-horror everyone felt.

'What happened?' Marcie spoke with urgency.

'He wasn't alone. Geraint Parry-Jones was with him, and he was armed,' Ann replied.

There was a shocked silence.

'Then what?' said Trot.

'They pushed Jack off *Manatee* at gunpoint and kept me as hostage. Then they set off for France.'

'Good grief.' Ralph expressed the horror they all felt. 'So how come you are back here now? How on earth did you manage to survive the night?'

Ann smiled. 'I drugged their drinks, and when they were both out for the count I tied them up and made contact with the lifeboat that had been tailing *Manatee* at a safe distance all the way from Aberystwyth.'

Briefly Ann told her friends about drugging Geraint's wine and Randall's refusal to have a drink until they were nearly at St David's Head; how it was only then that she had been able to drug him, strap him up, and make contact with the lifeboat; and how, once rescued, she had been taken back to Aberystwyth and reunited with Jack who, after a long wait in the freezing cold, had been joined by Ifor and the relative warmth of the hotel car.

Jack, who was still looking exhausted, smiled and thanked everyone who had helped them during their ordeal.

'I want to emphasise the fact that without Ann's courage, intelligence and resourcefulness, she would have been murdered last night. Another fact I want to emphasise is that although the lifeboat crew picked up Ann and handed Randall and Geraint over to the police, it was *you*, Don, who organised the rescue and saved the day. Ann and I want to thank you from the bottom of our hearts, and we also want to thank Ifor for bringing the car over and driving us back to Brinkley House.'

Although horrified by what Ann and Jack had told them, the whole group was overjoyed to learn that Randall and Geraint were now safely locked away at Aberystwyth police station, soon to be transferred to Wandsworth Prison.

'I wish I'd been a fly-on-the-wall when Randall and Geraint came round and found themselves behind bars at Aber police station!' Trot chuckled.

'Yes, I agree,' Marcie added. 'Now all we have to do is trap Cheryl.'

'Good point,' said Sally. 'I wonder how she'll react when she learns that Randall is in prison.'

CHAPTER THIRTEEN

Cheryl is Tricked

I

C HERYL GIBSON WAS annoyed when she woke up and remembered that she was stuck in Aberdovey without a car. Only a few hours earlier she had driven all the way from Llancoed to the Black Stallion to spend the night with Randall, only to watch him drive off to Aberystwyth in her car, leaving her stuck miles away from anywhere. Presumably he had parked it at their usual spot close to the harbour before meeting up with Geraint and sailing off to the Continent. So there was absolutely no point in trying to contact him. As for Fion, she'd probably be on her way to Spain to join Geraint or, more likely, being driven back to Paddington by Sam – a local man paid to drive her on an *ad hoc* basis.

Lying on her bed, Cheryl made a call to a local acquaintance requesting a lift to Aberystwyth, but the woman was unable to help her. Cheryl put down the receiver and considered her options. Then she remembered that Amy – or Annie, as she remembered she now called herself – worked at Aberdovey and looked up the telephone number she and her husband, Ifor, had given her.

'Hello, can I speak to Mrs Thompson, please?'

'I'm sorry, she can't take your call right now. Can I take a message?'

'Is that Ifor?'

'Yes – who's speaking?'

'It's Cora. We met at Llancoed yesterday. I just happen to be in Aberdovey and wonder if Amy would be free to meet me.'

'Hello, Cora. Brilliant idea! She's doing breakfast right now, but she could meet you later. When can you come over?'

'I'm afraid I can't come to you because I haven't got a car. Perhaps she could drive over to see me.'

'What's happened to your car?'

'My friend's been called away by her office – some sort of emergency. I've got to get back to Aber and thought maybe Amy could give me a lift.'

Ifor smiled at Cheryl's fib. He knew full well that Randall had taken her car, and why.

'I'm afraid Amy can't drive,' he explained, 'but I could drive you if you like. Where are you ringing from?'

'Don't worry. It doesn't matter.'

'Look, it's really no problem for me, Cora.'

'Yes, but it really doesn't matter.'

'Yes, it *does*. Where are you staying?'

'I'm at the Black Stallion.'

'Well that's easy enough. Why don't I pick you up in about half an hour? You could even be back at Llancoed in time for your elevenses.'

'That's very kind of you. Thank you. I'll wait by the car park exit sign so you don't have to park.'

'Perfect! See you soon.'

11

Ifor hung up and went to the office.

'Mrs Saunders, may I have a word?'

'Of course, Ifor.'

'Cheryl Gibson rang just now. She's stuck at the Black Stallion without a car and hoped that Annie might drive her to where Randall left her car at Aber last night. I told her that Annie can't drive but said I'd pick her up in about thirty minutes.'

'Now that could be very useful, but I'd better check with the others. Why don't you come with me to save time?'

'Okay, but don't tell Annie she called.'

'My lips are sealed,' said Sally as she led Ifor out of the office and along towards the rear of the hotel. Soon both employer and employee had entered the Conference Room where the group was congregated. Sally explained the situation.

Janey was excited by Ifor's news.

'If Cheryl could be lured over to Brinkley House it would give us a chance to confront her about all the criminal things she and Randall have done to us and our families over the years. The thefts, the deaths, the false names, the lies – the list is endless. We could hold her here until she started telling us the truth and then we could call the police.'

'The first problem is how to get her here.' Sally looked at Ifor. 'Is there any way you could lure Cheryl over here? Any ideas?'

'Yes,' Ifor replied, 'I've got one idea. It's based on a lie – which I don't like – but we might be able to build on it.'

'Go on then.'

'Well, yesterday, when Annie and I met Cheryl at Llancoed, she seemed quite taken by Braid. So perhaps I could tell her that Braid is unwell and that just after I put the receiver down she was sick and collapsed. Something like that. Then I could tell her that I suddenly remembered that our vet's practice is on the way to Aberystwyth and would she mind me returning to Brinkley House to pick up Braid from the annexe cloakroom. I could reassure her that Annie and I have our own private entrance and that it would only take a second to pick up Braid. Then, if some of you hide in the kitchen or annexe, you could wait until you see me get out of the car and walk over to the outside cloakroom to pick up Braid. At that point you could make contact with Cheryl while she's waiting in the car and invite her to join you all in the small Conference Room. I could leave the annexe doors unlocked so that you could wait for Cheryl in there, if you like.'

'Now that's a very clever idea!' Janey was delighted. 'A small group of us could lie in wait for her to arrive.'

'I like it, Ifor,' said Don, 'and may I say that using the little Conference Room as the venue is a great idea, because it has a side exit that opens on to the footpath leading directly to the annexe.'

Livia leaned forward in her chair.

'It's rather a dirty trick, though, don't you think? There's Cheryl thinking that Randall and Geraint are in Spain, while all the time they are in prison here in Aberystwyth. She needs to be told the truth so that she can visit them. If we lie to her and trick her, surely that makes us just as bad as she is?'

Ralph laughed. 'So if you set a trap to catch a rat, does that make you as bad as the rat? Cheryl and Randall, together and separately, have committed crimes of the most horrible, cruel, greedy and despicable nature against Marcie, Roxanne, Ann and Jack, Sally and Don, Janey – and even *you*, Livia – and so she richly deserves our criticism and resentment. Tricking her so that she has to confront her victims is a very good idea.'

'Well, I don't agree. Keeping the truth from her makes us complicit in a way . . . Honesty and openness is always the best policy. The Katie Gilbert who worked for me was a *good egg*!'

'I'll tell you what,' said Sally. 'How about a compromise? If Ifor tricks Cheryl into coming here, why don't *you* make it your business to tell her about Randall's arrest and offer to drive her to Aberystwyth so that she can pick up her car? Anyhow, Ifor, time for you to go and pick up Cheryl.'

'Right, I'm off now. I trust you not to tell Annie about this. After breakfast perhaps you could distract her with a job somewhere away from the kitchen area. I feel bad going behind her back, but it's best she doesn't know just yet.'

'Don't worry, Ifor, we'll look after Annie,' said Sally reassuringly.

'Okay. Bye then.' Ifor left the Conference Room.

Don stood up. 'Please, would you mind if I get back to the office? We open to the public tomorrow so there's lots to do. Sally? Are you coming?'

'No, not just yet,' Sally replied. 'I feel that I should know what the plan is before Cheryl gets here. The first thing I need to know is who's going to wait for Cheryl's arrival at the annexe and what the plan is once she's here. Any ideas?'

'I think I ought to wait for Katie,' said Livia. 'After all, I know her best.'

'What makes you think that?' Marcie stared at Livia with surprise.

'Well, I still think I should be there,' Livia insisted.

'Well, I don't,' said Janey. 'After all, we don't want her warned off. We want to trick her into joining us all in the Conference Room.'

'Why don't *you* decide for us, Sally?' said Judith. 'After all, this is your hotel and we are your guests. Why don't you pick the reception committee?'

'Okay, as long as everyone's happy with the idea,' said Sally.

'Yes, good idea.'

Everyone seemed in agreement.

'Right then, I'd like Janey and Trot to be waiting at the annexe, so that the moment Ifor leaves the car, ostensibly to pick up Braid, they are ready to block Cheryl so she can't run off. I'd also like Ralph and Judith to be waiting in the wings, ready to back up Janey and Trot, and help escort Cheryl to the Conference Room along the outside footpath.'

Everyone agreed that this was a sensible arrangement, after which Sally asked her friends what specific questions they wanted to ask Cheryl and in what order. Once everyone knew the plan, Sally left the room and returned to the office.

Meanwhile, when Ifor returned to the annexe, Braid greeted him with excitement.

'Sorry, old girl! It's the outside cloakroom for you – just for a short while. That's right! Good girl!'

He led Braid across the backyard to the outside cloakroom and set out water and a snack for her next to her basket. Braid, who was used to this temporary accommodation, went straight over to the food and ate greedily. Then Ifor set off for the Black Stallion.

III

It took Ifor fifteen minutes to drive to the Black Stallion and as he entered the car park he could see Cheryl standing by the exit. How strange it was, he thought, that only yesterday he had thought her attractive, and yet today he found her looks decidedly unappealing.

'Hello,' he said, with an insincere smile pasted on to his face as she climbed into the car, placing a large handbag beside her feet. 'It's good to see you again, and I'm sorry Annie isn't with me. The hotel opens to the public tomorrow, which means she's got lots to do . . . Look, I have a small problem and wonder if you can help me.'

Ifor quickly steered the car into an empty parking bay near the exit and turned off the engine.

'It's Braid, you see. Just after you rang me, she collapsed. I put my finger down her throat in case there was a blockage but I couldn't find anything there. She soon came round, but she's very sick and needs to get to a vet – urgently. It was only after I left the hotel and was on my way here that I realised that our vet's surgery is on the way to Aber. So . . . would you mind very much if we popped back to the hotel to pick her up? I can drop her off on the way to Llancoed and pick her up on the way back.' He looked at Cheryl, who seemed put out by the news.

'I don't know,' she said. 'I don't want to be taken to the hotel. I don't like crowded places. Drop me off at a bus stop. I can make my own way to Aber.'

'Oh dear, no, you can't do that. Besides, you won't be going to the hotel at all, because Annie and I don't actually live there. We have our own private annexe with a private lane leading up to it, you see. You could wait in the car while I pop over to pick her up. I'd be back in a jiffy.'

'Oh, all right then,' said Cheryl grudgingly, and Ifor immediately restarted the engine.

Fifteen minutes later, the car was heading down the small lane leading to the annexe.

'Here we are,' said Ifor, pulling up the handbrake. 'You sit tight while I pick up Braid from the cloakroom over there.'

'Will you be long?'

'No, I'll be back in two ticks,' Ifor lied.

Taking the car keys with him, he walked over to the far side of the annexe and disappeared from sight. Braid welcomed him excitedly.

'Hello, Braid, let's go for a nice long walk.'

Braid jumped about as Ifor opened the cloakroom's rear door, and seconds later both man and dog were heading out across the headland and up into the hills.

IV

Cheryl Gibson watched Ifor walk over to a pretty white cottage, and then disappear from view. Looking behind her and to her left she could see that he had parked the car at the rear of the hotel, and that the hotel and annexe were connected by a white-painted covered way. The general cleanliness of the hotel and annexe impressed her, and she wondered what it would be like to work alongside Annie – or Amy, as she had known her at the reformatory. It was an idea definitely worth investigating. She turned her attention back to where she had seen Ifor disappear and so did not notice a door open on the far side of the annexe.

Trot walked over to the car, opened the door, and sat down in the driver's seat.

'Good morning, Cheryl dear. I thought I might find you here.'

Cheryl glanced at Trot for a split-second and then hit the passenger door like a trapped bird hitting a window. In her blind attempt to escape she did not see Janey Collins standing there as the door swung open. Janey snapped at her like an irate schoolmarm: '*Kelly Graham, get back this instant!*'

Shocked into obedience, Cheryl did as she was told, and Janey slammed the passenger door shut and stood guard over it.

Trot tried to reassure Cheryl.

'Don't be frightened, it's only me – Trot – and we've met before. As you probably know, a group of us has been staying here over the weekend, so when Ifor asked Sally for permission to use the hotel car to pick you up from the Black Stallion, we thought it would be a lovely idea if we could all meet up with you. So we played a little trick on Ifor to get you here. Oh, and by the way, Annie doesn't even know you're here at Aberdovey. We thought it best not to tell her.'

As Cheryl listened to Trot's words, she bent forward in the passenger seat with her arms clasped protectively across her chest.

'Now,' said Trot. 'I wonder if you remember us as clearly as we remember you? In 1962, if you recall, you looked after us during the week we stayed at Redcliffe to celebrate Marcie's marriage to Randall Selkirk. So there was Sally – who now owns this hotel – Janey, Livia, Judith, Ann and me – and there was Marcie, of course, as well as Randall's sister, Roxanne Selkirk – though she didn't attend the wedding. In a moment Judith and her husband Ralph are going to escort us to a private Conference Room so that we can catch up on what you've been doing since we last saw you.'

As Trot spoke, Judith and Ralph came into view, crossing over from the kitchen via the covered way. As they approached the car, Janey opened the passenger door and crisply addressed Cheryl.

'Get out, please,' said Janey.

Cheryl remained seated.

'Please, we want you to get out now,' repeated Janey, but Cheryl made no attempt to comply with Janey's order. At this, Trot climbed out of the car, signalled to Ralph to stand blocking the driver's door, and walked around to the passenger door to lend support to Janey. Trot spoke to Cheryl in a no-nonsense voice.

'Now then, Cheryl, *please get out of the car*. You're quite safe.'

Observing Cheryl's demeanour at close quarters, Judith wondered if the blank expression and pursed lips were signs of distress, rage – or something else? Whatever it was, she reckoned, Cheryl's true feelings were not on display right now, and she reminded herself that Cheryl could change her persona at the drop of a hat and was probably weighing up her options. She watched as Trot tried again.

'Please get out of the car and come with us now.'

Cheryl sat still, staring straight ahead.

'I'm going to say this again. Get out of the car!'

Cheryl sat still, her arms crossed protectively over her body.

Trot tried again.

'I should warn you that if you refuse to get out of the car, I'll get the rest of the group to come over and drag you out.'

Cheryl's reply came swiftly between clenched teeth.

'Then I'll have you up for assault.'

'If you make a complaint, we'll simply deny that anything happened. So what is it to be? I'll say it once more: *Get out of the car.*'

Sulkily, and very, very slowly, Cheryl pulled herself upright, opened the car door, and stuck out one leg, then the other. Slowly the rest of her body followed until, after what seemed like an age, Cheryl was standing in front of them, an insolent expression on her face. Judith studied her demeanour – the tightly folded lips, the flared nostrils and the sulky expression – and was reminded of a spoiled brat suddenly deprived of its favourite toy.

At last, with Janey and Trot following closely behind, Judith and Ralph managed to frog-march Cheryl along the footpath to the side entrance where Sally and Don were waiting for her.

'Hello, Cheryl,' Sally said. 'I'm not sure how well you remember *me* but, as you know, Don and I know Randall very well indeed. Anyway, come on in and say hello to everyone.'

Everyone stopped talking as Cheryl was led into the Conference Room.

'Hello. Here you are at last,' said Livia. 'Please, my dear, sit yourself down. Which would you prefer, tea or coffee? How about a biscuit? Or a croissant?'

Everyone looked at Cheryl with curiosity, wondering how she would respond to Livia's courteous reception; but Cheryl was not responding to Livia at all. Seated at the table with her arms folded across her chest, she was staring straight ahead with a 'butter-wouldn't-melt-in-my-mouth' expression on her face. Looking at her self-satisfied demeanour, Judith suddenly felt such an acute rush of anger that she had to stop herself from jumping up and smacking Cheryl right then and there. She recalled the circumstances that had caused so much pain and misery to her friends: the destruction of Redcliffe and the Stanton-Gray family, the murder of the Saunders' unborn son and the theft of their parents' life savings, the appalling murder of Mrs Collins and the theft of her most valued possessions.

Judith turned towards Ann, who caught her eye and raised a quizzical eyebrow before turning her gaze back to Cheryl, whose blank stare intensified as she put into practice a trick that she had first learned at the reformatory.

V

Sitting in the Conference Room, surrounded by the very people she had cheated, robbed and betrayed over many years, Cheryl felt the need to run away, hide, disappear – *anything* to reduce the stress. She had been caught like a rat in a trap and her mind went back to her first week at the reformatory when a girl had called her 'child murderer' in front of the whole class. Afterwards there had been a vicious fight, after which she had been sent to a senior member of staff. The teacher was holding a cane in her hand.

'Now then, Cora,' she had said 'I'm going to ask you a question and you must tell me the truth.'

The teacher had pushed her face close to Cheryl's.

'Your attack on Marian was so violent you fractured her shoulder. Why did you do that? Tell me the truth now.'

'It was just a game.'

'And when you suffocated that little boy in the refrigerator, was that "just a game" too? No? I thought not. So . . . now I'm going to question you again and I want you to think very carefully before you reply. I want the *exact* truth about why you attacked Marian.'

Cheryl remembered feeling faint as she realised that *everyone*, both staff and pupils, knew the truth of what she had done to Peter Sims. It was unbearable. She fixed her eyes on the wall behind the teacher's head. The wallpaper was covered with pink roses, some open with frilly petals and dark centres and others still in bud with leafy stems. She focused her attention on one particular rose.

'Come on,' said the teacher. 'Tell me the truth!'

Cheryl remained silent.

'If you don't answer, I'll have to teach you the hard way.'

Cheryl stared at the rose.

'That's it then, Cora. Put your hand out. Not that one, your *left* hand. *Palm up*.'

Cheryl extended her left hand.

'I'll ask you again: why did you attack Marian so viciously? The truth, please.'

Cheryl stared at the flower and, again, said nothing.

Cheryl's hand immediately received a blow so sharp and agonising that she nearly collapsed. She stared hard at the large rose with its dark centre and imagined she was small enough to climb right into it. Once inside, she concentrated on the velvety softness of its sweet-smelling heart and tried to block out everything else.

'Keep your left hand out and tell me why you attacked Marian,' the teacher repeated. 'You have one more chance to tell the truth.'

Cheryl continued to concentrate on the pink rose and nothing else. She remained silent.

WHACK! This time Cheryl could see a red line

appearing across her hand as the blood squeezed out, but now somehow, she could cope better with the pain.

'Now then, Cora, this is your very last chance to tell me the truth about what happened. If you don't own up, there will be dire consequences.'

The teacher spoke to Cheryl in icy tones, but Cheryl was not listening to her; instead concentrated on her pink rose. Gradually, as she watched, the flower started to open up and out of its black heart came a small snake which swelled larger and larger, its jaws opening wider and wider as it swallowed first the teacher's cane and the hand holding it, then her yellow hair and horrid face. Finally the fat body of the teacher slipped altogether into the snake's reptilian maw. After consuming every part of Cheryl's torturer, the snake became tiny again and slid back into the flower.

WHACK! Cheryl felt no pain this time.

Later, after Matron had bandaged her hand, Cheryl knew that, not only had she won against the senior teacher, she had also learned how to use the power of her mind to shield herself from painful situations and over the ensuing years she had perfected the art.

Today she was putting all the lessons she had learned into practice.

VI

Marcie stood up to speak.

'Cheryl – *Cathie Brook* – when you ran our Chelsea house, my parents felt blessed to have you in their employ. We all trusted you implicitly. But recently I've come to realise that my marriage to Randall was arranged by the two of you so that you could enrich yourselves at the expense not only of my family, but also of the farmers who depend on the Redcliffe estate for their living. My parents died prematurely from stress, desperation, broken hearts and, I reckon, other causes that you may well know may know about, so please could you explain to me why you and Randall worked so hard to destroy us? I mean, what had we done to deserve such hatred?'

Everyone looked expectantly at Cheryl, who remained silent, her eyes fixed at some point just beyond the table where they were all sitting. Marcie sat down and then Sally stood up.

'The close connection you enjoy with Randall Selkirk puts you in the frame alongside him. So when Don and I accuse Randall of cheating us out of our hard-earned family savings we are accusing you too. Randall befriended us only to defraud us and then, when I confronted him about it, he shoved me down a flight of stone stairs and the baby he knew we were expecting was killed. We know that you and Randall are as thick as thieves – an apt description in this context – so please tell us all what on earth we could possibly have done to deserve such cruel treatment. Please tell us – Cheryl Gibson – because now is the time to make a clean breast of everything.'

Cheryl stared ahead of her, apparently unmoved, her expression registering utter boredom. Her manner was so strange that a feeling of unreality took over everyone seated around the table.

Janey leaned across the table to display her mother's ring.

'Yesterday,' she said, 'this ring was found at Llancoed lying on the ground between the house and the church. It is a Collins family heirloom and extremely valuable. Later yesterday, at Llancoed, we also found valuable paintings, tapestries and albums that had been stolen from my house during the period you were paid to look after my mother. You dismissed my staff, stole priceless heirlooms, murdered my mother, and then pulled this ring off my dead mother's finger. So – Kelly Graham – please could you explain your actions?'

Ann, listening to her friends' brief statements, watched Cheryl's lack of emotion with fascination. She observed that all the time Cheryl was being accused of carrying out these atrocities, she remained impassive, sitting stock-still, her arms folded protectively over her chest. It seemed clear to Ann that Cheryl was using some form of self-hypnosis to protect herself from having to face up to the cruel and seemingly motiveless crimes she had perpetrated against so many people, over so many years.

While she is on cloud nine, Ann thought, *she doesn't have to face up to her sadistic behaviour. Perhaps she learned to hypnotise herself at the reformatory. She watched, enthralled, as Cheryl lifted her conscious mind to a sanctuary of her own making, far away from the appalling crimes she had committed.*

From her safe place high up in the clouds, Cheryl could see and hear everything going on below her with amazing clarity, but nothing could touch her while she was up there. Down below she could see the Conference Room door open and a woman walk over and whisper to Sally. Then, high above the world of these little people, Cheryl idly watched Sally stand up and say:

'I'd like to have a quick word with you, if I may – Janey, Judith and Ralph. It won't take a second, but I need to keep what I have to tell you private for obvious reasons, just for a short while. All will be revealed very soon.'

VII

Sally walked out of the room, with Janey, Judith and Ralph following closely behind her. The rest of the group stayed behind, talking quietly to one another, all the while keeping an eye on Cheryl, whose behaviour seemed very strange indeed. Ann calmly looked around the table at her friends before whispering to Roxanne who was sitting next to her.

'She's hypnotised herself to avoid having to face up to what she's done – pass it on. I'll try to bring her out of it when the others come back.'

Roxanne silently acknowledged Ann's comment before repeating it to her neighbour. Soon the message had gone full circle.

Meanwhile, standing just outside the Conference Room, Sally was getting down to business.

'Janey,' she said. 'I've just been told that the police have found your missing cushion at the Parry-Joneses' Paddington house. It was found wrapped in a tablecloth, hidden at the back of the top shelf of a large tallboy.'

'What? Oh, but that's wonderful news!' Janey was overjoyed. Then her face froze. 'But . . . surely it wouldn't have been hidden away like that unless it was used to . . . to suffocate my mother?'

'Yes, it does seem suspicious,' Sally replied, 'which is why the forensic team have asked for the cushion's matching partner to compare it with. John Green wonders when you'll be going home so that the team can get started.'

'Ralph and Judith kindly drove me here,' Janey said, throwing a questioning glance in their direction, 'so I'm in their hands. I think we were planning to break the journey somewhere, weren't we, but . . . ?'

'Yes, we're booked in to spend tomorrow night at Ross-on-Wye,' said Judith, 'but we're in your hands, Janey. We'll happily fit in with whatever you want to do.'

'Look, I don't want to delay John's forensic team,' Janey replied, 'so I'd be perfectly happy for him to send someone over to my house to pick up the cushion whenever he likes. He's got a copy of my key, and I trust him implicitly. Oh, and Sally – please could you tell him that the matching cushion is in the drawing-room on a chair next to the piano. I'll be back home by around midday tomorrow, so it's up to John to decide what he wants to do.'

'Good,' said Sally. 'I'll get back to him just as soon as I can, but . . . I'm afraid I've got to mention something else, something important, that John told me to tell you all – including Cheryl. We need to go back to the Conference Room now.'

During the short interlude that Sally, Janey, Ralph and Judith were talking outside the Conference Room, Cheryl remained stationary, her eyes glazed as if staring at some object far out in space. Slightly awkwardly, the rest of the group had sat around making desultory conversation, waiting to be reunited with their friends who, as they re-entered the room, elicited a short burst of conversation, after which Sally addressed Cheryl.

'Cheryl, the police have been on the phone. You see, your employer, Mrs Fion Parry-Jones, has gone missing. Are you listening, Cheryl? Early this morning they called at Llancoed but Mrs Parry-Jones wasn't there and her car had gone. The police then contacted the London Met to see if she had arrived at her Paddington home, but she hadn't. As you know, Fion's health is seriously impaired and so we are asking you, as her housekeeper, to tell us where you think she might be.'

Everyone looked at Cheryl, but Cheryl was not responding.

'I'm talking to you.' Sally was annoyed.

No response.

'For God's sake, Cheryl, can't you show a tiny bit of interest in someone other than yourself?'

'I don't think she's quite with us at the moment,' said Ann. 'She's put herself into a trance.'

'What? How frightfully convenient! *Bloody hell!*' It was all too much for Sally, who was so busy and so stressed she felt she could strangle Cheryl.

Ann explained the situation as she saw it. 'Somehow Cheryl has learned – probably at the reform school – to disengage herself from her surroundings when things become unendurable. She has learned to lift her mind up and away from situations that upset her.'

'Well, what the hell am I supposed to do about *that?*' Sally replied. 'The police want her to help them locate her employer who has gone missing.'

'Well, I might be able to help,' said Ann. 'Bear with me, please, because I haven't done this for a while, and please don't interrupt me whatever you do.'

'What?' Janey stared at Ann.

'I said don't interrupt, *please,* all of you. Just for a moment. I'll see what I can do to gain her attention for you, Sally, but you must all shut up and let me get on with it.'

Ann stood up and walked around the table to where Cheryl was sitting. She picked up a chair and gently turned it around so that she was facing her.

'Hello, Cheryl, you know who I am. I am Dr Edwards, and what I have to say is very important . . . very important. You see, I need you to help me find Fion Parry-Jones and only you can help me . . . As you know, Fion is very, very ill . . . Today she drove off in her car and nobody knows where she is . . . She isn't at Llancoed, and she isn't at Paddington . . . You are the only person who can find her, Cheryl . . . We need you to help find her and so you need to listen very . . . very carefully to what I'm about to say . . . this is very urgent . . .'

As Ann spoke, every eye in the room was fixed upon Cheryl's face to see how she was responding. But Cheryl was not responding. She was staring ahead of her, her face devoid of animation, her eyes glazed. Again, Ann spoke very slowly and quietly.

'In a moment . . . I'm going to ask you to help us find Fion . . . As you know, she is very, very ill . . . she may even be dying . . . so the question I'm asking you is . . . crystal clear . . . and your insight will be . . . crystal clear . . . as you see how to help find Fion . . . You will see everything . . . in just a few moments . . . In a few moments' time you will tell us how we can help Fion . . . It will become crystal clear . . . when you listen very carefully . . . very carefully . . . to the words to help find Fion. You will listen very carefully . . . to help Fion . . . In a moment you'll hear my voice count down from *ten* to *one* . . . and because you want to help Fion . . . more and more . . . with each descending number between *ten* and *one* . . . you will become ever more alert and wide awake . . . with each descending number. Each descending number between ten and one will help you to feel more and more fully alert and wide awake . . . so that you can see how you can find Fion. So . . . ready? *Ten . . . nine . . . eight . . .* feeling more alert and focused on finding Fion . . . *seven . . . six . . . five . . .* that's it, Cheryl . . . you want to help find Fion . . . *four . . .*

three . . . you are waking up and . . . everything . . . is crystal clear . . . *two* . . . waking up . . . you are alert and ready to help find Fion . . . one . . . waking up, waking up and . . . *zero* . . . You are fully wide awake, wide awake, and your mind is crystal clear . . . crystal clear.'

Ann spoke these words very slowly and very gently and a few moments later Cheryl started to look around her, after which, to everyone's amazement, she explained the situation to the group.

'Fion seems to have disappeared.'

'Yes,' said Ann, 'and we are all hoping that you can tell us where she might have gone.'

Cheryl looked at a loss for a second and then she had a sudden inspiration.

'If she was too ill to go to Spain with Geraint, she might have gone to the Paddington Antiques Emporium to help run Geraint's business for him while he's away. She employs a man called Sam who drives her to London if Geraint is away or she's feeling too ill to drive. I haven't got his phone number – sorry.'

'Well, we can contact the Paddington Emporium right away. Do you have *their* phone number by any chance?'

Cheryl immediately gave Sally the Emporium's telephone number from memory and waited politely while Sally returned to the office to try to make contact with them. Then, as they all sat quietly waiting for Sally's return, everyone felt they owed Ann an enormous debt of gratitude, not only for her amazing courage and resourcefulness on *Manatee*, but also for her brilliance in waking Cheryl out of her trance.

A few minutes later, Sally returned shaking her head. 'The Emporium is open and I spoke to the manager, Carl Johnston. Carl doesn't know where Fion is, and there is no sign of her car either. So now we are all getting rather worried about Fion because, as you know, she needs urgent medical attention. Is there anywhere else she might have gone?'

'I can't think of anywhere at the moment, but I'm trying to put myself in her shoes. If she's feeling really ill she may have driven herself to the hospital at Aberystwyth.'

'No, the police have checked Bronglais and she's not there. They've also put out information about her on local radio, but there have been no replies. I've also been asked to confirm that your employer's first name is *Fion*?'

Cheryl made eye contact with Sally and shook her head.

'No, it isn't.'

'Who is she, then, and what is her real name?'

'Her real name is Fiona.'

'Thank you. And would you happen to know her maiden name?'

'Gibson.'

'But isn't Gibson your surname?'

'Yes.'

'How come?'

'Fiona is my sister.'

VIII

There was a stunned silence, followed by a clamour of questions. Roxanne was the first to make herself heard.

'I don't recall a Fiona Gibson at Dicester Heath when I was growing up. I remember *you*, but no sister called Fiona.'

Cheryl looked at Roxanne and, to everyone's amazement, she smiled enigmatically.

'The reason you don't remember a family called Gibson living at Dicester Heath is because we didn't live at Dicester Heath. We lived three miles out at Eastworth. Eastworth was our family home, and my father, grandfather and great-grandfather were born there. I used to bicycle to school at Dicester Heath, cross-country, but Fiona wasn't allowed to because she was too little. Fiona was only seven years old when Peter Sims died and I was sent to the reformatory. After that my father died – I think that the shock of my mother's love-affair with Mr Sims and my crime were too much for him. So my mother took over my father's estate but after a while she sold up and bought the house in Paddington. That's it!'

Janey Collins sat forward in her chair.

'Where in Paddington?'

'You see,' said Cheryl, ignoring Janey's question, 'my mother lived on her own in Paddington for several years, but during that time Fiona had some serious health problems. Our mother simply couldn't cope and blamed me for everything, so I wasn't wanted there. After I left school, I took a job as a housekeeper in Norfolk and during that period my mother met Geraint Parry-Jones who latched on to Fiona. A short while later he married Fiona and moved into our Paddington house. Then our mother died of cancer and Geraint used our inheritance to build up his business. That's it, really. My sister, Fiona Gibson, became Fiona Parry-Jones, or Fion, and it's been a miserable marriage.'

'It sounds as if both you and your sister have had a pretty rough time,' said Marcie, 'and it strikes me that if Fiona is feeling desperately ill she may have decided to drive to Aberystwyth where there are people who can help her if she collapses. Without you and Geraint at Llancoed, there's nobody around to help her, so I reckon she's gone somewhere where she is known.'

'Yes,' said Cheryl with urgency, the wonderful and reliable housekeeper emerging in front of their very eyes. 'You're right. There are places in Aberystwyth she likes, but I can't remember their names. If I could pick up my car from the harbour I could drive around and check on her.'

'Well, that poses a slight problem,' said Sally. 'Normally we could give you a lift down to Aberystwyth but this is our last day together. Later this afternoon we all go our separate ways and Brinkley opens her doors to the public again tomorrow. So we've got our work cut out.'

'Yes, of course.' Cheryl looked downcast.

'Don't worry, Cheryl,' said Livia, playing her role flawlessly, 'I'd be very happy to drive you to Aberystwyth. Right now if you like.'

Cheryl turned towards Livia. 'Yes please. That would be marvellous. I'm so worried about Fiona. Thank you.'

'Is that all right with all of you?' Pretending to be surprised, Sally looked around the table at her friends, receiving nods of affirmation from everyone. There was a general feeling of elation at the thought of getting rid of Cheryl, especially now that Randall was safely locked up in prison.

IX

Livia and Cheryl stood up together and walked around the outside of the hotel to the car park, where Livia's shiny new car was parked. Expertly Livia steered her way down the lane to the T-junction where she turned left on to the coast road.

'Thank you for helping me out in there, Livia.'

'I was pleased to help.'

'Well, thank you anyway.'

'There was an ulterior motive to my offering you a lift.'

'Why? What was that?' Cheryl sounded surprised.

'I have bad news for you, I'm afraid. The others didn't want me to tell you this, but I won the argument, which is why I offered to give you a lift.'

'What do you mean?'

'Right then, here goes . . . Brace yourself for a shock.'

'What's happened?'

'Last night Randall and Geraint hijacked a yacht with the owners on board. They pushed the husband off the yacht at gunpoint and kept the wife on board as hostage. Then they headed for the French coast but, somewhere near St David's Head, a lifeboat crew boarded the yacht and Randall and Geraint were arrested and taken to Aberystwyth police station. They are being transported to a London prison today.'

Livia looked sideways to see how Cheryl was taking this news, but Cheryl's face was blank. She was giving nothing away.

'Wandsworth, I suppose,' said Cheryl thoughtfully.

'Would you like me to drop you off at the police station when we get to Aberystwyth? You might just catch them before they leave for London.'

'No, I don't think so. I think my top priority is to find Fiona. She needs to know what's happened to Geraint.'

'Yes, of course. Another thing . . . I'm told that Randall's yacht is still moored at Aberdovey, is that so?'

'Yes.'

'Well, getting his yacht returned to its Aberystwyth mooring is one thing you could do for him. I gather that if everything is taken into account, Randall might receive a long sentence. Geraint too.'

'Yes, I see.'

'Well, let me know if there is any way I can help.'

'Thank you.'

The two women continued their journey to Aberystwyth. Once there, Livia dropped off Cheryl at the harbour before driving back to Aberdovey. She felt relieved to have got rid of the woman she had once loved so much, the woman who had tricked her and wounded her so cruelly. Livia felt pleased that she had countered cruelty with kindness and now the whole episode was closed.

CHAPTER FOURTEEN

Judith Speaks Out

|

AFTER LIVIA AND Cheryl left the Conference Room, there was a clamour of excited comments, mainly directed at Ann.

'What on earth was that all about?' Trot asked. 'What happened to Cheryl? One minute she was totally *out of* it and the next minute she was totally *with* it; so what happened, Ann?'

'Well, it seems to me that when Cheryl found herself being confronted by the very people she had abused, she found the situation too much to bear. So, rather than face up to what she had done, she put herself into a trance and took herself off to cloud cuckoo land.'

'Well, I get that bit – but how did she do it?' Trot persisted.

'I suspect,' said Ann, 'that at some point in Cheryl's past she was confronted by a situation so unbearable that the only way she could protect herself was by transferring part of her conscious mind to an imaginary place where she could retain a safe distance but also, at another level, listen in to what was being said.'

'Yes, but what about you? How did you know what to do?' Trot was not going to let the subject drop.

'Well, I used a very, very basic technique I learned as a student to bring her mind back to the present situation using Fion's – or Fiona's – disappearance as the key to reaching her. I was lucky, that's all.' Ann closed the interview.

'Well, the whole process proved highly satisfactory,' said Roxanne.

'All thanks to you, Ann,' said Janey, 'and at least Cheryl has gone. Praise be!'

II

Janey's comment was followed by a brief silence during which Judith sat wondering when she could broach a subject that, though unpopular, she felt compelled to raise. When Sally returned to her seat in the Conference Room, Judith knew that, although Don was working in the office and Livia had not yet returned from Aberystwyth, she had to speak now. If she left it until after lunch it might be too late; members of the group might already be leaving the hotel. Standing up, Judith forced herself to make eye contact with her friends, who looked up at her with surprise.

'There's something I have to say that I couldn't say with Cheryl here. As you know, while we were at Llancoed yesterday, I was the only one to get a glimpse of Fion, the woman we now know to be Cheryl's little sister, Fiona Gibson. I think I told you that she looked very thin, even emaciated, and that it occurred to me that she wasn't destined to remain in this world much longer. We now know that Fiona is three years younger than Cheryl which makes her forty-six or forty-seven years old: the same age as our year-group, though she looks more like ninety.

'This morning I had a dream that was so vivid I could still see images of it even after I'd opened my eyes. I was back here at Brinkley House and we were in the gym, skipping. We were doing "double bumps" and in my dream, Marcie, you held the record at two hundred! At the same time as we were skipping, some of us were having fun at the expense of a girl who had joined our class at the start of our second year at Brinkley. This new-girl was so fat she couldn't jump at all, with or without a skipping rope. She had a fat bottom, and as her surname was Fanshaw, we decided to call her "Fat Fanny". I'm sure you all remember "Fat Fanny", I know I do.'

Judith's eyes took in the table where her school friends were sitting forward, staring at her. She carried on.

'Well, it was then that I realised that the tiny, skeletally thin woman I had seen creeping around at Llancoed yesterday and the skinny woman creeping around in my dream were one and the same person: Fion Parry-Jones. That is to say, Fion Parry-Jones, Fiona Gibson, Fiona Fanshaw and "Fat Fanny". Four names for one individual.'

There followed a shocked silence, broken by a common-sense request from Ann.

'All this is quite a leap, Judith. Please could you tell us why you think your nightmare can be trusted as fact, as opposed to the usual kind of rubbish we dream up? You need to draw the threads together a bit more.'

'I'll try to be brief. I don't want to hold up lunch. My first point is this – that when I saw Fion at Llancoed yesterday, I vaguely recognised her but couldn't place where I had seen her before. Geraint had told us that Fion was suffering from a tummy-bug and yet there she was, fully dressed, creeping along outside the house, trying not to be seen. It was the manner of her creeping that jogged my memory, and, of course, we all know why Fion – or Fiona, the girl we used to call "Fat Fanny" – didn't want to show her face yesterday. Why would anybody want to be confronted by the people who bullied them at school? And yesterday, while we were impudently strutting around her house as if we owned the place, she must have felt extremely threatened. After all, as children we were told that Fat Fanny had been removed from Brinkley House for her own safety.'

Sally broke in. 'What do you mean? I dimly remember Fat Fanny, but I don't recall her being bullied.'

'Rubbish,' said Trot, 'we all bullied her to some extent. Some more than others, I admit, but that's not the point. The point is this: what does all this have to do with Randall Selkirk? After all, the reason we were invited here was because Randall was posing a threat to those of us who happened to be guests at his wedding. So how come, now that he is safely locked up in jug, we are chewing our fingers to the nub because of his relationship with Cheryl Gibson and her little sister?'

'Good point, Trot,' said Judith. 'The importance of raising this subject is to find answers to the questions that brought us all here in the first place. So the facts as they stand are that Mrs Gibson had an affair with a Mr Sims and moved out of the family home. Then, aged ten, Cheryl killed Peter Sims and was sent to a reformatory, which brought shame upon the Gibson family and probably exacerbated Mr Gibson's premature death. A year or two later, Mrs Gibson fled Eastworth and moved to

Paddington, where she changed her name to Fanshaw. Then, the year after we were sent to Brinkley House, Fiona joined us and, as we know, was badly bullied. Subsequently Mrs. Gibson removed Fiona from Brinkley House, and a few years after that, she married her off to Geraint Parry-Jones, letting the Gibson family fortune slip through her fingers.'

Janey interrupted angrily.

'What the hell are you implying, Judith? You're talking total gibberish! Please change the subject before we all start flagellating ourselves about things that have no relevance to today's issues. Raking up all these things from the past is not only irresponsible, but also a total waste of our time. Please, shut up, Judith!'

There was a shocked gasp, and Ralph leaned forward, ready to step in if necessary, but Judith stood her ground.

'So, what's the significance of recalling beastly stuff best forgotten? Well, I think that if one examines the facts and asks the right questions, the truth is bound to shine forth. So here are some questions which should reveal some elements of the truth we came here to find out this weekend.

'Marcie? Why did Cheryl gain employment with your family under a false name and why did she engineer your marriage to Randall Selkirk? Why did she stand by while Randall stole from you and your family, wrecked Redcliffe, broke your parents' hearts and health, and caused you to have a major breakdown? Is it possible that Cheryl's actions were motivated by some warped idea of avenging her little sister who was bullied at Brinkley House School?

'We know that Livia was devoted to Cheryl, or *Katie Gilbert,* and that when Cheryl left her employ Livia was very upset. Suppose, however, Cheryl purposely sought employment with Livia in order to hurt and rob her? She failed to rob her, but she did treat her appallingly and it's just possible that her cruel behaviour was motivated by her sister's unhappy experiences at school.

'Sally. Why did Randall befriend Don only to cheat him and cause him to lose his job? Why did he steal from your family, and what motivated him to attack you even though he knew that you were pregnant? Answer: because, *at Cheryl's behest,* he wanted to punish you for the cruel treatment meted out to "Fat Fanny" at Brinkley House. What other motive could there possibly be for such despicable behaviour?

'Janey. The apparently motiveless murder of your mother – why? What possible reason could there be for murdering Mrs Collins? And how did Cheryl manage to get the agency to recommend her services just at that critical moment in time when you needed to find a carer to look after your mother? Did Cheryl actually murder your mother? If she didn't, who did? Again I suspect, though I could be wrong, that Geraint and Randall helped Cheryl to obtain false papers, false references and a false name, so that she could access your house as your mother's trained carer. So what was their motivation? Clearly, for Geraint it was the chance to steal valuable paintings, tapestries and albums – but who actually murdered Mrs Collins and why? I can only guess along the following lines … That all those years ago, when Mrs Gibson first moved to Paddington, Mrs Collins was kind enough to help her. Perhaps Mrs Collins encouraged her to change her name from Gibson to Fanshaw, or, guessing again, perhaps Mrs Collins told Mrs Fanshaw about Brinkley House School, where her own daughter was happy, and suggested that Mrs Fanshaw send Fiona there. Finally, I think it's just possible that when Mrs Fanshaw found that Fiona was being bullied at Brinkley House, she confided this news to Mrs Collins and Mrs Collins advised her not to remove Fiona from Brinkley House but rather to encourage her to hang in there and earn the respect of the other girls. Of course this is pure guesswork as I haven't any evidence for any of this, and doubt any of you have either. All we can say is that, tragically, the murder of Mrs Collins may have been the manifestation of a sadistic desire on the part of Cheryl to destroy the one person who was helpful and supportive of Mrs Gibson.'

'I can see you've got the whole thing buttoned, haven't you? Quite the little sleuth,' sneered Janey, looking daggers at Judith, who ignored her and calmly carried on saying what she had to say.

'Thankfully Randall and Geraint are out of the picture now but this morning when I glanced at the sports section of the *Cambrian News*, the names G. Parry-Jones and F. Parry-Jones popped up several times in the list of participants in the local rifle-shooting competitions. So perhaps it wasn't Randall who shot your horse, Marcie. Perhaps it was Fiona! I don't know who it was, but had either of them decided to shoot you, I doubt they'd have missed.'

Marcie sat forward in her chair. 'Good grief, it doesn't bear thinking about. What a dreadful possibility. Yes, "Fat Fanny" was bullied at Brinkley House but, sadly, lots of children are bullied at school and yet their families don't carry out full-scale vendettas against the bullies and their families, year after year after year. The whole idea is preposterous.'

'Yes, Marcie, you are quite right,' said Judith, 'and the whole saga has put a new and unwelcome slant on everything we thought we understood. I only mention all this now because it supports Ann's suggestion that Cheryl may be a very clever sadomasochist who, with her psychopathic sidekick, Randall, may have used the fact that Fiona was bullied at Brinkley House as the excuse for a lifetime of revenge, criminality, and even murder.

'We are all guilty of bullying "Fat Fanny" to some extent, but remember, we too were victims . . . just a bunch of 'war-babies' sent away from home for no apparent reason – or rather, no reason we were old enough to understand. We too were deprived. Nobody kissed *us* goodnight or read *us* a bedtime story. Nobody comforted *us* when we were bullied, or felt lonely, or sick, or sad, or homesick. Some of us came from broken homes, or had parents living abroad. Most of us had hardly any experience of normal family life, and the staff at Brinkley House were an idle, negligent bunch. They must have known what was going on, but turned a blind eye.'

Judith sat down, and for a moment nobody spoke, but then Trot stood up.

'Thank you, Judith. I think you've done the right thing in raising these points. Of course it's not pleasant to be reminded of the way we treated "Fat Fanny" all those years ago but, as you rightly say, there was nobody around to check our behaviour during the many hours a day we were left entirely to our own devices. None of us had chosen to be sent away from home and none of us had chosen to be sent to Brinkley House. We had no parents to support us and we were all homesick and lonely to some extent. It was vital for us to keep in with the crowd because to do otherwise would probably cause *us* to be bullied too. It was the law of the jungle and the need to conform was very strong. Yes, I think that what you've just said is very important and you've helped us in another way too, Judith. The fact that Randall and Geraint are locked up doesn't mean that it's all over. We still have the Gibson sisters to contend with. And to cap it all, we can't rule out the fact that Fiona may be a "crack shot" like her husband, so we need to keep on the alert.'

'Thank you, Trot,' said Judith turning towards Sally, who was standing up to make an announcement.

'Lunch is served in fifteen minutes – but, Judith, before we go in, would you object if I telephoned Tom Mortimer to tell him everything you've just told us? Actually I think that both Tom and John Green should be put in the picture, assuming nobody objects. The facts need to be checked out, don't you think?'

'Good idea,' said Judith. 'I leave that to you and Don. Thanks.'

Stiffly, everyone stood up. Sally left the Conference Room first, followed by Trot, who saluted Judith as she passed. Then Roxanne left the room, followed by Ann and Jack, and the three of them smiled fondly at Judith as they left. Then Ralph stood up, put his arm around Judith's shoulders, and lovingly escorted her out of the room. Marcie and Janey left together and headed for the cloakroom.

II

Janey muscled her way into the small cloakroom, checked the lavatories to make sure they were empty, and gave Marcie the thumbs-up. Marcie then went inside and stood leaning against the closed door, both to prop herself up and to block any unwanted visitors.

'That was awful.' Marcie gripped her walking stick, her body stiff with exhaustion.

'I'm sorry I overreacted back there, it was stupid of me, because we need to keep a sense of proportion about all this.' Janey looked at Marcie apologetically. 'After all, what we did to Fat Fanny was nothing but a storm in a teacup, the storm having been greatly stirred up by Fat Fanny herself. Mind you, it could have been so much worse.'

'Yes, but to think that my parents employed Cathie Brook for all those years without knowing that she was *Fat Fanny's sister. It's appalling!*'

'Yes, but if you think about what we did back then, the whole situation is crazy. I know we were naughty, but surely the hour that Fat Fanny spent locked up in the sports hut doesn't warrant all the misery heaped upon our families over the years. It's bloody ridiculous!'

'In actual fact she was shut in for less than an hour and, as we know, the 'sports pavilion' was really just a hut, a prefab with a skylight; quite cosy in its own way. So there has to be some other, far greater, motive for all the criminal stuff Randall and Cheryl heaped on my family over the years and for your mother's murder. Besides, Livia, and Sally and Don, have been victimised too, and they had nothing whatsoever to do with locking Fat Fanny in the hut.'

'I know that Mrs Fanshaw made a big fuss, and that our parents were contacted, if you recall?'

'Yes, you're right!' Janey replied. 'Mrs Fanshaw wanted us to be expelled, but our parents made damn sure we weren't. Instead Mrs Fanshaw removed Fat Fanny from Brinkley House and the whole episode was handled with great tact and kept from the others – at least, I think it was. I know that Judith has no idea because if she'd known the truth she would never have raised the subject out of loyalty to me. No, at one time or another, everyone bullied Fat Fanny. What we did was cruel and hateful, but children are only children and surely Cheryl, having murdered Peter Sims at a similar age, should have appreciated that fact. Anyhow, may I suggest that we continue to keep this under our hats for the time being? I don't want my friendship with John Green, or my career as a CPO, jeopardised. So, Marcie, shall we agree to keep our mouths shut? . . . Yes? Good. We'd better go now.'

III

Ralph and Judith went up to their room. As soon as they were inside, Ralph put his arms around Judith and held her close.

'You were wonderful, but how come you didn't tell me about it earlier?'

'I tried, but you were so sound asleep I couldn't get you to take it on board, but anyway it was Cheryl's strange behaviour this morning, and finding out that Fiona was her little sister, that clarified the situation for me and made sense of my nightmare.'

'Brinkley House must have been a dreadful school.'

'Yes, I suppose so, although it seemed all right at the time. We had nothing to compare it with and didn't know any better. We were so young when we started there. Actually, I preferred being at Brinkley House during the term than being stuck on my own with Granny Fielder during the holidays. I had no social life in the holidays, so going to school was a great relief. As you know, Ma and Pa came home from India when I was thirteen and after that everything was perfect.'

'You were so deprived. It pains me to think of you, hardly more than a baby, all alone with your grandmother and then stuck at a school where bullying was condoned. Your teachers were criminal in their neglect. Poor Fiona Gibson! Poor little girl! But why did her mother allow her to get so fat? Mrs Gibson must have been a truly stupid woman.'

IV

The moment she left the Conference Room, Sally strode purposefully to the office, where she found Don working.

'I've got to make an urgent telephone call. Listen in and I'll explain later.' She dialled a number.

'Hello, I believe this is Detective Sergeant Tom Mortimer's private number. Is he there? My name is Sally Saunders and I'm the proprietor of the Brinkley House Hotel at Aberdovey. Thank you, I'll hold on . . . Hello, Tom? This is Sally Saunders.'

'Hello, Sally, what's up?'

'It's about the Gibson sisters. We've just been presented with a worrying fact that seems to make excellent sense. We now believe it's probable that Fiona Gibson (that is, Fion Parry-Jones), apart from being Cheryl's little sister, was actually at school with us right here at Brinkley House for a short while. She joined the school at the start of our second year, aged around nine years old, and her surname at the time was Fanshaw, not Gibson. I'm afraid that, because she was enormously fat and her surname was Fanshaw, we called her 'Fat Fanny'. She wasn't with us for long because her mother, Mrs. Gibson (or Mrs. Fanshaw) took her away.'

'Hang on . . .' Tom echoed Sally's words with horror. 'So you're saying that Fiona is Cheryl's little sister and that she was at Brinkley House while you were there, but had to be removed because she was so badly bullied?'

'Yes, I'm afraid so. We were very young at the time and our teachers must have known what was going on, yet did nothing. We've only just realised that at some point after Cheryl had been sent to the reformatory, her widowed mother – who had changed her surname from Gibson to Fanshaw – moved to Paddington and, a year or two later, sent Fiona to board at Brinkley House School. We now wonder if all the pain and misery we've suffered at the hands of Cheryl and Randall over the years might be some kind of distorted vendetta carried out against us because we bullied Fiona all those years ago.'

'Yes, I see . . . You know, I'd really like to lock Cheryl up for the all the malicious tricks and falsehoods she practised on you over the years *and* for her possible part in Mrs Collins's death, but we need hard evidence to make an arrest. Hearsay evidence isn't enough. I'll try to find out more about Fiona. What year was she at Brinkley House?'

'The school-year 1952 to 1953, I think. Anyhow, during our second year. She was nine years old when she joined us and left just a few months later.'

'If you lot are forty-six or forty-seven years old now, your teachers will be well over the seventy mark. Do you happen to know if any of them are still alive? If so, have you got any names?'

'I still keep in touch with a Mrs Gwen Morgan who lives within walking distance of Brinkley House. We enjoy speaking Welsh together. She was a peripatetic dancing teacher at Brinkley House and a few other local schools. So yes, Gwen Morgan.' Sally passed Gwennie's details to Tom.

'Thanks. Incidentally, the Met has asked for everyone's contact details and, where relevant, a brief account of any criminal activities Cheryl Gibson and Randall Selkirk perpetrated upon you. John Green wants to weigh up the evidence as soon as possible, so can I ask you to be an angel and collate this information for me to pass on to him before everyone leaves your hotel?'

'Of course. I'll pass on your request over lunch. I already know everyone's contact details, so it's only the details of what Cheryl and Randall did to some of us over the years that need to be recorded before we all go our separate ways.'

'Thank you, Sally. Oh, and if Fiona Parry-Jones turns up at Brinkley House, please contact us immediately. She needs to be hospitalised as soon as possible.'

'Of course.'

'Thank you, Sally. You've been very helpful. Gotta go. Be in touch.'

'Okay. Bye.'

Don stared at Sally, curiosity getting the better of him. 'That was interesting. Tell me more about what Judith told you. Fiona Parry-Jones was at your school?'

'Yes, but don't worry – I'll explain everything over lunch.' Sally rushed off to the little dining-room, leaving Don to hand over the running of the office to Janet, who worked for them on a part-time basis.

V

At the back of the Bara Brith Tea Shop in Aberystwyth, a haggard-looking woman sat staring at a cup of tea. Fiona (or Fion) Parry-Jones was casting her mind back to the days and nights she had spent as a boarder at Brinkley House School.

The bullying had started with teasing and name-calling: 'Fatty', 'Fat Fanny', Doughnut' and 'Piggy'. These names had been popular with her classmates but then, because none of the teachers had intervened, the bullying had become more aggressive. On one occasion a letter from her mother had been intercepted by a humorous member of her class and read aloud in the quivering, falsetto tones of an elderly drama-queen, amidst howls of laughter. *'My darling, darling little daughter . . . my sweet . . . What a clever girl you are! Well done . . . my special little Fee-fee . . .'*

Fiona remembered sitting there, scarlet with embarrassment, with her heart breaking; yet dormitory life was even worse. Where was Matron when her 'dorm-mates' made her an 'apple-pie bed', or when they pulled one of the legs off Bruno, her furry bed-companion? Where was Matron when, 'after lights', she became victim to ghostly apparitions and strange voices that, even though they were often accompanied by repressed giggles, frightened her considerably. No adult seemed willing to take responsibility for her welfare and so she had been left to face her enemies alone.

From her bent position Fiona slowly leaned down to her shoulder bag and, with the aid of a walking stick, hooked out two letters tied together with red ribbon. One letter, dated 1953, was one she had sent to her mother; the

other letter was her mother's reply. Fiona's letter had
started well but ended with the usual heartfelt plea.

Dear Mother,

Thank you for your lovely letter. I'm glad
you had a nice time in Spain. I'm sorry I wasn't
able to see Aunt Jennifer.

I am working hard and have started
French, but I'm not happy. Please take me away
from here. The food is horrible and there is not
enough. Please take me away, I'm really
unhappy. After lights is worse. Please. They call
me names,

Love, Fiona.'

The reply from her mother repeated the same old mantra.
Fiona scanned the familiar lines.

Darling little Fee,

You are privileged to be at such a well-known
and successful school. A lot of girls would give
their eye-teeth to have an education like yours,
so take advantage of the opportunity and for
goodness sake stop moaning about everything.
Silly girl . . .

Fiona found it hard to recall all the everyday events that
had made life at Brinkley House so stressful. Being called
'Fat Fanny' was upsetting enough and it was humiliating
when nobody wanted to be her partner at games, or to
have her on their team. She could not run, jump, or skip
rope like the other girls. She was utterly useless at netball,
and had not been taught to swim. On one occasion, a

group of girls waited for her in the changing-room and sang a song they had made up about her. Fiona tried to remember the words, but she was feeling so ill and weak that she could not recall them. There was one occasion, however, that Fiona could recall only too well.

It was a cold January afternoon and, just as she was crossing the lacrosse pitch on her way to the dining-room for tea, Janey Collins and Marcia Stanton-Gray had waylaid her, pushed her into the sports hut and locked her in. Left alone, and having failed to open the door, Fiona recalled how she had tried, but failed, to open the skylight using the window pole. It was getting dark, and Fiona recalled the anxiety she had felt when it suddenly occurred to her that she might have to spend the night there, all alone. Soon everyone would be enjoying supper, after which there would be free time and 'lights out'. Would anyone miss her? Would anyone come to let her out? Fiona remembered shouting until she was hoarse, but to no avail; so she stopped shouting and sat quietly listening for footsteps. After what seemed like an age she heard someone approaching the hut and shouted at the top of her voice. Fortunately, a part-time teacher called Mrs Morgan heard Fiona's cries but was unable to unlock the sports hut door as the key was missing. So Mrs Morgan had had to leave Fiona alone again until a spare key had been located; only then had the door finally been unlocked.

Eventually Fiona had been escorted to Miss Castleford's study by Mrs Morgan, and her mother had been contacted. Marcie, and Janey (who had been caught with the key in her blazer pocket), had been read the riot act and threatened with expulsion. Both Lady Stanton-Gray and Mrs Collins were contacted, and when Fiona heard of this she realised that she now had enough ammunition to force her mother to take her away from Brinkley House for good. She knew her mother could now no longer stay on friendly terms with Janey's mother, Mrs Collins.

Fiona was glad that Janey and Marcie had not been expelled. In retrospect she realised that, in the long term, Brinkley House had even done her a favour, although it had taken her a long time to realise it. After leaving school she had started a fitness programme that involved eating less and exercising more, and slowly she had lost weight and changed her lifestyle for the better. She admitted to herself, however, that latterly she had rather overdone it and let herself get too thin but that wasn't their fault. Forgive, forget, and die happy! Smiling to herself, Fiona asked the owner of the Bara Brith Tea Shop if she could use their telephone to make a quick call.

VI

Don was just heading off for lunch when the telephone rang.

'Brinkley House Hotel?' Don answered automatically, inclining his head to one side as he struggled to make sense of the thin, squeaky voice on the line.

'Have they gone?'

'Sorry, have *who* gone?'

'The private party?'

'Do you wish to book a room?'

'Yes, but only after your weekend guests have gone.'

'Don't worry, the private party will be leaving today and we are re-opening tomorrow. Please may I know your name and how long you wish to stay . . .'

The line went dead.

VII

Sally crossed the hall and joined the rest of the group in the dining-room. A minute or two later Don arrived.

'Is Janet looking after the office?' Sally whispered to Don.

'Yes,' Don whispered back.

'Good.' Sally banged on the table. 'Everybody, just a couple of points. Firstly, welcome back, Livia! How did you get on with Cheryl?'

Livia stood up. 'The whole trip was uneventful – although, surprisingly, Cheryl rejected my offer to drive her to see Randall at Aberystwyth police station. Instead she got me to drop her off at the harbour where Randall had left her car.'

'Now why doesn't that surprise me?', said Sally. 'Anyhow, changing the subject, I've got a couple of messages from Tom Mortimer. You'll be sorry to learn that, as yet, the police have no legal grounds for arresting Cheryl. If, however, the forensic team finds saliva on the golden cushion, then they will probably carry out further tests. Tom thanks us for updating him about Fiona Parry-Jones, née Gibson. Thanks to Tom, the relevant facts have been checked out and, yes, Fiona Gibson – Fanshaw – was definitely at Brinkley House. The fact that Fiona is Cheryl Gibson's little sister is now also on record. Bearing all this in mind, John Green has asked us for our contact details and written summaries of any antisocial or criminal acts carried out against us by Randall and/or Cheryl over the years, with dates, *et cetera*. He asks if you would mind if Don and I forward your details to him today, please. If you'd rather not, Tom Mortimer's and John Green's contact details are available at the office.'

Sally sat down, but to her surprise, Don stood up.

'Just one more thing. I think I should tell you that just now, literally five minutes ago, I received a phone call from a woman with a quivering voice asking when the "private party" was leaving. I told her that the party would be leaving late this afternoon, and I'm afraid the penny didn't drop until after she hung up. I realise now that the caller could have been Fiona Parry-Jones.'

'I'll get Ifor to look out for her. What does she look like, Judith?'

'She doesn't walk, she creeps,' said Judith. 'She is very small and thin. She uses walking sticks and has a sickly appearance. Her hair is short, grey and dishevelled. Not very appealing, but remember to be very careful not to approach her, as today may be her last chance to get her own back for what we did to her at school.'

'Thank you,' said Sally.

'Janey, are you armed?' Don spoke quietly, looking Janey straight in the eye.

'Yes. Well . . . no, not at this precise moment,' Janey stammered. 'I'm packed and ready to leave after tea. My firearm is in my shoulder bag along with my luggage, on my bed.'

'Well, don't you think we'd all feel safer if you had it with you – just in case?'

'Yes, I suppose so, though I very much doubt "Fat Fanny" will come here.'

Janey stood up and reluctantly walked over to the door. She felt embarrassed, not only because Judith had raised the subject of Fiona's victimisation at school but also because, as a CPO, she had been issued with a firearm for the specific purpose of protecting her friends and should not have left it lying around in her bedroom. She headed for her room on the second floor where she checked her weapon. She then put the pistol into her handbag and retraced her steps. She met Sally in the hall.

'Nobody's seen Fat Fanny, so that's good,' Sally informed Janey.

'Phew, that's a relief! Janey replied.

The two women rejoined their friends in the little dining-room where an excellent buffet lunch had been set out for them.

CHAPTER FIFTEEN

The Letter

I

CHERYL WAS PLEASED to find her car in its usual spot at the harbour, but having found it, she was not quite sure what to do next. She walked over to Valkyrie's mooring even though she knew that it would be empty. One of Randall's sailing friends waved at her.

'Hello,' Cheryl called.

'You'll not find him here.'

'Who?'

'Randall.'

'What a pity! Where is he, d'you know?'

'Arrested.'

'Good heavens! What for?' Cheryl feigned shocked surprise.

'Him and a man with a gun hijacked Jack Edwards's yacht and took his wife as hostage.'

'Good heavens! Is she all right now?'

'Yes, she was rescued by the Coastguard.'

'She was lucky then. What's she called?'

'Ann. Surely you know Ann and Jack? Regulars from

Chichester? Owners of *Manatee*, the boat that was hijacked?'

'But that's terrible! How did Ann survive the ordeal?'

'Well, she was brilliant, you know. Everyone's talking about it. From what I gather she drugged the two men and called in a lifeboat.'

'Clever Ann! Thank you for putting me in the picture.'

Thanking the chatty old seafarer, Cheryl thought about the information she had just received. A woman clever enough to drug Randall and Geraint and call a lifeboat . . . Ann Edwards . . . *Ann Edwards*? Why did that name sound so familiar?

Suddenly the words 'I am Dr Edwards' popped into her head. Of course! Little Miss Clever-Clogs, currently showing off her skills as a hypnotist at Brinkley House. *Ann Edwards* – that's who she was! And wouldn't you know that Randall and Geraint would fail to be on their guard on account of her being a mere woman. Well, while those two chauvinist pigs were mouldering away in prison, she, Cheryl, would have to settle the score for them. So Dr Ann *Smarty-Pants* Edwards – WATCH OUT!

By the time Cheryl had crossed the harbour and entered Randall's favourite pub, she was badly in need of a drink. She went straight over to the bar and ordered a large glass of whisky which she downed in one; then she bought another large whisky and walked over to the telephone booth, glass in hand. So where was Fiona? She called the Llancoed number: no reply. Then she tried the number for the Paddington house: no reply. She stood still for a moment trying to work out where Fiona might have gone. There was a local tea shop she visited regularly, but she couldn't remember what it was called. She flicked through the local telephone directory. What was it? Of course! The Bara Brith Tea Shop. There it was, right in front of her nose. Cheryl dialled the telephone number and the call went through.

'Bara Brith Tea Shop, good afternoon,' said a female voice.

'Hello. My name is Cheryl and I'm wondering if you have my sister, Mrs Parry-Jones, with you. I know she frequently visits your tea shop, so I hope she is with you now?'

'Yes, of course. We have Mrs Parry-Jones here. I'll put her on.'

'Thank you.' There followed a short pause while the telephone was taken over to Fiona's table.

'Hello?'

'Fiona? Cheryl here. Are you all right?'

'No, I'm not. Where's Geraint? He should have contacted me by now.'

'Look, I'm in Aberystwyth and would like to see you.'

'Well, come on over. You can't stay long as I'm meeting a friend in less than an hour.'

'I'll be with you in five minutes.'

'See you soon, then.'

Cheryl left the telephone kiosk and walked over to her car. She checked the petrol gauge and was pleased to note that Randall had left the tank almost half full. Then she drove over to the Bara Brith Tea Shop, parked, and went inside.

II

As she entered the Bara Brith Tea Shop, Cheryl saw Fiona's skeletally thin body hunched over a table down at the far end. She looked very frail. Cheryl ordered herself a cup of coffee, walked over to Fiona's table, and sat down.

'Hello, little sis', she said, smiling at Fiona.

'Hello, Cheryl,' Fiona replied anxiously. 'Have you heard from Geraint yet? He always telephones me when he gets to Madrid, but so far not a word! Have you heard anything?'

'Yes, I've just received news. Not good, I'm afraid.'

'Why? What's happened?'

'After Geraint left Llancoed yesterday, he set off for Cardiff Airport but at some point he must have changed his mind. He then contacted Randall and asked him to sail him to France.'

Then Cheryl told Fiona how Randall and Geraint had hijacked a yacht, kicked off the owner and kept his wife as hostage before setting off for France, explaining how the wife had managed to drug them both and had called in the RNLI.

'I'm afraid that both Randall and Geraint have been arrested. They're to be transported to a London prison today.'

There followed a long silence while Fiona absorbed this information.

'God, how awful! The poor owners of the yacht. The husband must have been terrified that his wife had been killed, her body thrown overboard . . .' Fiona was momentarily speechless.

'The funny thing is,' added Cheryl, laughing, 'they had sailed over here for the Brinkley House School reunion.'

'Do you mean that the wife might be a contemporary of mine?'

'Possibly. Ann and Jack Edwards – ring any bells?'

'Do you know,' said Fiona, 'I think I do remember an Ann at Brinkley House. Ann? A tall, fair-haired girl with glasses? Ann *Ross*? She was always nice to me. What a shame she had to be kidnapped and abused by louts like Randall and Geraint. Still, thanks to her, they are prisoners now. Thank you, Ann Ross. Thank you, Ann, my very dear friend.'

Cheryl looked decidedly peeved as Fiona continued to praise Ann's quick thinking.

'I wonder how long Geraint will get now that "hijacker" and "kidnapper" have been added to his criminal record. The policemen who came to Llancoed yesterday told me that his stash was large enough to fill two police vans, so now that the police have locked the little bastard up, hopefully they'll throw away the key. Wouldn't that be wonderful news?'

Fiona giggled, making a gurgling noise deep down in her throat. Then she raised another issue.

'The tragedy is that Geraint's arrest has come too late for me. If I had my health, I'd enjoy running the Paddington Emporium on my own. As it is, all I'm in charge of is Geraint's emergency *nest egg*.'

'What? Are you telling me that Geraint has transferred everything to you?'

'No, of course not. All I am is the proud owner of a special "Parry-Jones piggy-bank", or emergency account, set up in my name in case I am left all alone. Like now. *Boo-hoo!* All in all, he's always been the most stupendous chump and such a nasty piece of work too.'

'So who gets everything when you die?'

'Aha! That's my secret.'

'But what about me? Do I get anything?'

'You must think me awfully stupid, Cheryl dear. I know I'm dying, but I've still got my wits about me!'

'What do you mean?'

'Well, how long do you think I'd last if I told you that I'd left everything to you? Five minutes?'

'That's not fair.'

'Okay then, ten minutes?'

'Ha ha. *Not* funny!'

'But you know what's wonderful, Cheryl? I'll never ever see Geraint again. Hip hip hooray! He is the most loathsome man, and I sincerely hope he gets the prison sentence he deserves. Mind you, though, there is one thing I'd like to do before I die.'

'What's that?'

'I'd like to say goodbye to my old Brinkley House chums. Good friends like Ann Ross – although I gather they're all leaving the hotel this afternoon.'

Cheryl looked confused.

'But Fiona, surely they're not your "old school chums" – not after everything they did to you?' Cheryl stared at her little sister.

'Yes, I know they teased me for being fat, but in the long term, they did me a great favour.'

'But surely you can't forgive them for what they did!'

'Forgive them for what? Calling me "Fat Fanny"?'

'Yes.'

'But I *was* fat, in fact I was *enormous*. Our dear mama spoiled me rotten, especially after you were sent away to the reformatory. She gave me far too much to eat, and I reckon, in retrospect, going to Brinkley House saved my life. I'd have died of fatty degeneration ages ago if I hadn't been sent there.'

'I'm totally amazed by what you say. I got the

impression that you loathed the three girls you wrote to me about.'

'Wrote to you about? What girls? Who do you mean? Why, what did they do?'

'Don't you remember writing to me about how Marcie, Janey and Sally rowed you out to sea in a dinghy and left you to drown? And how you were rescued and flown to hospital in a helicopter?'

'What dinghy? What helicopter?'

'The dinghy you wrote to me about.'

'I haven't a clue what you're talking about! I never, ever, went out in a boat or swam in the sea the whole time I was there. You're not making sense.'

'But you sent me a letter from Brinkley House telling me all about it. Randall and I have read it so often we know it by heart. After all, it was my fault that you were sent to Brinkley in the first place.'

'I can't remember writing anything like that.'

'Well I can remember reading your letter . . . and, besides, I've kept it. It's in my handbag and goes everywhere with me. Look, I'll get it out for you.'

Cheryl rifled through her bag and produced a scruffy envelope with childish writing on it. Then, carefully, she pulled out a well-worn letter with peeling corners and stains all over it, and proudly held it out to Fiona, before reading it out loud.

Dear Cheryl,

I don't really like it at school. You'll never guess what. Marcie, Janey, and Sally took me out to sea. To start with I only thought we were having fun in the two row boats. I thought they were my friends. Marcie and Janey were rowing, but about a mile from the beach Janey got in with Marcie and Sally and took my oars. Then they left me. I was all on my own going right out to sea. I cried for help but nobody heard me. Then I saw lightning and heard thunder. One time it happened, I got so scared, I stood up and it went over, I was sinking. Then someone got me on a yocht with people looking after me, they took me to where a helichopter flew me to hospital I want to leave school, away from them.

Fiona.

'There you are,' Cheryl said, 'it's definitely your handwriting. *Now* can you remember writing it?'

'No I can't, but surely you could see that it wasn't true. It was just my way of getting back at you. I wanted you to feel bad for killing Peter Sims and getting me sent to boarding school. Surely you can see that.'

'But why else would Mummy have taken you away from Brinkley House at exactly that time? So, if your letter to me wasn't true, what really happened?'

With great difficulty, Fiona dragged her body upright in her chair and leaned forward over the table. Staring at Cheryl, she struggled to speak.

'Janey and Marcie locked me into the sports hut one afternoon. A teacher found the key and let me out. I used what happened to put pressure on Mummy to take me away from Brinkley House. So yes, I was teased about being fat, but then my gross appearance was our dear mother's fault, and your fault too. If you hadn't murdered poor little Peter, Daddy wouldn't have died. If Daddy hadn't died, Mummy wouldn't have moved to Paddington and chummed up with Mrs Collins and sent me to Brinkley House, and I'd never have become Mrs Geraint bloody Parry-Jones and got so bloody ill. Everything is *your* fault.'

'Yes, I know. But before you decide to contact your old school friends, I think I'd better try to explain to you what your letter meant to me then and still means to me today.'

'Oh dear, I don't think I like the sound of this.'

'Well, to cut a long story short, I kept your letter with me for the remaining years I was at the reformatory. I read it and re-read it every day, and it inspired me to struggle on because if you could survive that, then I could survive the reformatory when everyone seemed turned against me. Then, after I left there, I used your letter as the inspiration for two highly successful, interlocking careers – mine and Randall's. The qualifications I had acquired at the reformatory enabled me to manage households to the benefit of both my employers and myself, and a while later I heard of Marcia Stanton-Gray – through Randall's sister Roxanne – and realised that she was the "Marcie" in your letter. It didn't take me long to get a job running the Stanton-Grays' Chelsea house, and together, Randall and I became a successful team: *me* the trustworthy housekeeper, and *he* the sexy lover-boy.

'As predicted, Marcie fell head over heels in love with Randall, who, once they were married, joined me in a brilliant money-making double act: *he* the hard-working husband struggling – but failing – to run the Stanton-Gray estate, and *me* the trustworthy housekeeper supervising the whole operation from Chelsea. Fortunately for us, the Stanton-Grays were too stupid to work out what we were up to, so later we adapted the same, highly successful, formula to enrich ourselves at the expense of Sally Griffiths – Sally Saunders, as she became – and her husband Don, as well as Janey Collins and her interfering old mother, who provided us with our greatest prize.

'Randall and I have spent many happy hours plotting and planning different ways to get back at the girls who bullied you for being fat: the girls you told me had taken you out to sea and tried to drown you. It became the motivating force behind everything Randall and I did together.'

Fiona stared at Cheryl, her face a haggard mask.

'But why pick on *my* school friends? They were part of *my* life, not yours. If you had taken me into your confidence, I could have told you what really happened all those years ago and stopped you.'

'But don't you understand? We didn't want to be stopped. Even Geraint understood how we felt. He knew how to keep our secret and, in fact, he helped us and benefited financially from us on several occasions. For example, he and Randall worked together to obtain the paperwork I needed to get the job of carer looking after Janey Collins's mother, and while I was working there he was able to steal several valuable antiques and Collins family heirlooms. Geraint even shot Marcie's horse for Randall, which is probably why Randall felt obliged to sail him to France last night. We couldn't tell you all this because you'd have stopped us, and we didn't want to be stopped. We kept you out of it on the basis that the less you knew the safer we'd be.'

'I see. Well, that was kind of you. I must say, all this must have required an awful lot of organisation and planning. You must be very pleased with what you and Randall accomplished together.'

'Well, yes, we're very pleased, because we've been able to benefit financially by building on our individual talents.'

'So how would you describe your own particular talents?'

'Well, I suppose that the fact that I'm a very good cook-housekeeper is my greatest asset, but I'm also very good at planning and organising staff. I'm one hundred per cent reliable and can cope with any eventuality.'

'So, in terms of your partnership with Randall, which of the following terms do you think suits your particular attributes best: thief, cheat, liar, or murderer?'

'That has nothing to do with what we're discussing.'

'God! You disgust me. I can't bear even to look at you. How dare you take it upon yourself to trick and defraud your fellow human beings out of their hard-earned money using my very short connection with them as motive and justification? They were only children, for God's sake, and they were my friends. Poor Marcie – poor Janey – poor Sally. Please go away. Just *go*. You sicken me.'

'I only did it for you, Fiona.'

'No, you didn't. You did it for yourself. You enjoy hurting people and stealing their money. You're a criminal and a nutcase and should be locked up like Randall. You don't give a fig for the fact that Randall's been sent to prison; you only care about yourself.'

'Well, you'll be dead soon and I don't suppose you'll leave me anything in your will now, so I might as well go.

Oh well! Goodbye, Fiona dear!'

Cheryl stood up. She felt annoyed by Fiona's negative response to what she had confided to her. She stood up and walked out, banging the door behind her. *Oh well*, she reflected, *Fiona always was a rotten little killjoy*.

As she walked over to her car, Cheryl suddenly knew what she was going to do next. She was going to drive back to the peace and quiet of Llancoed and do some housework. All those nosey people in the house yesterday would have left a dreadful mess. Yes, she felt better now that she knew exactly what she was going to do and there would be no more trouble from Fiona if she turned up at Llancoed – *she'd* see to that.

III

After watching Cheryl walk out of the tea shop, Fiona felt so ill she thought: *This is it – I'm dying*. Then, out of the corner of her eye, she saw the door open again and Gwen Morgan walk in.

Thank God! she thought as she watched Gwen walk straight across to her table and sit down close to her.

'What's happened?' Gwen asked. 'You look upset.'

'Oh, Gwennie, I'm so relieved to see you. Something awful has just happened and I must tell you about it before I peg out. You need to know this.'

Gwen Morgan, now in her eightieth year, looked like a spring chicken compared with Fiona. Years of teaching dancing at schools in the Aberdovey area had kept her fit and youthful, whereas Fiona, who had been just a fat little girl when they had first met in the sports hut at Brinkley House School, looked old and emaciated. For it was Gwen who had rescued Fiona from the sports hut after Janey and Marcia had locked her up all those years ago. Years later, after her move to Llancoed, Fiona had looked up the kind teacher who had helped her that day and they had become firm friends.

'What on earth has happened?'

'Cheryl dropped in just now. She showed me a letter that I had written to her from Brinkley House in 1953 while she was still at the reformatory – you know, the place they sent her after she suffocated Peter Sims. I can't remember writing the letter, but it's definitely my handwriting.'

Fiona recounted to Gwen the details of the letter she had written to Cheryl all those years ago.

'But that wasn't true, surely!' Gwen exclaimed.

'No, of course it wasn't. It was a total lie. I expect I was trying to hurt Cheryl, as it was because of her I was sent to boarding school. Unfortunately my letter to her coincided with my removal from Brinkley House, and Cheryl, who didn't know about the sports hut incident, thought there had to be a connection between my removal from Brinkley House and the imagined dinghy episode.'

'So what happened?'

'Cheryl decided that, whether or not my letter was true, it nevertheless justified a life-long vendetta against Marcie, Janey, Sally and their families. Cheryl's objective was to suck up to my friends and infiltrate their lives so that she could parasitise them from within. Just now, before you came here, Cheryl was swanking about all the happy times she and Randall had spent stealing from my friends while pretending to be their allies. Randall even married one of my friends so that he could steal from her family and ruin their lives. It was a just a game to Cheryl, a childish excuse for cruel and criminal behaviour.'

'But that's appalling!'

'Yes, I know. Cheryl just sat there, proudly boasting about the cruel and crazy things she and Randall had done to my totally decent school friends in order to pay them back for the *silly* stuff I wrote in a *silly* letter when I was nine years old.'

Watching in horror as tears filled Fiona's eyes, overflowed, and trickled down her emaciated face, Gwen put her arm around Fiona's shoulders and held her close while Fiona struggled to finish what she had to say.

'Janey, Sally and Marcie in particular are . . . the main victims of Cheryl's and Randall's criminal behaviour. Acts of revenge based on – nothing! Cheryl even seemed hurt by my reaction to what she was telling me, and went off in a huff. I honestly don't think she has any genuine conception of what she and Randall have done. Another thing, Gwennie: Geraint and Randall are in prison.'

'In prison? What for?'

'Hijacking a yacht.'

'Good grief, you can't be serious! Are you very upset, my dear?' Gwennie stroked Fiona's bony arm.

'No, actually I'm delighted that they've been caught. I'm sure that you already know that Geraint is a blackguard.'

'You poor dear,' said Gwen. 'You've had a very nasty shock. I'm not surprised you're upset. What would you like to do now? Would you like me to drive you to see Dr Jameson? Have you got your medication with you?'

'Thank you, Gwennie. I'll be all right in a minute. It's just the shock. Actually I'm tougher than I look.'

'So what are you going to do now? Are you going to visit Geraint in prison? Or is Sam going to pick you up and drive you to your London home today? If so, what can I do to help you?'

'Ah, if only everyone were as loving and true as you are, Gwennie. Thank you for your friendship – especially now, as there is a very big favour I'd like to ask you.'

'Ask away,' said Gwen.

'I'd like to add a codicil to my will. Today. Right now. So I'm wondering if you and the owners of the Bara Brith Tea Shop, who are old friends of mine, would act as my witnesses so that I can die confident that my sister inherits nothing from me and that my friends Janey, Sally, Marcie *and* Ann Edwards are compensated for the pain, misery and financial loss that my sister caused them in my name. Would you mind?'

'Of course not, Fiona dear. That's the very least I can do. Would you like me to go over to ask your Bara Brith friends to come over and join us? Sorry, I don't know their names.'

'Mr and Mrs Lewis.'

Fiona watched Gwen walk over to the counter where Mrs Lewis was standing. The two women talked briefly before Mrs Lewis called her husband in to join them. Then the three of them walked over to Fiona's table and sat down. Gareth Lewis smiled affectionately at Fiona.

'Well, well, Mrs Parry-Jones, Rhona and I would be honoured to help you with your will.'

'Thank you so much, Mr Lewis, but if anyone comes into the Bara Brith, please don't hesitate to serve them. Please, don't lose business because of me.'

'No worries. We've already closed up, so we're empty anyway. Besides, you are more than a customer; you are our dear friend and we are happy to help you in any way we can.'

'Thank you. Thank you. Do you have any legal experience, Mr Lewis?' Fiona asked.

'No – and please call me Gareth. But we had our own will done recently and we've got a typewriter, carbon paper and good quality stationery at the back, so we can make copies if you'd like us to.'

'Yes, good. That would be perfect. Thank you.'

Fiona, seated around the table with her old friends Gwennie, Rhona and Gareth, explained why she wanted to add a codicil to her will based on information she had just received. She wanted her sister, Cheryl Gibson (alias Kathryn Booker of Llancoed), to be written out of her will. Instead, she wanted all the money previously earmarked for Cheryl to be divided up between four school friends. These friends were: Marcia Stanton-Gray; Janey Collins; Ann Edwards (née Ross); and Sally Saunders (née Griffiths), the owner of the Brinkley House Hotel in Aberdovey. In addition, an extra lump sum – the amount was listed in the codicil – was to be transferred from her personal, private bank account (details given) and divided up between the same four school friends listed in the codicil. The contact details for all those listed in the codicil could be obtained from Mrs Sally Saunders at the Brinkley House Hotel, Aberdovey, and also from Detective Sergeant Tom Mortimer of the Aberystwyth Police Force. All items in the will not related to the codicil were to remain unaltered.

These adjustments took some time to organise, but once the codicil was drawn up, Rhona walked over to her office to type it out. Then, once each copy had been signed and witnessed, Rhona inserted the top copy into the envelope addressed to Fiona's solicitor while the other copies were duly passed on to Fiona and the witnesses of the codicil: Mrs Gwen Morgan of Aberdovey and Mr and Mrs Lewis of the Bara Brith Tea Shop, Aberystwyth. Finally, Gareth posted the codicil to Fiona's solicitor in plenty of time to catch the late afternoon post.

Gwen asked Fiona if there was anything else they could do for her.

'Yes, I think I'd better telephone my solicitor to tell him about the codicil and give him personal details of my wonderful witnesses, just in case the codicil goes astray in the post.'

'Good idea,' Gwen agreed, and Rhona and Gareth showed Fiona to the telephone.

After the whole process had been successfully completed, Gwen asked Fiona what she intended to do now.

'I think I'll go back to Llancoed now. I'm feeling much better. I'm so glad that the codicil has been drawn up. I cannot thank you all enough. You have been truly wonderful and I really appreciate the time and effort you have put in on my behalf. Thank you. So yes, I'll toddle off now.'

'Who's driving you home?' Gwen asked.

'My car is just outside. I'm feeling so much better now. I'll be fine.'

'Are you sure you don't want a lift? I'd be very happy to drive you,' said Gareth.

'No thanks. The three of you have given me a new lease of life. I'm so lucky to have you as my friends.'

Rhona smiled fondly at Fiona.

'Are you sure you'll be all right?'

'Yes, absolutely. I'll have a proper rest when I get home.'

Gwen, Rhona and Gareth helped Fiona into her car and watched her drive off down the road.

IV

After Fiona had driven off, Gwen Morgan walked over to her car and, waving goodbye to Rhona and Gareth Lewis, drove northwards to Aberdovey and her little cottage, which lay just outside the grounds of the Brinkley House Hotel. She needed to update her dear friend, Sally Saunders, on recent events, but even though she lived right next door to the hotel, she knew better than to drop in on Sally uninvited. Telephoning was a much better way of communicating with her busy friend.

'Hello? Sally? Gwennie here.'

'Gwennie, hello!'

'Look, I'll keep it brief. I've just been with Fiona Parry-Jones at the Bara Brith Tea Shop.'

'Oh, thank God! She's found! Everyone's been looking for her. I must telephone Tom Mortimer and let him know.'

'Of course, but first you need to listen to what I have to say because it relates to you, Janey and Marcia.'

'I'm listening.'

'When I arrived at the Bara Brith, Fiona's big sister, Cheryl, had just told Fiona about Geraint's arrest for hijacking a yacht. Although this news came as a shock to Fiona, what really distressed her was learning about a letter she had apparently sent Cheryl from Brinkley House School in 1953.'

'Fiona sent a letter to Cheryl at the reformatory?'

'Yes. Fiona has no recollection of writing it, but apparently Cheryl actually got it out of her handbag and showed it to her.'

'I don't understand! What on earth could Fiona have said to Cheryl that was so important?'

'Well, I suspect that Fiona's real motive for writing to Cheryl was to rub in the fact that it was because of *her* that she'd been sent away to Brinkley House.'

'So what did her letter actually say?'

Gwen passed on the substance of Fiona's childish letter to Sally.

'What? But that's ridiculous!'

'I know. Fiona says she never went anywhere near the sea the whole time she was at Brinkley House and the idea that the staff would ever allow pupils to row out to sea at all, let alone in a storm, is utterly ridiculous – it would never have happened. It's pure fantasy. Regardless of all that, however, Cheryl and Randall used this fabricated saga to justify all the criminal acts they perpetrated upon you and Don, and Janey and Marcie over the years.'

'Good grief!'

'Yes, exactly, and unfortunately the arrival of the letter at the reformatory coincided with Fiona's sudden removal from Brinkley House and so Cheryl may have seen this new information as extra ammunition for carrying out a prolonged series of criminal acts against you, Janey and Marcia: her little sister's enemies.'

'That's appalling! We couldn't understand why Cheryl kept picking on us. Now we have a better idea, although it does seem tragic to think that so much pain and misery has been caused by one stupid letter written by an angry nine-year-old to her big sister – a big sister who, unfortunately, happened to be a sadomasochist.'

'I totally agree, but there is another important part of this issue that I need to pass on to you before you hang up.'

'Fire away.'

'Fiona was so distressed to learn of Cheryl's treatment of you all – including the hijacking of *Manatee* – that she

263

has written a codicil to her will. In this codicil, which I witnessed along with the couple who own the Bara Brith, leaves each of you a sum of money as compensation for all the distress Cheryl caused you. We finished the job just before I drove back here.'

'Good heavens! What an incredibly kind thing to do. Poor Fiona having to worry about all this when she is so ill.'

'Yes . . . I'm afraid she doesn't have long to live, which is why she wanted the codicil drawn up today. Oh, and by the way, Fiona insisted on driving back to Llancoed on her own. God willing, she arrived safely.'

'Gwennie! Gwennie! Thank you so much for telling me all this. Look, I've got to go. Duty calls and I must tell Tom Mortimer where Fiona is, but thank you for everything you've passed on to me. I'll get back to you later today, after my friends have left. Goodbye, and thank you very much.'

'Goodbye, Sally dear.'

Both Gwen and Sally hung up. Then Sally telephoned Tom Mortimer.

V

'Tom? It's Sally Saunders ringing from the Brinkley House Hotel . . . Yes. I have news about Fiona Parry-Jones . . . Cheryl found her at the Bara Brith Tea Shop . . . Anyhow, I've just been talking to Gwennie Morgan, the friend I told you about. . . She met Fiona at the Bara Brith, and apparently Fiona insisted on driving back to Llancoed . . . Yes, alone . . . No, she was offered a lift, but refused to take it . . . Now, you've got everyone's contact details now, plus written accounts from Marcie, Janey, Livia, Don and me, describing the ways Cheryl and Randall tried to wreck our lives. So John Green is bang up-to-date? . . . Good, that's a relief. There's another subject I want to raise with you after everyone's left . . . It's to do with Fiona Parry-Jones . . . So you will keep in touch with Don and me, won't you? . . . Thank you again . . . Goodbye.'

CHAPTER SIXTEEN

Reparation

I

ON HER WAY to the drawing-room, Sally Saunders peeked into the little dining-room and was relieved to see that Annie had done a good job of clearing away the tea things. The room was back to its normal, pristine condition. Then, walking across the reception area and opening the drawing-room door, Sally's eyes focused on a cluster of her friends sitting around the fire, talking quietly, while, near the window, Don and Jack were sitting on a sofa laughing with gusto. It seemed a pity to interrupt them when they were enjoying themselves so much, but Sally had important information to impart. She walked over to the window.

'Don . . . Jack. I'm sorry to break in here, but I need to talk to both of you in the office.' Don looked up.

'Right now?'

'Yes, I'm afraid so.'

'Okay.' The two men stood up and walked over towards the door with Sally. As they passed the fireplace, Sally stopped and casually addressed Ann, Janey and

Marcie.

'Oh, and can I have a quick word with you three as well?'

'What, *now*?' Janey asked querulously.

'Yes, Janey, right now please. In the office.'

'Do you need more information to pass on to Tom Mortimer?'

'Indirectly, yes.' Sally was used to dealing with Janey.

'Right-ho.'

The six of them headed over to the office where Janet, who was helping Sally and Don to prepare for the hotel's reopening the following day, was holding fort. Sally spoke to her courteously.

'Can we have a moment please, Janet?'

'Of course.'

'Thanks.'

After Janet had left the office Sally turned her attention to Don, Janey, Marcie, Ann and Jack.

'I'll be brief,' she said. 'Firstly, Fiona Parry-Jones has been located at the Bara Brith Tea Shop in Aberystwyth. I've notified Tom Mortimer.'

'Was she all right?' Marcie asked.

'No, I'm told that she was far from all right. Apart from feeling very ill – she is, as you know, at death's door – she had just had a visitation from her *dear* sister Cheryl, who had sat there bragging about all the criminal acts she and Randall perpetrated against us over the years. Poor Fiona was shocked to the core, but what distressed her most was finding out that it was she herself who had unwittingly provided the motive for Randall's and Cheryl's crimes against us.'

'Why? What had she done?'

'Well, while she was at school here, she sent a letter to

Cheryl at the reformatory.'

Sally briefly outlined the contents of Fiona's childish letter.

'But that's ridiculous!' Janey exclaimed.

'Utterly!' Sally agreed.

'So what you are saying is that Cheryl and Randall stole from us, terrorised us, persecuted us, murdered my mother and your little boy, Sally and Don, all because of a ridiculous letter that Fiona sent to Cheryl when she was nine or ten years old? Surely there has to be more to it all than *that*?' Janey was incredulous.

'Yes, I agree, it *is* completely ridiculous,' said Sally. 'But, Ann, if Randall is a psychopath, and Cheryl is a sadomasochist, then maybe Fiona's letter acted as a sort of catalyst, or switch perhaps, that turned them both on, allowing them to express their inherent urges while, at the same time, providing them with a pseudo-excuse for what they were doing. Once they got started, they became addicted to their antisocial and criminal antics and Cheryl became expert at covering up her crimes by moving in and out of different jobs and presenting herself with a different disguise and alias each time. Working together, both she and Randall were each perfectly in tune with the aberrant behaviour of the other, and even Geraint Parry-Jones helped out when needed. To put it bluntly – *they were having a ball at our expense.*'

Marcie and Janey looked at Sally with interest.

'Good gracious!' exclaimed Janey.

'Yes. Well, anyway', Sally continued. 'There's more.'

'Good heavens, *more*?'

'Yes. Hear me out, please, as Don and I've got lots to do today.'

'Sorry!'

'It transpires that Fiona knew nothing about the crimes that Cheryl and Randall perpetrated against us over the years. She only found out today, and so the moment Cheryl left the tea shop she added a codicil to her will. This codicil, which was duly witnessed and sent to her solicitor this afternoon, states that when Fiona dies – which could be any minute now – we are each to be financially compensated for what Cheryl and Randall did to us over the years.'

There was a stunned silence, followed by a sharp question from Janey.

'What about Ann and Jack? You've forgotten them.'

'No I haven't: I'm coming to them. Today, when Fiona found out what Randall and Geraint had done to the pair of you, she was utterly appalled. My friend Gwennie, who helped Fiona write her codicil, told me that Fiona clearly remembered an "Ann Ross" from Brinkley House, a girl who was always kind to her. And when she learned what happened to the two of you last night, she *wept*. So you two are included in the codicil.'

Jack and Ann were delighted to learn of Fiona's extraordinary generosity, but Sally brought them back to earth with a relevant question.

'So now . . . Do we tell the others?' Sally looked at Don and her friends. 'Personally, I'd rather we kept this news to ourselves for the time being, because it mightn't come off. What do you think?'

'I agree with you,' said Marcie.

'Yes, me too.'

'And me.'

'Right then. It's just between the six of us? Incidentally, Gwennie told me that Fiona has her own money and is "comfortably off", whatever that means. Well, that's it.'

After calling Janet back into the office, Sally and Don escorted their friends back to the drawing-room.

II

After everybody had packed, vacated their rooms and put their luggage into their cars, they returned to the drawing-room to take last-minute photographs, exchange addresses and make plans for future meetings. As the afternoon wore on, everyone knew that it was time to say goodbye.

Ann and Jack had already popped over to the annexe to say goodbye to Annie and Ifor.

'But don't you want me to drive you to Aberystwyth?' Ifor had asked. 'I assumed you'd like a lift.'

'Don't you think we've given you enough hassle?' Jack had replied.

'No, you haven't,' Ifor had insisted. 'I'm driving you both to the harbour, and that's that!'

'Okay, I give in.' Ann and Jack thanked the couple and fixed a time to meet. As they left the annexe, Ann and Annie exchanged friendly hugs.

As with Ann and Jack Edwards, Judith, Ralph and Janey were under no time pressure to leave Brinkley House, knowing that Ross-on-Wye was not far from Aberdovey, whereas Livia, who was due back at her office early the following morning and was facing a five-hour drive, was itching to get started. Her voice cut through the general chatter.

'I'm sorry, everyone, I hate to break up the party, but I think I'd better start heading home now. As it is, I probably won't get home until after midnight, so, Sally and Don, thank you so much for organising this weekend for us –

it's been quite an adventure! Thank you both very much, and please thank Annie for producing such excellent meals for us all.' Livia smiled at Sally and Don, who were standing together with their backs to the drawing-room door, blocking the exit.

'Before you go, Livia,' said Sally, 'Don and I just want to thank you all for everything you have done to protect us from Randall's criminal behaviour. We don't yet know how long Randall's prison sentence will be, but at least he'll be locked up long enough for our children to leave home and go their separate ways. As for Cheryl, well, she's on her own now, and *she* knows that *we* know what she's been up to. The police, both here and in London, have her well in their sights, and Don and I can honestly say that thanks to you, this weekend has been an amazing success and all of you have been wonderful. Well, *you* know how we feel, Ann and Jack, Marcie, Janey and Roxanne, Judith and Ralph, Trot, and you, Livia. Thank you all for helping to bring justice for Mrs Collins, the Stanton-Gray family, and for us and for our unborn son. Thanks to your courage and your tenacity, the threat hanging over our heads has been lifted. Altogether, this weekend has been a fantastic success. So thank you all.'

Stepping aside to make room for Livia as she made her way out into the hall, Sally and Don wished her a safe journey and watched her leave the hotel via the glass doors. A few minutes later Livia had left the car park and was on her way back to London.

III

Judith and Marcie sat together by the fireside.

'I assume that Roxanne is driving you home tonight?' said Judith.

'Yes, and I'm really pleased, because she is going to stay with me for a while. We are going to start putting into practice plans that will increase productivity and put more money into my tenants' pockets.'

'Excellent news and now that Randall is in prison you can relax and get your health back.'

'Absolutely. In fact I'm already feeling much better. I can do things now that I couldn't do before this weekend. It just shows the effect of mind over matter. Being back with you again has made me feel so much stronger, and so much happier. You will stay in touch with me, won't you? You will come and visit me often, won't you? Please say yes. I couldn't bear to lose you again.'

'Of course I will, and when you are up and running, you must come to stay with me. I'm so relieved and comforted to have you back as my friend.'

'I feel the same. With you back in my life, and Roxanne kindly helping me, things are really looking up. I'm actually looking forward to getting home now. So, what about you two, and Janey?

Judith looked over towards Ralph who caught her eye, raised an eyebrow, and looked meaningfully over to the window where Janey was locked in deep conversation with Trot. Somehow they would need to separate those two or they would never get away.

Judith found it very hard to say goodbye to her friends. It was one thing to thank Annie for the wonderful meals she had cooked for them, but quite another to find the right words to express the admiration and gratitude she felt towards Don and Sally, Ann and Jack, and Roxanne and Marcie. Eventually, after Judith had said goodbye to everyone, she walked over to the car, accompanied by Ralph and Janey.

IV

As Judith and Ralph drove away from Aberdovey there was tension in the air. Judith had forgiven, but not forgotten, the way Janey had verbally attacked her when she had identified Fion Parry-Jones as 'Fat Fanny', and Ralph was finding it even harder to condone Janey's ill-manners. Whereas on the outward journey to Wales Janey had sat in the front seat of the car, today Ralph had shown her into the back. As Judith and Ralph chatted to one another, Janey was acutely aware that she had behaved badly towards her friends. She leaned forward in her seat the better to be heard.

'Well,' she said, 'that was one hell of a weekend. Frankly I found it quite exhausting. How do *you* feel now that it's all over?'

'Well, considering how many things could have gone wrong,' Judith replied, 'it's been a terrific success. Think of it: Ann could have been killed, Marcie could have failed to notice your mother's ring by the stile, the church could have been empty, and, of course, without John Green we might never have found out that Cheryl is *Cathie, Katie, Kathryn* and *Kelly* – that, in itself, is amazing.'

'Another thing,' Ralph added pointedly. 'If Judith hadn't had that horrid nightmare, we would never have known that Fion was "Fat Fanny" in the first place, so we've been incredibly fortunate.'

'Yes, I agree,' said Janey, 'and the future looks much brighter now that Randall and Geraint have been locked up. I imagine that they'll receive long sentences, so we're safe for a while.'

There was an awkward silence, and then Janey apologised to them both.

'I want to ask you both to forgive my stupid outbursts when you were recounting your nightmare, Judith. I could kick myself for speaking out as I did when you were raising issues of real importance. I lost it, I'm afraid, and so I owe you both an apology and an explanation for my offensive behaviour. You see, I was afraid that a secret that Marcie and I have shared ever since we were at Brinkley House might come to light and damage not only my career as a CPO but also my personal relationship with John Green.'

Judith and Ralph made no comment, so Janey carried on with her explanation.

'One day at school, Marcie and I locked "Fat Fanny" in the sports hut. After an hour she was rescued by a teacher who just happened to be passing the hut, and later that day I was found with the key in my pocket. Fiona's mother kicked up an enormous fuss and as a result Marcie and I were told that we were going to be expelled. Fortunately our mothers joined forces to put pressure on Mrs Gibson – or Mrs Fanshaw, as she was then – to remove Fiona. The whole incident was most unpleasant because, as you correctly presumed, it was my mother who had advised Mrs Gibson to send Fiona to Brinkley in the first place. Marcie and I decided to keep quiet about the whole thing, but as I grew older, secrecy became even more important to me because I didn't want John Green to find out. You see, John is crucial to my career as a CPO as well as being my lover, so I'd hate him to know that I once bullied a fellow pupil so badly she had to be taken away from school.'

Ralph and Judith listened to Janey with interest. So John Green was her lover. Life was full of surprises.

'There's more. Again, this is just between us, *please*! This afternoon Sally told Don, Ann and Jack, Marcie and me, that Fiona Parry-Jones has added a codicil to her will. She is leaving money to the six of us as compensation for the crimes Cheryl committed against us and our families. As you can imagine, because I locked Fiona in the hut that day, I feel excruciatingly guilty about it all, but Sally says that Fiona bears no ill-will towards any of us. So that's it.'

'But that is marvellous news!' Judith exclaimed. 'Ralph and I think you are wonderful and we promise never, ever, to mention this news to anyone. Actually, I have to confess that on our outward journey to Brinkley I felt quite worried about how boring your life seemed to be. Vicarage tea parties and knitting circles . . . it all seemed so dreary. Now that Ralph and I know more about your career as a gun-toting CPO, and about your relationship with John Green – well, d'you know, I think you are wonderful. Let's look out for somewhere where we can celebrate your brilliance over a cup of coffee. Besides, Janey, it's your turn to sit in the front – you've been in the back seat long enough.'

V

After stopping for a coffee-break, Judith and Janey swapped places. Reclining in the back of the car, lulled by the familiar voices issuing from the front seat, Judith's mind went back to her friends at Brinkley House. She was relieved to know that Roxanne was going to help Marcie run Redcliffe. Marcie certainly needed her help, and Roxanne, despite having Randall as her older brother, had come through her childhood difficulties extraordinarily well.

Imagine having a psychopath like Randall as your brother, or a sadomasochist like Cheryl as your sister. Judith felt sorry for both Roxanne and Fiona having such hellish siblings. *Why on earth had Cheryl decided to use a silly letter sent to her by Fiona as the justification and motivation for years of cruelty, theft and even murder meted out to totally innocent people?*

Suddenly the term 'chaos theory' popped into her mind. She tried to remember what it was, something about the 'butterfly effect'. Yes, she remembered now. A butterfly flapping its wings in Brazil could cause a tornado in Texas; or a small change in one area could cause a violent reaction in another. *Very apt*, thought Judith. *The butterfly in this case was a flimsy little letter and the tornado was the horrific damage it caused.*

Then another thought struck her: *Cheryl and Randall were both popular and attractive people. Cheryl was a hard-working and efficient cook-housekeeper, while Randall was funny and popular, as well as being an excellent sailor. It was no surprise that their victims never saw them coming because they seemed so genuine.*

Judith then thought about Fiona. She was worried about what Cheryl might do, now that she had been written out of her sister's will.

CHAPTER SEVENTEEN

Homecomings

I

CHERYL KNEW THE route from Aberystwyth to Llancoed so well she reckoned she could have driven home blindfold – well, *almost*. As it was a Monday afternoon, there was very little traffic, so she could concentrate her mind on what she was going to do when she got back. She needed to plan her housework because, as she knew, there was no point in starting on the cleanest parts of the house first, as the process of cleaning the dirtier parts of the house would only muck them up again. No, Cheryl thought, she would start upstairs on the bedrooms and gradually clean her way downstairs to the drawing-room, dining-room, kitchen, and utility room beyond. There would be no need to clean her own quarters: they were already spotless – naturally! Once the whole house was clean, she would reward herself with some food and a couple of strong drinks.

After entering Llancoed, Cheryl drove around to the back and parked her car outside her garage before walking over to the kitchen. She unlocked the door and let herself in. As usual, Geraint and Fiona had gone their separate ways leaving a mess for her to clear up. Cheryl walked around the house making a mental inventory of the total clean-up job. Two hours to tidy and clean up the house, during which time Fiona would probably turn up exhausted, needing to lie down.

She'll be dead soon, she thought, *and what's the betting I'll be expected to organise her funeral now that Geraint's in prison? Typical! It's always ME! I have to do everything, and for what? Not even a decent wage. In all honesty, considering the way I've been treated, a slice of Geraint's stash is mine by rights!*

As she carried the vacuum cleaner upstairs, Cheryl reflected on Fiona's harsh words at the Bara Brith Tea Shop. She wondered why she had been cut out of the will, considering everything she had done for her sister.

She was gazing over the banisters at the front hall below when the truth of her situation suddenly hit her. With Randall and Geraint locked up in a London prison, and Fiona more dead than alive, what on earth was she doing here? Was she mad? Randall and Geraint were no use to her now, and Fiona had just written her out of her will – *the cow!* So what had she been thinking of? Had she been asleep? It was time for her to leave Llancoed and find a new position, somewhere where she was unknown. Scotland, perhaps. Edinburgh? Once there, she could become a . . . Morag McLaughlin? Or a Kirsty Monroe? Yes, one of those names would do. A new hairstyle? Short, and blonde again, perhaps . . . and a handsome Scottish lover? Yes, things were definitely looking up.

It wouldn't take her long to pack, as experience had taught her always to have just the right amount of clothing and personal possessions to fill her two suitcases. She was an expert at speedy departures.

As Cheryl carried the vacuum cleaner back down the stairs, she realised that she would have to spend the night at a bed-and-breakfast on her way to Scotland, so there was no great hurry to get going. Having hardly eaten anything since her breakfast at the Black Stallion, Cheryl went into the kitchen to cook herself a very late lunch and make sandwiches for her journey.

While she was preparing a meal for herself, Cheryl popped outside to check the coal shed. Yes, her spade was still there. Good! She could hardly dig up her precious metal box without it.

'It's a good thing I've had the wit to feather my own nest while working here,' she said out loud to the empty house. 'After all, nobody was going to feather it for me. So let's see now, my name is Kirsty Monroe, and soon, with my exceedingly valuable treasure trove, I'll be the best catch in the whole of *Bonnie Scotland!*' Cheryl smiled at the idea.

II

Fiona was feeling very ill, but she reminded herself she had often felt worse than this. She liked her little car, and was grateful for the fact that the seating was comfortable. She felt pleased that she had decided to change her will, and even though no amount of money could heal the wounds that Cheryl had inflicted upon her friends, at least she had done the decent thing. Earlier, listening to Cheryl gloating about the criminal acts she and Randall had committed on the basis of one childish letter, Fiona wondered about Cheryl's threat to call on *Manatee* to pay Ann Edwards back for drugging Randall and Geraint and calling in the RNLI. It was now clear to Fiona that her sister was not right in the head and, in that respect, anything was possible.

Until today, Fiona had not really considered the possibility that Cheryl might be insane. Maladjusted, yes, but not *mad*. But then, looking back, she realised that after Cheryl had been sent to the reformatory and she had been sent to Brinkley House, the two of them had seldom met. Even after Geraint had employed Cheryl to look after Llancoed, Fiona had never really got to know her sister; after all, Cheryl lived at Llancoed and she lived mainly at Paddington. So who was this woman who had wormed her way into the lives of her old school friends in order to cheat them, abuse them, break their hearts, and even murder them? What sort of nutcase would do that? Reluctantly, Fiona realised she had answered her own question. Yes, Cheryl was a nutcase – a heartless, sadistic person who derived pleasure from inflicting pain on others. She was a danger to all who knew her.

Fiona was just approaching Llancoed when an extraordinary notion popped into her head. It was an idea so appalling that she was forced to slow down in case she fainted at the wheel. She took some deep breaths and took command of her mental processes.

'My idea *does* makes sense,' she said to herself, 'and if I could carry it out, it would stop Cheryl from committing any more crimes against any more innocent people.'

Fiona recalled the self-satisfied look on Cheryl's face as she proudly recounted the details of how she and Randall had carried out their cruel and avaricious vendetta against Marcie, Sally and Janey, *and* managed to get away with it over the years. While Cheryl had gloated, Fiona had nearly fainted with the horror of what she was hearing.

Driving along the lane, Fiona weighed up the pros and cons of carrying out her plan. Soon she would be dead, but if, before she died, she committed the sinful act that she was now contemplating, all her hopes of heaven would be forfeit and she would be lucky to end up in purgatory . . . but then, she thought, her life had already been purgatory, and surely that counted for something. She had really tried to be a good wife to Geraint, even though he didn't love her, or even like her. Fiona prayed for Geraint, and then, as she approached Llancoed, she prayed for her own salvation.

III

Fiona purposely drove past the entrance to the cut-through leading to Llancoed, and continued along the lane to the cul-de-sac. She did not want to bump into Cheryl, and although the track around the back of the oakwood was rain-sodden, over the years she had become used to this short cut. She parked behind the hedge to avoid being seen by Cheryl, and sat mentally preparing herself for the first stage of her plan.

With difficulty, leaning over to the glove-compartment, Fiona pulled out a pen and a small slip of paper. On one side she had started to write a shopping list, the other side was blank.

In a small, angular hand Fiona wrote on the blank side of the piece of paper:

Llancoed, Monday.

My name is Fiona Parry-Jones. I am the younger sister of Cheryl Gibson. I am terminally ill, and today may be my last day on earth. My sister, Cheryl, has committed numerous crimes and will go on doing so unless she is stopped.

I have decided to use my training and experience as a rifle marksman to prevent my sister from committing any more crimes. I pray for accuracy, and for forgiveness for my very great sin.

Please contact Cheryl's partner, Randall Selkirk, at Wandsworth Prison, to let him know of her death.

Tom Mortimer, Aberystwyth Police, also needs to be informed.

Fiona Parry-Jones

Fiona sat still for a while. She then folded her note and put it into her jacket pocket.

'This is where I must be very careful not to fall,' Fiona warned herself as she slowly eased her body out of her car. Using one walking stick, she struggled into Llancoed's rear parking area, her heart pounding and each breath agony. She started to feel dreadfully sick.

'Pull yourself together, old girl', she said to herself, 'and get on with it.'

Creeping along the gap between the two garages, Fiona saw Cheryl's car parked outside, but no sign of Cheryl. The boot was open. Why? What was she up to? Painfully, Fiona struggled over to Cheryl's car and looked inside.

'Good God! She's moving out!' she gasped.

Neatly strapped on to the back seat were two large suitcases. Two empty boxes sat side by side in the boot. This sight warned Fiona that Cheryl might appear any moment, so she'd better keep out of the way.

Now feeling even more determined to go through with her plan, Fiona made her way back along the gap between the two garages. Then she opened a door at the side of the larger garage and slipped inside.

It took a few moments for Fiona's eyes to adjust to the darkness but then, having worked through a series of security procedures, she unlocked the rifle cupboard, took out her rifle and strapped it over her shoulder. She then took out a single round of ammunition and put it in her pocket. All was quiet.

Armed with her rifle, Fiona could see no sign of Cheryl, so gently touching the garage walls to guide her steps, she crept down to the far end and listened. Then she heard the kitchen door slam and heard Cheryl walking towards the church side of the house. Fiona limped out from between the garages just in time to see her big sister climb over the stile, stride along the path and disappear into the oakwood. She was carrying a spade.

Slowly, and in great pain, Fiona eventually made her way to the stile and sat down on the middle step. After a terrible bout of nausea, followed by shooting pains all over her body, she took her rifle off her shoulder and leaned it against the side of the gate. Then she prepared herself for action. Trained to shoot lying prone which, to some extent, negated her physical disabilities, today she would have to shoot from a standing position – or would she?

The little gate was kept padlocked, so to get back home Cheryl would have to climb over the stile, thereby walking right into the rifle's firing range. Fiona realised that where she was sitting right now offered certain advantages because, not knowing how long Cheryl would be, she could wait for her in relative comfort. In addition, she realised that if she edged herself along to her left and lined up her rifle on a bar of the gate, she could set her sights directly on her target.

As she took the round of ammunition from her pocket and loaded her rifle, Fiona prayed that her years of competitive target-shooting would stand her in good stead. She knew that, in order to prevent Cheryl from seeing her, she would have to pull the trigger as soon as she appeared on the footpath.

At last Fiona saw Cheryl emerge from the oakwood carrying a heavy metal box. She was looking triumphant, and the expression 'the cat that got the cream' popped into Fiona's head as she aimed her rifle at her sister's head and gently squeezed the trigger.

Cheryl fell to the ground, the box spilling its shiny contents over the path, as startled birds flew out of the trees.

A feeling of numbness came over Fiona.

She lay against the stile, and waited.

THE END